MAIDEN GENERAL

How 17-year-old Joan of Arc Saved France at Orléans:
A True Story

D0806995

Mike MacCarthy

Illustration by Victor Guiza

outskirtspress

DENVER, COLORADO

Maiden General
How 17-year-old Joan of Arc Saved France at Orléans:
A True Story
All Rights Reserved.
Copyright © 2016 Mike MacCarthy
v2.0

Outskirts Press, Inc.
http://www.outskirtspress.com

ISBN: 978-1-4787-6351-2

Library of Congress Control Number: 2015912898

Outskirts Press and the "OP" logo are trademarks belonging to Outskirts Press, Inc.

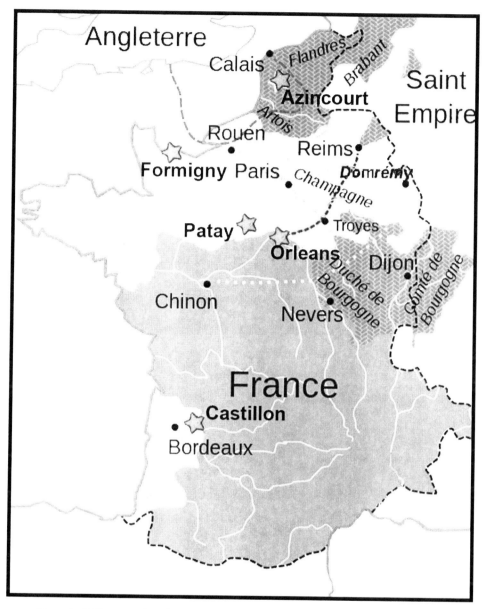

Map of all France showing the areas controlled by the English and French

Anglaterre

Calais

Flandres

Brabant

Saint
Empire

Azincourt

Rouen

Reims

Domrémy

Formigny

Paris

Champagne

Artois

Patay

Orleans

Troyes

Dijon

Comté de Bourgogne

Chinon

Nevers

Duché de Bourgogne

France

Castillon

Bordeaux

This book is dedicated to Saint Joan of Arc:

In the face of your enemies, in the face of harassment, ridicule, and doubt, you held firm in your faith. Even in your abandonment, alone and without friends, you held firm in your faith. Even as you faced your own mortality, you held firm in your faith.

I pray that we all may be as bold in our beliefs as you, Saint Joan. I ask that you ride alongside us in all our own battles. Help us to be mindful that anything worthwhile can only be won when we persist. Help us hold firm in our faith. Help us to believe in our ability to act well and wisely.

Amen.

Table of Contents

Table of Contents for Maps and Illustrations

* Used with permission from
Xenophon Group Military History Database:
http://xenophongroup.com/montjoie/orleans.htm

All other maps and illustrations are from sources
published before 1924.

"Joan was a being so uplifted from the ordinary run of mankind that she finds no equal in a thousand years. She embodied the natural goodness and valor of the human race in unexampled perfection. Unconquerable courage, infinite compassion, the virtue of the simple, the wisdom of the just, shone forth in her. She glorifies as she freed the soil from which she sprang."

—Sir Winston Churchill in
A *History of the English-Speaking People.* (1956)

 # Note to the Reader

This book differs from other books about Jehanne d'Arc because it chronicles each small and large step of her journey from farm girl to knighthood in the French army. *Maiden General* also presents seemingly sudden personality changes in Jehanne leading up to the Battle of Orléans. The alterations in Jehanne's persona over the course of this book usually attract scant attention because so much else is going on in her life.

Maiden General presents who Jehanne was when she ran away from home—gloriously innocent, incredibly focused, naïve, hot-tempered, quick to tears, and miraculous, yet exceptionally humble and committed to the service of God. But there was more to her than that.

This is the true story about a French peasant girl, most commonly known as Joan of Arc. She came to public notice at a pivotal moment in the Franco-English war, later named the 100 Years' War. The names of those in her story (see "Cast of Major Players," next page) are real and have not been changed or invented; their personalities and character are also fully documented. The records show that the people surrounding Joan actually met and spoke and acted in specific ways in response to those conversations, but seldom did anyone make notes. Where documentation actually does exist in French public records, those conversations have been included, but sometimes edited for clarity.

In *Maiden General*, I most often refer to the main character as

Jehanne in honor of how she chose to be addressed during her public life. My hope is that, by the end of the book, you will come to see this young woman as someone you care about and that what she accomplished is an epic piece of history more amazing than fiction.

—*Mike MacCarthy*

Cast of Major Players at the Beginning of 1429

(Alphabetical by First Name or Place of Title)

Legend:

E = *(Players loyal to the Crown of England)*
U = *(Players loyal to their own perceived best interests)*
V = *(Players loyal to the Houses of Valois/Armagnac/Orléans/the French Crown)*

(V) Bastard de Orléans, age twenty-six—Named Jean at birth, the illegitimate son of Duke Louis d'Orléans—King Charles VI's younger brother—had asked to be addressed as "the Bastard" since childhood. He and Charles VII grew up together as children.

(V) Bertrand de Poulengy, age forty-three—close friend to Jehanne.

(V) Boussac, maréchal de [aka Jean de Brosse], Seigneur de Sainte-Sévère (age fifty-four)—A veteran and courageous field commander, he was made marshal of France in 1426 in exchange for considerable funds advanced to Charles VII. He later became commander of Charles VII's special bodyguard of 100 men-at-arms.

(V) Charles de la Valois, age twenty-six—After learning of his father's death (King Charles VI) in 1422, Charles VII, the Dauphin (Crown Prince), wept uncontrollably for weeks and then, reluctantly, began the seemingly impossible task of throwing the English out of France.

(V) Charles I Duc de Bourbon, age twenty-eight—Known as the Comte de Clermont, he had recently been an aggressive leader of the Armagnac Party forces that supported Charles VII.

(E) Duke of Bedford, John Plantagenet of Lancaster, age fifty— Youngest brother to King Henry V of England, he was appointed guardian of England and the infant Henry VI by the then dying Henry V. When Philip of Burgundy refused to accept the regency of France from Henry V on behalf of the child-king (Henry VI), Bedford also became the English regent of France.

(V) Étienne de Vignolles, age thirty-nine—Nicknamed "La Hire" ("the Anger"), he was a courageous, hard-fighting, and trusted field captain known for his violent temper and foul mouth.

(U) Georges de la Trémoïlle, age forty-four—Supported the House of Burgundy in his early years and later entered their employ until his capture by the English at Agricourt in 1415. After the House of Valois organized his ransom, he professed allegiance to Charles VII. Two of his wives mysteriously died, leaving him incredibly rich, which then led to his appointment as grand chamberlain of France in 1427 and "most trusted" status of all advisors to Charles VII.

(V) Jean II, Duc d'Alençon, age twenty-five—A close friend of the Dauphin, D'Alençon was recently released from an English prison in exchange for ransom. He was handsome, dashing, and fierce.

(V) Jean de Metz, age forty-two—close friend to Jehanne.

(V) Jean Poton de Xaintrailles, age thirty-nine—Like La Hire, de Xaintrailles was appointed captain because of his valor. La Hire and Xaintrailles usually entered battle together.

(V) Jehanne la Pucelle, age seventeen—A peasant farm girl from Domremy (northeastern), France, on a mission for God. After her powerful love of God and family, her country came next.

(U) Sir John Stewart, age forty-nine—Entered France in 1419 as commander of 6,000 fierce Scottish troops in support of King Charles VI. In 1427, Stewart returned to Scotland seeking more troops, which he brought to France in 1429. Known as the Constable of Scotland, he had great difficulty following orders from French field commanders.

(V) Louis I Bourbon, Comte de Vendôme, age fifty-three—A well-known and revered member of the Armagnac Party, he was generally recognized as a reliable and hard-charging field commander with enthusiastic loyalty to the Valois cause.

(U) Sir Philip Burgundy, Duc of Burgundy, age thirty-three—Assumed head-of-the-family status in 1419 after the death of his father Sir John Burgundy (aka John the Fearless). The House of Burgundy was a powerful and wealthy French family with vast land holdings in France and across Europe.

(U) Queen Isabeau, age fifty-nine—Mother of Charles VII and openly unfaithful and gluttonous wife to Charles VI. She was also the "moving force" behind the Treaty of Troyes of 1420 for which the English provided her with lands and considerable personal wealth.

(V) Queen Yolande of Sicily and Aragón and Duchess of Anjou, age forty—The beautiful wife of Louis II of Sicily, mother of Marie who became betrothed to Charles VII in 1413; Yolande later became mother-in-law to Charles VII in December 1422.

(U) Raoul de Gaucourt, age fifty-eight—Publicly pledged to Charles VII. Appointed military governor of Orléans by Charles VII in 1428. Subject to delusions of grandeur.

(U) Regnault de Chartes, age forty-nine—Appointed archbishop of Reims in 1414 by Avignon Pope John XXIII despite the fact that de Chartes had never been to that city. He was also one of Trémoïlle's most willing pawns.

(V) Robert de Baudricourt, age twenty-nine—The governor of Vaucouleurs and loyal captain of the royal garrison there. He successfully defended that city in 1428 against an Anglo-Burgundian invasion, thus earning the eternal gratitude of Charles VII.

(E) Earl of Shrewsberry I, Sir John Talbot, age fifty-six—Throughout his service to England, he modeled honor and chivalry in all things. He was also known as a daring and aggressive soldier; some thought him the most audacious captain of the age. His trademark was rapid aggressive attacks. He had already served in France under the regent Duke of Bedford, and by his exploits rendered his name more terrible to the foe than that of any other English military commander.

(E) Earl of Suffolk, William de la Pole, 4th Earl of Suffolk, age thirty-three—When the Earl of Salisbury died in battle at the beginning of the Orléans campaign, Suffolk succeeded to his command on the 3rd of November 1428.

(U) Robert Le Maçon, age sixty-four—Overtly loyal to Charles VII, but subject to manipulation.

(E) Lord Thomas de Scales, age twenty-nine—Became one of Bedford's field commanders in 1422 and beginning November 1428 assumed technical equal authority along with Suffolk and Talbot.

(E) Sir William Glasdale—A twenty-year veteran who had been part of the English invasion forces alongside the Earl of Suffolk since 1423, and considered one of the "first lords of England." When Suffolk assumed command of Orléans in November 1428 following the death of the Earl of Salisbury, he placed Glasdale in charge of the defense of Les Tourelles (a vital bridge). Upon his arrival in Orléans, Glasdale swore that it was his intention to kill everyone in the city.

(E) Sir William de Moleyns, age twenty-four—Born in Stoke Poges, Buckinghamshire, England, in 1405. He had fought side by side in France with Glasdale since 1424.

(E) Les Goddams (aka, the Goddams, the Goddons, etc.) a nickname given the English soldiers by the French people because they didn't understand their language well, but heard them using the word "goddam" so often. The French had no clear idea what 'Goddam' meant in French, only that it was a word the English used often, no matter the situation.

Chapter I
God's Work

A BYWAY TWO MILES SOUTH OF VAUCOULEURS, FRANCE
MONDAY, JANUARY 12, 1429
1000 HOURS

Peasant farmer Durand Lassois and his seventeen-year-old niece, Jehanne d'Arc, sat side-by-side in a wooden cart inching their way through the latest blizzard. The dangerous storm didn't really concern Jehanne. She'd grown up on a farm and knew to expect winter whiteouts this time of year. But what her uncle had said about the possibility of a wolf attack bothered her a lot—especially since it meant she could die before completing her mission for God.

In these rolling hills of the Lorraine region of northern France, the weather of the new year had continued from that of late December—blizzard days followed by a period of dark, foreboding skies and gusting winds followed by yet more snow. In such harsh conditions, the prey herds such as deer, mountain goats, moose, and elk wandered and migrated toward southern France, and the local gray wolves in particular found themselves trying to survive on mice, birds, or fish. But when blizzards bombarded this region, one after another, even the small prey disappeared, forcing the starving wolves to search for food much closer to human populations.

1

Experienced local farmers knew to be on constant "alert" to protect their stock during such conditions. Safeguarding their animals could be as heart-felt as protecting family members. Without livestock—both sources of food and beasts of burden—most peasant families would soon find themselves destitute. Their animals were considered members of the family.

Before leaving for this journey, Uncle Durand had spoken to Jehanne in unusually harsh language, warning her of the very real dangers that might lie ahead—even during a short trip like this. "I hate traveling to Vaucouleurs in such dangerous weather," he told her, "but I made you a promise, and I'm going to keep it."

Right after that, he loaded his crossbow and hunting clubs in the cart, alongside his best hunting dog.

As his matched team of Rouncy plow horses—named Michelle and Jacques—labored to pull their squeaky wooden cart along the drift-covered road, their best guide was instinct. These powerful pulling animals had made the journey to the county seat dozens of times on behalf of their forty-three-year-old owner, but usually in less dangerous conditions. At the moment, Durand held the reins loose, squinting into the gusting storm, searching for any unusual movement or a strange snow mound. Ravenous gray wolves would sometimes burrow into snowdrifts and ambush unsuspecting animals or humans. Jehanne's uncle had insisted that she sit beside him, soothing his large male Alaunt that now rested on the cargo bed, totally at peace from the girl's attentions while the blizzard continued to blow and swirl in all directions.

Coated with snow and ice and huddled under thick woolen blankets, the two lonely figures were making their way toward the largest city in the region. Durand couldn't help but think about the wolves and his niece. Jehanne had celebrated her seventeenth birthday barely six days ago, but acted older than her years.

Standing barely over a meter and a half, she was no longer the docile daughter of his sister and her tyrannical husband. The once-quiet little girl had, during the last year, become a sturdy, strong young woman—accustomed to and unafraid of hard physical labor.

Although Jehanne considered herself ordinary in appearance, her large blue eyes seemed to attract the gaze of animal, friend, and stranger alike. Concealed beneath her long black hair, a dark red birthmark ran down behind her right ear ending at the nape of her neck—something she tried to conceal, especially from sniggering classmates.

Two things dominated her thoughts for the moment: the possibility of a wolf attack and the important secret that she needed to share with her uncle. But that would have to wait. Turning in her seat to look back at the massive dog, still resting peacefully under heavy blankets, Jehanne continued to pet his large head with one gloved hand. Her uncle had nicknamed him Shepherd Dog, but his real name was Francis, and Durand used him to round up live-stock and hunt large game, including marauding wolves.

When they finally had left from her uncle's farm about an hour before, he began schooling Jehanne about what she was to do in the event of a wolf attack. "Whatever you do, don't let Francis charge the wolves. He's a good strong dog and can handle most wolves one-on-one, but when they gang up on him, he won't back off unless I really yell at him. He doesn't know his limits."

Jehanne had since wrapped a long, thick rope, tied to the dog's collar, around her nonpetting hand, trying not to slacken her grip despite the numbing cold. She stared out at the storm looking for wolves through a small opening in the wool scarf covering her neck and face. Her mother had made it for her birthday as she did for all Arc family members, and Jehanne treasured the gift—especially now for the warmth it provided.

Like most who lived in her village, Jehanne, her parents, and three older brothers each owned but one set of clothing. Her father and his sons usually wore coarse tunics and long stockings while her mother and she wore long woolen dresses with stockings. Like most peasant women, Jehanne wore linen undergarments to offset the uncomfortable wool, but her discomfort had no place in her thoughts at the moment. A possible wolf attack and working up the courage to share a big secret she'd been keeping since her thirteenth year were the only thoughts she could entertain.

Please, God, help me hear your words and find the courage.

Durand broke the silence.

"I still don't understand why we're doing this," he said, eyes fixed on the struggling team. "I promised I'd get you another appointment with Governor Baudricourt, so why must we travel in such conditions? There can't be any meeting if we freeze to death before we arrive."

The girl looked away. "We've already been over this," she said. "The snow keeps falling and falling. Who knows when it will stop? God's work has waited long enough."

"God's work? How is risking our lives and those of my animals in a blizzard doing God's work?"

Jehanne shook her head in frustration and looked up at the sky. "We went through all this last May," she said, creating an opening in the scarf to be better heard. "That's why I went to see Baudricourt back then—to do God's work. I needed a meeting with the Dauphin. You knew that." Her words shot out as a steam cloud and darted away in the wind.

"Yeah, yeah, God's work," Durand said. He scowled and faced her. "But you never explained to me how you knew what God wanted you to do. Are you certain you haven't just been dreaming?"

Now's the time . . .

"Uncle," she began, meeting his gaze. Snow had blanketed his

4

thick beard and turned to ice. "Can I trust you?"

At first Durand frowned. Jehanne usually avoided serious conversations with him, and he liked it that way. He took a deep breath and nodded.

"Of course, you can trust me."

"I mean, can I trust you to keep a promise, no matter the consequences?"

"What kind of a question is that? Why else are we out in this godforsaken blizzard?"

"If I tell you something no one else in the world knows, will you promise to never tell another living soul, including family or anyone else in Domremy?"

He took a deep breath and exhaled into the swirling storm. "If that's what you want, I can and will keep such a promise."

She continued to study him. "Do you promise to God in heaven that what I am about to tell you will never be read or heard by another?"

Again, he nodded, but this time almost imperceptibly, raising his right hand, a tradition recently established by the nobles of France; if someone broke the law, their right hand would be branded with a letter to show their crime.

"I promise," he said.

Jehanne gazed back into the storm, staying quiet for longer than she intended.

"Well," she said finally, "it is now all in the hands of our Father in heaven."

Don't tell him everything—no need for that.

Just then, high-pitched squeals filled the air as both horses reared, legs pawing at the air, tails whipping in all directions. Eyes wide with terror, they thrashed in the snow to break free, but the buildup made it impossible—hoofs sank deeper with each new leap.

Jehanne's eyes darted through the white and saw dark shapes slinking closer from a distance.

Wolves.

Francis bolted from under his blankets, barking and growling as he bounded down the back of the cart, jerking Jehanne with him into a windswept drift.

Jehanne couldn't breathe but stood and quickly unwound her face scarf.

The accumulated snowpack also prevented Francis from gaining traction, his movements were sluggish and stilted, and his barks quickly became screams of rage. Jehanne scrambled back to the cart and locked one arm around a wheel.

Dear God, help me.

Her hands shook like leaves in a wind. A strong urge to vomit swirled in her stomach as she gasped for air, but she focused on what she needed to do.

Over the howling wind, Durand shouted. "Stay near the cart! If a wolf comes, back away slowly, facing him, but don't make direct eye contact. If it looks like it might attack, shout and wave your arms—you'll appear larger. Whatever you do, don't run—the wolf will think you're prey."

The two horses continued their screaming and rearing, so her large, muscular uncle jumped onto Jacques's back and yanked hard on the reins, which stopped his rearing. Durand then turned to her and pointed at a nearby embankment where three gray wolves stood, leering down at them. He then jumped down from the horse and grabbed the reins of both horses.

"Let go of Shepherd Dog," he yelled to Jehanne, "and bring me those weapons!"

Her hands still shook.

Durand let out a piercing whistle. Francis stopped scrambling toward the wolves and headed for his master, growling and barking with each trying step. Jehanne released the rope, pulled herself up into the cart, and gathered the crossbow, her frozen fingers fumbling with the clubs. Falling snow blew hard in her face, and she could barely see the way to her uncle.

Durand took one of the clubs and the arrow quiver. He handed her the reins, having already looped them tight around the cart's brake handle. "Hold onto these," he said, "and don't let go."

As he loaded the crossbow, the horses began bucking, rearing, and screaming again, ears flattened.

"If they get past me and Shepherd Dog, don't be shy about using that club," he shouted above the din. "You're a lot stronger than you think. Understand?"

She nodded without thinking.

The three ravenous wolves had already begun to scamper down the embankment, quickly closing the distance between them and their prey. Durand and his large dog moved quickly, planting themselves between the wolves and horses.

Jehanne jumped down from the cart, still holding the reins with all her strength while soft-talking the horses through dry, trembling lips.

The wolves stopped in their tracks, snarling and growling through clenched teeth at the man and dog blocking their path. Durand bellowed at the top of his lungs at the wolves. He took dead aim with the crossbow at the dominant wolf, who now stood stiff-legged and tall. The animal's ears perched erect and forward. Its tail was held vertical and curled toward its back.

"Hold, hold," her uncle shouted to his dog.

Francis yelped, growling, quivering with rage at having to wait for a signal.

"Steady, Michelle. It's okay, girl," Jehanne cooed, hands trembling. "Everything's going to be fine. Jacques, come on, big boy, help Michelle—show her you're not afraid. You know Durand and

Francis are going to keep us safe."

As she stroked their heads with her stiff-gloved hands, the horses stopped rearing, but their tails still swished, and they continued to whinny and snort, desperate to flee.

Saints Michael, Catherine, and Margaret, I don't know what to do.

At some unseen signal, the largest and smallest wolves broke away from the leader, the larger headed toward Francis while the other charged Durand.

"Go! Go!" he shouted to the dog as he fired his crossbow. His arrow lodged into the charging wolf's throat, dropping it to the ground amid sharp yowls and an expanding red stain in the snow.

The larger wolf locked now in mortal combat with Francis, teeth bared, filling the air with primal growls and yelps. Jehanne couldn't take her eyes away, uncertain if the big dog really could handle such a large wolf.

"Jehanne!" Her uncle's scream snapped her eyes from the dueling animals.

The third wolf—the leader—now crept slowly toward Jehanne.

Her mind seemed to empty amidst the swirling storm and fast-moving events.

Durand kept shouting, raising his hands high and running toward her.

"Drop the reins, wave your arms and yell!"

Right. No eye contact—just wave.

The girl did as she'd been told, jumping and shouting and waving her arms, but the third wolf kept coming. The horses were again rearing, kicking, and screaming. Jehanne chose to ignore them. Through the white of the storm, she could see the approaching wolf's ribcage. He was starving.

Waving and shouting aren't enough.

The large wolf crouched near the ground, edging closer,

inch-by-inch, as the wind swirled and whipped from all directions. Less than three meters away now, the growling wolf showed no interest in her, eyes riveted on the frenzied horses, coiled for the perfect moment to strike.

Durand was running toward her as fast as he could, but was too far away to help.

It was up to her. Her uncle's words remained sharp in her mind. She knew she had to act quickly.

You're a lot stronger than you think.

Jehanne tightened her grip on the club and sprang at the wolf, swinging the weighted hunting weapon down on the snarling animal with all her might.

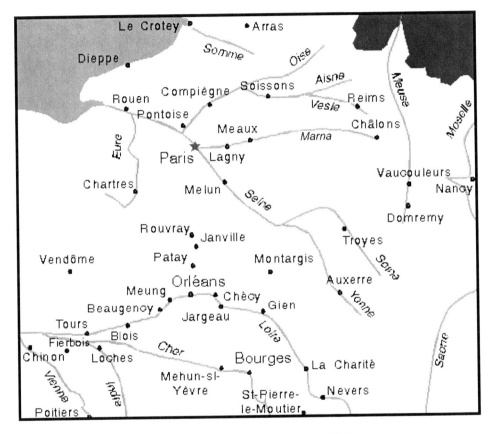

Map of 1429 Northern France & the places of Jehanne's story

CHAPTER II
𝔍𝔢𝔥𝔞𝔫𝔫𝔢'𝔰 𝔖𝔢𝔠𝔯𝔢𝔱

A BYWAY TWO MILES SOUTH OF VAUCOULEURS
MONDAY, JANUARY 12, 1429
1100 HOURS

𝔇 urand couldn't believe his eyes. "Jehanne, get away!" he bellowed, hopping through the knee-deep snow.

But she kept clubbing the wolf over and over until the animal lay still, a bloody stain swelling in the white.

When Durand finally arrived at the cart, he grabbed the reins, attempting to still the horses. "Jehanne, are you all right? Are you hurt?"

But his voice was inaudible to the girl—her attention fixated on Shepherd Dog, still growling, snarling, and rolling in the snow with the last wolf. With barely a moment's hesitation, she ran at the two blood-covered animals, club at the ready.

"What are you doing?" Durand screamed, running after her, crossbow in hand. "Jehanne! You'll be killed!"

But she was quicker than her uncle. When at last she spotted a gap between the snarling animals, Jehanne swung as hard as she could. Her blow caught the wolf on the side of his snout, knocking him sideways into the snow. Shepherd Dog pounced and bit into the wolf's exposed throat, puncturing and tearing at it with his powerful jaws. The wolf yelped and thrashed for a few moments, then went limp.

Jehanne fell to the ground, face in her hands. Durand knelt beside the girl and wrapped a large arm around her shaking shoulders.

"Don't cry, Jehanne," he said. "It's over."

She made no response.

Durand's ears rang in the silence with the brays of the still terrified horses, the whisper of the falling snow, and the whistle of the blustering wind.

His heart leapt to his throat as Shepherd Dog flung the dead wolf to the ground, growling and poised to renew his attack at the slightest provocation. A moment passed and the wolf remained still. Francis turned and limped slowly toward them, whimpering with each step.

"Oh, Francis, you're hurt!" Jehanne cried out.

Before Durand could say anything, she rose to her knees and wrapped both arms around the big dog, searching for his wounds.

He joined her in probing the dog's fur. There were several gashes across his neck and torso. Shepherd Dog would need to rest and get away from this evil snow.

"Let me take him," he said softly. He wrapped both arms around Francis and hurried as best he could through the deep snow toward the cart, his brow creased with worry about the severity of the dog's wounds.

Still flailing in their harness, the horses saw him coming, and seemed to know the danger had passed. They quieted significantly.

"It's all right, Michelle, it's okay, Jacques," Durand said in as soothing a tone as he could manage. "Nothing's going to hurt you."

He heaved Francis gently onto the back of the cart and covered him with thick blankets. He smiled and stroked the big dog's head. "I'm so proud of you, Shepherd Dog," he said, kissing his wet snout. "Wait until I tell my friends what you and Jehanne did today." He could practically see the amazement on their faces when he related the tale of his seventeen-year-old niece and his hunting dog killing two gray wolves by themselves. "They're going to think I've had too much to drink," he whispered to himself.

Durand thought it best to lead the team on foot the rest of the way to the city. He explained to Jehanne that he could better ensure they stayed on the road; it also put him in a better position to defend against further wolf attacks.

Jehanne remained in the cart with Francis, petting and reassuring him that all would be well once they reached Vaucouleurs. She tore away some of the undergarments from beneath her tattered red dress and used them as bandages to stem the flow of blood from the dog's head and legs.

"My beautiful Francis," she repeated between strokes. "You were so brave."

Though her uncle had assured her of her own bravery, she cried silently, alone in the cart, at having to kill the poor starving wolves.

They had only done what God created them to do.

And any courage previously mustered to confide her secret to Durand had now left her.

In April of 1428, Jehanne had visited her uncle's family to help with chores around the Lassois house and to get away from her own family. Her father had been having nightmares about her and, upon waking, shouted at her and accused her of indecency. Her mother, sister to Durand's wife, thought the visit with her aunt a good idea. When Jehanne arrived at the Lassois home, she asked to accompany her uncle when he made his next visit to Vaucouleurs. She "needed to be about God's work," she told him in confidence, but offered no further explanation. And, at the time, Durand asked no further questions.

On Ascension Thursday a week later, after Durand and Jehanne had finally arrived in Vaucouleurs, Jehanne told her uncle that God had given her a mission involving the crown prince of France—the Dauphin. At first Durand laughed at her and told her that was ridiculous, but she would not be put off so easily.

The French war with England began nearly a century before when the English decided to annex France, and had dragged on ever since. It now fell to the Dauphin, Prince Charles VII, to organize the French defense from a seemingly unwinnable position. The English controlled most northern territories and Orléans stood as the only obstacle to a total English victory.

All France knew the situation.

At the time, Jehanne couldn't tell if her fervent insistence that her mission came from God convinced her uncle or if she had simply touched his heart. Either way, he eventually came to believe her and took the girl looking for the governor of Vaucouleurs.

As they searched, her uncle told her all he knew about Sir Robert Baudricourt from years of buying and selling horses with him. Durand explained that as governor of the region, Sir Robert assumed responsibility for all the people's safety. Toward that end, those in charge of overseeing his governance provided him with a castle, from which he organized the local militia and defended the city from the invading English and their allies.

"He's been known to kill wolves with his bare hands," her uncle said with a smile.

"Does he do a good job?" Jehanne asked.

Durand laughed. "Well, he knows not to take on a whole pack at once, so he does it better than Shepherd Dog."

She gave her uncle a playful shove. "I meant fighting off the English."

He nodded, a gleam of admiration for her filling his eyes. "He does a very good job." They finally caught up with the governor riding back to his castle after the Ascension Thursday Mass.

Governor Robert de Baudricourt was a massive bear of a man with a nose like the beak of a vulture and hard eyes. Jehanne could easily picture him tackling a wolf and crushing it in his arms. But beneath the man's soldierly exterior and lanky black hair was a mouth that warmed upon seeing an old acquaintance. Durand introduced Jehanne and asked Baudricourt to listen to what she had to say.

"Jehanne," her uncle said, "please tell Lord Baudricourt what you told me."

Once she did, the knight stared at her and Jehanne could almost see herself through his eyes—a teenage farm girl with long, dark hair and an old, fraying red dress. She knew he would laugh at her, as her uncle had, but would prove much harder to convince.

After a brief silence, Baudricourt's laughter came, and Jehanne felt blood rush to her face. But the Dauphin's knight quickly got his amusement under control. "Monsieur Lassois," he began, "thank you for introducing your niece. She seems a credit to you and your family. I've always known you to be a serious businessman, but . . ." He threw back his head and let out another robust bark of laughter.

Jehanne took a deep breath, but said nothing.

"Do you really believe that your niece is on a mission from God?"

Durand shrugged. "I don't know . . . In her entire life, I've never known her to tell a lie, neither has my wife or the girl's parents."

Jehanne appreciated her uncle's words, but could see they hadn't worked.

Baudricourt shook his head. "I can't help you, Jehanne, and I don't know where you got the idea that God Himself has sent you on a mission." He chuckled again, but caught himself. "Durand," he continued, "I suggest that you take this girl back to the home of her father, and have him give her a good smacking."

With that, he galloped toward his castle, leaving Jehanne in the cold, despite the bright sunlight.

After a seven-month absence from Vaucouleurs, Jehanne and her uncle once again proceeded to the home of Henri and Catherine le Royer, close friends of Durand. Seeing the hunting dog's injuries, the le Royers directed them to the nearest medical woman, who stitched and bound Francis's wounds. The woman asked to keep the dog a few days to allow the gashes to start mending and to make sure he hadn't caught rabies from the wolves.

The blizzard had not abated and the drifts seemed to be growing five centimeters every hour. On their way back from dropping off Francis, Durand and Jehanne rode quietly through the thick snow.

Once again her uncle broke the silence. "Jehanne, I want to ask you something. Before the wolves came, you made me promise—you said, 'It is now all in the hands of our Father in heaven.'"

Just then another small tornado of snow and wind buffeted their faces.

Jehanne nodded. She had hoped he would let it be. "You have a good memory," she said.

"What did you mean? What's in the hands of God?"

She took a deep breath and shivered. "It's a long story. We will need someplace private. And out of the cold."

Her uncle nodded. "I will make sure Henri and Catherine do not disturb us."

Jehanne did not respond; she still wasn't going to tell him everything.

Once bundled up inside the le Royer home and alone with her uncle, Jehanne commenced her story. Her secret began in the summer of her twelfth year. She'd been in the fields tending the family sheep with girls from the village. Often, to pass the time, they would run foot races with one another, chasing each other across pastures and up and down the grassy hillsides. Jehanne loved these races because she always won. After one race, when the other girls had gone home, she rested by herself in the shade of a solitary tree.

As she did, a peasant boy her own age crossed the field to her and said, "Jehanne, go home. Your mother is in need of your help."

New families and children visiting in Domremy had become commonplace in recent days because of marauding soldiers in nearby regions, so Jehanne thought nothing of it at the time. She ran home and reported to her mother, who was quite surprised— she had not sent any such message, and instructed her youngest to go back to the fields and pay no attention to messages from children she did not know. It was probably a prank.

Once out the door, Jehanne decided to stop at Saint Remy, the village church, to pray. Saint Remy stood beside the d'Arc property, just beyond their vegetable patch. As the girl ran past the garden, a chorus of ortolans, orioles, and chickadees from the trees surrounding her home broke into such melodious song that she stopped and looked up. A brilliant, shimmering, domelike cloud of white light approached and, within seconds, glided over and completely enveloped her.

She could no longer hear the birds—there was total silence— and a man stood in front of her. He was handsome and tall—much taller than any man she had ever seen—and dressed in French battle attire. She wasn't sure if he was an angel or a demon.

"Jehanne the Maid, daughter of God," he greeted her in a deep, commanding voice.

She fell to her knees, terrified.

"Do not be afraid," he said. "I come from God to help you live a good and holy life. And to serve our Lord."

She took a second look—he seemed familiar to her. She had often seen paintings in neighboring churches when visiting friends or her uncle. A similar figure was often shown in the guise of a handsome knight with a crown on his helmet, wearing a coat of mail, and bearing a shield. Today, he wore no helmet; only long, dark hair covered his head, but she still recognized him. It was the angel Saint Michael.

The angel gazed at her for a moment. "Do not fear, Jehanne. Do you not know who I am?" he asked.

Jehanne stared up at him unable to speak, legs numb. She couldn't even nod.

"Jehanne, have you no questions for me?" His query went unanswered. "As you wish; I will not press you now." He turned to leave. "Before I return, two others will visit you. They, too, come from the Lord."

The prospect of other apparitions finally pulled Jehanne from her silence. "Who . . . who is coming?" she asked, tentatively.

"Saints Catherine and Margaret."

"But why?" She was astonished she could speak at all. "Why are you here? Why are they coming?"

"God commanded us. *You* have been chosen by Him for a divine mission."

Still kneeling, she looked up and asked, "What? What mission?"

"All will be made clear to you in time. Be good, Jehanne, and God will assist you." With that the angel dissipated and, with him, the shimmering light.

Now alone, Jehanne sprinted all the way to the church. On her knees, she prayed, *Deus meus, ex toto corde poenitet me omnium meorum peccatorum . . .*

"O my God, I am heartily sorry for having offended thee and I detest all my sins, because of thy just punishments, but most of all because they have offended thee, my God, who are all good and deserving of all my love. I firmly resolve, with the help of thy grace, to sin no more and avoid the near occasion of sin. Amen."

"I have kept all of this secret," she finally concluded with Durand. Her heart was in her throat, but even if her uncle thought her mad, it was a relief to finally tell someone. She watched as he considered her, staring off into a dark corner of the room for several moments.

"And did Saint Michael come back?" he asked at last.

Jehanne nodded. During the intervening years, she received daily visits from at least one of the three—most often in a bright cloud of light. Occasionally the three presented themselves as a group, but Catherine and Margaret visited the most—usually one at a time. Once in a while, other angels came to visit—even the Archangel Gabriel—but mostly just the original three. They spoke in her native tongue and, many times when they were to depart, she would throw her arms around their legs and weep and beg them to stay. They were beautiful.

"As I grew older," she explained, "they became more pointed in their suggestions from God. 'You must come to the immediate help of the king of France,' Catherine and Margaret kept saying. 'You must obey our instructions. They have been sent by the ordinance of our Lord.'"

The blizzard raged outside. Her uncle continued to study her. She swallowed the knot in her throat and shrugged.

"And that's how I came to learn my sacred duty," she said. "As you can see, I . . . I need to meet with the Dauphin right away. I don't have much time to complete my mission."

After a full minute of silence, her uncle leaned forward and rubbed her trembling shoulders, kissing her forehead. His generous gesture of kindness caught her off guard, and she teared up again.

"It's going to be all right, Jehanne," he said. "It won't be like last May. We'll stay with the le Royers for as long as it takes. This time, Baudricourt will listen, and he will listen carefully. I will see to it. I promise."

He stood up from his chair, stretching and cracking his back.

"And you don't have to worry," Durand said softly. "I'll never tell your secret." More to himself, he added, "No one would believe me anyway."

CHAPTER III
The Prophecy

The coming of a savior virgin for France had been foretold for hundreds of years, before the current nations of England and France yet existed. From tales passed through Merlyn, the Sybil, and the Venerable Bede, it was said that, *"France will be lost by a woman and saved by a virgin from the oak forests of Lorraine."*

In war-ravaged France, this prophecy was nearly as sacred as the Word of God. Men and women, the clergy, and itinerant peddlers alike, looked eastward, to the furthest Marches of France—Lorraine—for the arrival of the virgin, their savior.

In 1429, even Charles VII, the Dauphin of France, prayed for such an intercession. To Prince Charles, his country was defined by war. The Anglo invasion of France had begun in 1337 when British King Edward III asked for and received approval from his Parliament to unite France and England under one crown—by whatever means necessary. Since then, France and England had taken turns gaining the upper hand in their ceaseless battle.

After more than forty years of brutal campaigns and barren coffers, an exhausted Charles V, then king of France, died in 1380. Charles VI, eleven years old at the time, was immediately elevated to the throne for the House of Valois. But because of his age, the running of France was left to others. Once he assumed power at age fourteen, he ruled well, building up the national treasury and leading the fight against the English invaders with such brilliance that, at age twenty-three, he became known as "Charles the Well-Beloved."

It was a period of celebration. The new king had married Isabeau of Bavaria, who gave birth to their first son in 1386. But the young king's mental capacities began to weaken, and in 1392, he suffered a crippling mental breakdown—the first of many—a symptom of the disease that would devastate his health and reign.

The administration of the country and its war against the English now fell to Charles VI's wife and two uncles, Philip the Bold, the then Duke of Burgundy, and Jean, Duke of Berry. This proved disastrous for France as Isabeau, a greedy woman, sought both power and lovers without consideration of the consequences for the House of Valois.

In 1403, the king and Isabeau had their eleventh child and final son, Charles VII.

When Charles turned ten, his mother betrothed him to nine-year-old Marie of Anjou and sent him to live with the girl and her mother, Queen Yolande of Sicily and Aragon, known throughout Europe for both her beauty *and* her wisdom. Charles grew quite close to Queen Yolande, eventually coming to refer to her as his "good mother."

At that age, Charles had never thought about the throne. His two older brothers stood ahead of him in line and were being molded for politics under the influence of their mother, together with their uncle, John the Fearless, Duke of Burgundy. But under the tutelage of Yolande, Charles sought active involvement in the affairs of the realm. In 1416, he became captain general of Paris and began to participate in the royal council. In one of his father's final lucid stretches, the king appointed Charles lieutenant general of the kingdom in 1417. By April that same year, both of his brothers had died.

As lieutenant general, Charles received authorization to open negotiations with the House of Burgundy, seeking ways both families could cooperate against the English. John the Fearless had a reputation for trying to manipulate all parties to serve his own expansionist agenda. But Charles was determined not to let his own family down. Until now, Burgundy had been unwilling to commit to engaging in a formal dialogue with the House of Valois under any circumstances.

To everyone's great surprise, the Dauphin reached an agreement with the Duke of Burgundy on a bridge near Melun, France, in July of 1419. The two sides shook hands and signed an official document of friendship, agreeing to meet in September, in the town of Montereau, to further develop their alliance with an eye toward defeating the English.

Nearly ten years later, the memory of that day still made Charles sick to his stomach.

━━◦❋◦━━

THE TOWN OF MONTEREAU
SUNDAY, SEPTEMBER 10, 1419
1700 HOURS

Despite the meeting having been scheduled for two months, tension hung like an invisible fog, pierced gently by the light rain that fell on the narrow footbridge that crossed the Seine. The span connected two cobbled boulevards that paralleled the water and were heavily populated with armed guards for the mutual security of the parties: John the Fearless, Duke of Burgundy, and sixteen-year-old Charles.

The signing of a friendship agreement between the two French factions in July seemed to have stalled the English offensive. Launching an assault against this new alliance would be foolish.

A blessed opportunity beckoned for France—or at least that's how Charles and Queen Yolande saw it—to finalize a united front against the English. The Dauphin's personal hatred and distrust of Burgundy—ensuing from the murder in 1407 of his uncle Louis I, Duke of Orléans, and the attempted kidnapping of Charles during Burgundy's invasion of Paris—weighed heavy in the teenager's thoughts. Also, both Queen Yolande and Charles thought that his brothers had died under suspicious circumstances. The Dauphin could never fully trust Burgundy, but knew he had to put the good of the country ahead of his personal feelings.

Nonetheless, Charles half-suspected that these negotiations might very well be a trap. Witnesses to the negotiations in July had predicted that, in the end, the Dauphin would have to give ground to the blustery Burgundy who had a reputation for getting his way and caring more for retaining his own lands than defeating the English.

Four years before, the English had appropriated some of the duke's holdings in northern France, and the veteran warrior raged he would get revenge against "those arrogant Celtic bastards" who had sought outrageous ransoms for Burgundy's own property.

Charles made sure that he and his entourage arrived on time, knowing full well Burgundy would not. The Dauphin knew by now that the duke made arriving late for negotiations a ploy to create an impression of indifference to the outcome—especially with a relatively inexperienced teenager. But the Dauphin had long ago been schooled by his mother-in-law to expect such provocations and treat them with infinite restraint. He must now take a deep breath and relax.

In expectation of the drizzle, Charles had ordered a temporary wooden enclosure erected in the center of the bridge with one door at each end for entrance and exit to each side; the interior would barely hold twenty men. As he waited for Burgundy on the bridge, Charles cast his gaze in the direction of those advisors he had brought with him to guarantee his safety. To his right stood Sir Robert le Maçon, the forty-four-year-old chancellor of France and one who had saved him during Burgundy's failed attempt to take control of Paris in May of last year. His other two rescuers—Sir Tanneguy Chastel, age fifty, and Sir Jean Louvet, age forty-nine, now stood side by side along the back wall along with six younger, taller, thick-chested men with swords, battle-axes, and maces hanging from their waists.

<hr />

Charles rubbed his temples and closed both eyes, haunted by that night in Paris—May 29, 1418. As usual, he'd had trouble going to sleep in the Paris hotel owned by Queen Yolande; it reminded him too much of his childhood. As the night progressed, the rioting and fighting on the city streets, punctuated by occasional canon and small arms fire, reminded him of how close he had come to losing his life in that same city when he was ten. He couldn't possibly go to sleep as long as the commotion in the streets continued.

An hour after midnight, Maçon knocked on his door and brought him a glass of warm milk laced with "a little brandy," he had whispered with a conspiratorial smirk. Each of the servants chosen by Queen Yolande kept close track of the boy's every move.

"Drink it all and you should be sound asleep within the hour," the older man counseled.

The next thing Charles knew he had been wrapped in a blanket and rug, and tied face-first over the saddle of a galloping horse with the blanket covering his head. His eyes wouldn't open and he couldn't talk. All he could hear was the sound of at least a half-dozen horses galloping at full speed along a dirt road and men muttering to each other about those in pursuit. Soon the group split up and the number of hooves lessened—three horses by Charles's count.

Suddenly the group slowed and trotted into a building, the horses' hoof-falls dampened by the thick air. Somewhere a large door quietly rolled shut. Powerful hands lifted him off his horse and stood him on his feet. They pulled the blanket off his head, and there in the faint light of dawn stood Sir Robert de Maçon, Sir Tanneguy, and Sir Jean all staring at Charles.

Sir Robert smiled and took a deep breath. They were in a barn.

"What happened?" Charles said.

The three men looked at each other for a moment.

"Well, my lord," Tanneguy began, "let's just say that the duke sent several men to find you."

"What for?"

"To take you back to your mother so she *could take care of you,*" added Sir Jean. "You know—like she took care of your brothers."

Charles could barely keep his eyes open. "Where are we?"

Sir Robert stepped forward and wrapped one arm around the boy's shoulders. "Safe. That's what's important. We're going to rest here a while until it's time to begin our sojourn to Bourges—where you'll be completely safe. It's about a three-day ride; we'll travel mostly by night. Meanwhile, you should lie down in this hay and get some rest."

⟶ ⇌✷⇋ ⟵

The sound of approaching hooves on cobblestones echoed up and down the waterway where the Dauphin awaited. Charles looked out over the water to the Burgundy side of the bridge and saw that John the Fearless would soon arrive for the scheduled negotiations. The Dauphinists inside the shelter began muttering amongst themselves, anger lacing their every breath. Charles knew they were remembering Paris too, but did his best not to be swept up in their sentiment. He would remain diplomatic, just as Queen Yolande had trained him.

The duke strolled up his side of the waterway toward the meeting enclosure with ten of his own men directly behind. Charles thought he looked like a man who had just left the arms of his secret lover. Unfortunately, Charles knew Burgundy's lover—the wife of Charles's best friend; the mental image revolted the young man, but he made sure to conceal his roiling disgust of the approaching head of the House of Burgundy.

Once inside the shelter, both men exchanged a slight nod. The duke knelt out of respect for the office of the Dauphin. Rising, Burgundy put his hand on the hilt of his sword.

"You put your hand on your épée in the presence of His Highness the Dauphin?" Lord Jean Louvet shouted.

In the blink of an eye, Tanneguy Chastel lunged forward and delivered an ax blow to the duke's face, crying "Kill, kill!"

Blood splattered in all directions.

Charles's stomach did a somersault before his jaw could even fall open. No no no! How had things gone so wrong so fast?

Sir Robert grabbed Charles, threw him over his shoulder, and ran out of the enclosure on the Dauphin's side, past men-at-arms rushing in.

"Stop!" Charles screamed, heaving down the back of Le Maçon. "This is the wrong thing, you fools! Stop them! Make them stop, please!"

But Sir Robert kept running.

Charles began weeping. "Don't you see? We can never win now!

Burgundy will align with the English. Everyone will blame me."

From inside the enclosure, the clashing swords and stabbing of flesh, like a butcher pounding at meat, filled the autumn air. Burgundy's final scream pierced the late afternoon, followed by a momentary hush.

Horrified, the boy made a hurried sign of the cross.

Deus meus, ex toto corde poenitet me omnium meorum peccatorum . . .

After the assassination of John the Fearless, the war had escalated and the life of Charles had careened into chaos. Queen Isabeau seized the opportunity to ensure her own financial and political future and, the next year, signed the Treaty of Troyes—betraying Charles, her own husband, her family, and all of France.

The treaty struck a major blow against the Valois claims to the French throne, awarding it instead to Henry V of England via an overnight marriage to Catherine de La Valois, Charles's greedy older sister.

The first part of the prophecy had been fulfilled; France had indeed been lost by a woman.

Queen Yolande, out of the country when John of Burgundy died, refused to let her future son-in-law and political protégé be disinherited, refused to let him give up hope. "We have not nurtured and cherished you for the queen to make you die like your brothers," she told Charles, "or go mad like your father, or become English like her. I will keep you here for my own. Let her come and try to take you away, if she dares."

But by August of 1424, the English had hardened their efforts and at Verneuil, Charles's army suffered a devastating defeat. According to most reports, the combined Franco-Scottish forces lost 15,000 men that day, even though they had outnumbered the English better than two to one. The loss left Charles so disheartened he began to wonder if his legacy would ever be anything but death, if his country would ever be anything but torn apart by war.

"O my God," he prayed, "I am heartily sorry for having offended thee, and I detest all my sins, because of thy just punishments, but most of all because they have offended thee, my God, who are all good and deserving of all my love. I firmly resolve, with the help of thy grace, to sin no more and avoid the near occasion of sin. Amen."

Meanwhile, in the fields of Lorraine, a sweaty twelve-year-old farm girl sat resting in the shade of a solitary oak tree.

CHAPTER IV
Miracle In Vaucouleurs

By the time Jehanne and her uncle had fully settled in with the le Royer family in late January 1429, the snow had stopped and the girl began to notice a difference around the city. Word of her mission had gotten out, and people began following her every move. They knew when she slept and when she arose; with whom she spoke and who came to visit her; and, of course, when she went to church and how long she prayed. They even knew how often she went to confession and communion.

All this new attention didn't bother her. Instinctively, Jehanne knew the passion of the local citizens had already made a difference in the governor's attitude. He'd stopped laughing at her and seemed to be giving her some genuine consideration.

She also knew from the cheers of encouragement as she walked about town that the people now believed in her. In less than a month, their attitude toward her had become one of enthusiastic and open support, even among some of Sir Robert Baudricourt's staff. But somehow their excitement had to be channeled into convincing the governor to act.

His words to Durand last year still brought an aching in her heart. "Take this girl back to the home of her father," he had said, "and have him give her a good smacking!"

Jehanne had met with Baudricourt yesterday; her biggest obstacle remained getting him to see her as more than just a girl. The rumors circulating through town that she fulfilled some prophecy were certainly helping in that regard—some of his staff had even reported that he regretted treating her so rudely in May—but this would not be enough.

After her uncle had a few conversations around town, leading merchants and tradesmen began openly organizing donations of men's clothing for Jehanne, as well as chain mail and armor for her expected journey to Chinon, where the Dauphin currently held court—assuming Baudricourt would eventually give his blessing. Some generous noble had even donated a horse!

Alone, in front of a mirror in the le Royer house, Jehanne tried on the trousers, tunics, shirts, and armor that had been collected for her. Even the best of them were ill-fitted to her short stature, and nothing made her look like anything more than a girl playing dress-up. Her nostrils flared. She burst through the door, startling her hosts, and rushed to the kitchen, seizing a knife and disappearing back into the room before they could say a word.

Five minutes later, her long, black locks lay in a heap on the floor. She nodded at her reflection, satisfied. She'd have to find a way to conceal the birthmark on her neck, but mostly she looked like any other young French soldier.

Baudricourt burned with frustration. He had grown accustomed to being well-liked by the people he'd sworn to protect. In addition to making sure his sentries remained ever-ready against a possible Burgundian attack and staying well-informed of the local war situation, he would also—from time to time—go out to lie in wait for wolves on the outskirts of the city. Under cover of darkness, the wild beasts would creep close enough to town to slaughter anything that smelled fresh and edible and afraid.

In the past, whenever the governor had shown up just after daylight, dragging wolf corpses behind him, the populace cheered and thanked him for his courage. But since the arrival of Jehanne, the cheering had turned to indifference. Not only was this change in public enthusiasm disappointing, but puzzling, in that it also seemed to coincide with his discovery of three dead gray wolves he hadn't killed. Who would do such a thing and not brag about it?

With respect to Jehanne d'Arc, Baudricourt knew what the people wanted: to arrange a meeting for her with the Dauphin—nothing more, nothing less. And so, as a cold winter rain pummeled the walled city, the governor paced the stone corridors of the castle from which he governed his district, considering the girl from Lorraine.

For several hours after morning Mass, he had been contemplating his next move with Jehanne. Several days ago, he went ahead and sent a messenger to Chinon to inquire of the Dauphin court. Should Baudricourt find her acceptable, would the Dauphin see her?

He had yet to receive a response, but what could he do to make sure she really was sent by God? At first, he thought he could expose her as a fraud, so he sent a priest to question her. To his surprise, the cleric concluded she was a good Catholic girl—well versed in her faith and most definitely not a witch.

But he had to be certain. If he sent her to the Dauphin and she later proved to be a fraud, his reputation would suffer. But if he failed to arrange a meeting for her, and she really was from God, it might cost not only his job, but his life—maybe even the country. Since she had arrived, Vaucouleurs had been filling up with visitors from as far away as Orléans, Chinon, and Bourges—just to see her, talk to her, touch her. So desperately did the people of France want this girl to be their savior that there was no predicting how they might react if he decided not to send her to Chinon, never mind what the Dauphin might do. He thought back to his brief meeting with Jehanne yesterday.

Once she had arrived, he asked the girl to sit down, remove her still wet hat, cloak, and mittens, and join him in front of the huge crackling fireplace for a short chat. Her long dark hair glistened in the firelight.

"Are you warm enough?" he asked once she looked at ease by the fire.

"Yes, thank you, Sir Robert, I'm quite comfortable."

"Would you like something warm to drink?"

"No, thank you, my lord," she insisted. "As you know, I don't eat or drink very much."

He nodded. "You're probably wondering why I decided to meet with you after sending you away so many times."

The girl shrugged. "You're the governor; you have many demands on your time."

"You know that I really want to send you to Chinon, don't you? That I really want to please the people of this town and send you to meet the Dauphin?"

"How could I know that?"

He sighed. "Because I've told you so, many times, but I still need a concrete indication from God. Something that is a clear sign that the Dauphin and his council would have to agree was undeniable proof that God sent you! Otherwise, you're asking me to take too big a chance. Can you understand that?"

The girl stared at him for a long while, then stood and put on her wet cloak, trying to hold her tongue. "Sir, I must pray. If our Heavenly Father so decides to send a sign, I'll get word to you. I thank you for seeing me and for your kind hospitality."

Before he had time to say anything more, she was gone.

And pray she had. Two members of Baudricourt's military staff, Sir Jean de Metz and Bertrand de Poulengey, had been standing guard in the rain while she prayed. They had reported to Baudricourt late last night, informing him that Jehanne had requested another meeting.

"She says she has what you need."

Baudricourt had nodded.

"She says she will await word from you at the le Royer home."

"You have my grateful thanks, both of you," he told them. "I will call on her tomorrow."

It was all in the Lord's hands now.

Henri and Catherine le Royer were a humble couple in their late thirties. They had enthusiastically agreed to have Jehanne stay with them while visiting in Vaucouleurs. Their friendship with Jehanne's uncle went back to their childhood.

Anytime Jehanne voiced apologies at intruding upon their home and hospitality, they would throw up their arms in protest.

"Nonsense!" Catherine would say. "We have been blessed with this opportunity to assist in God's work!"

Like most of their Vaucouleurs neighbors, the le Royers had required little convincing that their houseguest had been sent by God. They too had grown up with the prophecy about a virgin from Lorraine, destined to save France. But they had learned not to bring it up, lest they embarrass Jehanne.

The main room in their house was one of subtlety and comfort. The doorway to the outside stood in the center of the outside wall, and it held a thick oak door that when opened led down stone steps to today's rain-covered streets. Inside and to the right of the huge doorway hung a crucifix made by Henri, a wheelwright by trade; in fact, he had made nearly all the room's simple and carefully crafted furniture.

Henri sat in one corner of the quiet room, whittling a small figurine. Catherine and Jehanne sat in another, spinning wool together.

Heavy hooves clattered through the narrow streets outside, the sounds stopping at their door. Disciplined boot steps clamored up the front stairs. The door burst open and Bertrand de Poulengey charged in, breathless.

"My Lord Baudricourt," he announced, "is mounting the steps this moment!"

The le Royers and Jehanne stood, her hair still damp from her morning walk back from the chapel.

Baudricourt came through the open door, followed by Jean de Metz.

"You honor us with your visit, my lord," Jehanne said, blue eyes wide. "How may we be of service?"

The governor looked at Catherine and Henri. "I would like both of you to permit me and my two most trusted soldiers to be alone with Jehanne d'Arc."

The le Royers quickly withdrew, shutting the door behind them, and each soldier moved to stand guard at one of the entrance doors.

Baudricourt started to pace, eyeing her sideways.

"My men say that you have a sign for me. What sign? Surely, you cannot mean to sway me with a boy's haircut."

Jehanne chewed her lip and sat down, hands clasped in her lap. "Sire," she began, "you told me at our last meeting that you would arrange a meeting with the Dauphin if you only had a sign that I had been sent by our Father in heaven, something I could only know from Him—that if I gave you such a sign, you would immediately dispatch me with an escort to Chinon. Is that not so?"

Baudricourt continued to stroll, alternately studying the well-crafted floor and the faces of de Metz and de Poulengey. "Aye, I recall speaking similar words."

"Right now, Sire, as we speak, the forces of the Dauphin are fighting a monstrous battle with the English in a town close to Orléans. The Count of Clermont and Sir John Stewart, constable

35

of Scotland, have both been badly wounded. Our forces far out-number theirs, but we are being crushed." She paused and glared at him, watching intently as the confused expression on his face shifted to one of incredulity. "I should have been there to help," she said, crossing herself, bowing her head, and falling to her knees in silent prayer before the crucifix on the wall.

Sir Robert stopped walking and stared at her. He knew there was no logical way for her to know the names of any of the field commanders for the French or the English. She lacked military training, political knowledge, and tactical expertise. She'd never been further away from her village than Vaucouleurs.

No one spoke as rain pounded on the building and streets. Nearly a minute had passed and Robert de Baudricourt continued to stare, jaw hanging open.

"How could you possibly know that?"

CHAPTER V
Rouvray France

300 MILES SOUTHWEST OF VAUCOULEURS
FEBRUARY 12, 1429

𝕿 he Duke of Bedford had been the English regent in France for the last seven years. He had spent most of the winter in Paris where he received frequent reports from his field commanders that, because of the harsh weather, the morale of the French people inside Orléans had reached new lows. Furthermore, his captains claimed, if Bedford could devise a strategy to raise the morale of the English troops, Orléans would be theirs for the taking—more food and weapons would be a brilliant beginning.

The supply convoy consisted of three hundred carts and wagons carrying cannons, ammunition, crossbow shafts, provisions, and hundreds of barrels of herring—appropriate, as the Lenten season approached. Sir John Fastolf, known to French commanders as a ferocious enemy, had been given command of the English resupply detail, along with a thousand mounted archers, southbound from Paris.

Now in his early fifties, Fastolf's military prowess had risen to the point where he had been elevated to the Order of the Garter. Fastolf had little regard for French military acumen—they seemed to lack discipline and patience, something the English military had learned long ago.

On February 11, 1429, Commander Fastolf's convoy reached the village of Rouvray and bedded down for the night, their camp a mere eight kilometers above Janville and no more than thirty-two kilometers north of Orléans.

"Sir," said one of Fastolf's officers, "what if the French attack from the south?"

Fastolf raised an eyebrow at the man. "If they do, we'll just have to hope they don't make things too easy for us, won't we?"

◆━◈✳◈━◆

While heavy winter rain pummeled Vaucouleurs and Jehanne prayed for a sign from God, the weather in central France turned sunny and clear. The ground was still frozen north of Orléans making it a good day to smash the English—at least that's what the Bastard told the other field commanders of the new French army he had assembled, now poised to strike the English at Rouvray.

The Bastard—Jean d'Orléans—had taken two hundred of his men to Blois the day before and redistributed them amongst the thousand Scottish soldiers under the subcommand of the constable of Scotland, Sir John Stewart of Darnley—a staunch French ally with a disconcerting reputation for undisciplined and independent action during battle. Two more veteran field commanders from Orléans, the foul-mouthed Étienne de Vignolles, and his close companion Poton de Xaintrailles, had led their men to join the French and Scottish forces in Blois.

Yet the battle plans had changed. Word came of an English supply detail moving south from Paris headed for Orléans and the Bastard and his men had been ordered to intercept the convoy. He and his two trusted associates, de Vignolles and de Xaintrailles, had been fighting together for Charles VII for years, and on the evening

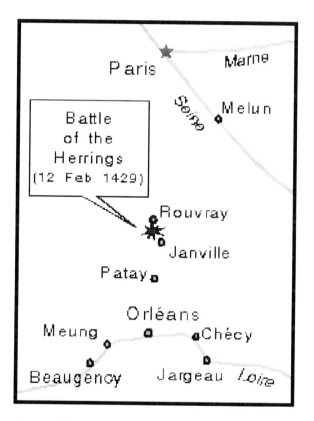

Battle of Herrings battlefield locale north of Orleans

of February 11th, the three comrades-in-arms gathered around a fire in front of the Bastard's tent for some after-dinner libation and private conversation—out of earshot of the other commanders.

The Bastard stood and eyed his guests. "Noble lords and friends," he said, raising his cup, "please accept my deepest gratitude for your joining me in an attempt to keep this new army intact for Orléans—now so badly needed. This entire war may hang in the balance of what takes place in the next few days."

Étienne de Vignolle rose from his chair. Nicknamed "La Hire" (meaning "anger"), he now vented his ire at the endless politicking that was, in his mind, imperiling the future of Orléans and the future of France.

"*C'est tellement stupide!* If Orléans falls, there is nothing to prevent the English swine from flooding south, infesting all of France! Yet we are being asked to divert forces away from the city for what? A supply train? Dammit, my lord!" He hurled a dagger into the ground, emphasizing his point. "By the blood of our Lord Jesus, I want to strangle these politicians and royal councils. They hide behind their closed doors and make infantile decisions that get good Frenchmen killed. They have no idea what it takes to win a battle—let alone a war—and it's our men who pay the price of their incompetence!"

Poton de Xaintrailles cleared his throat. "I completely agree. What is the Dauphin thinking? Sending four thousand men after an English supply train that may or may not exist—and who knows where? Orléans' defense is why this army was put together. Without us, the city has no chance against *Les Goddams!*"

The Bastard nodded slightly and glanced about to see if anyone else was near. "Of course you're both right, but there's no turning back. The decision is made. The only thing we can do now is make certain these men arrive in Orléans in one piece." He carefully studied the scarred faces of his two companions. "Until that happens, we keep our men in line—especially Clermont and Stewart. Are we in agreement?"

The older men remained silent for a moment, exchanged a quick glance, and then began nodding. "Indeed, we are, *mon ami,*" they solemnly agreed. "Indeed, we are."

As the Bastard made his way north with the rest of the new French army, he found himself thinking a lot about his cousin, Charles VII, and what he must be going through these days. Since childhood, the two had stayed in touch and worked closely on many campaigns for the realm.

At age fifteen, the Bastard had taken up arms against the forces of John the Fearless, but the Burgundians had taken the boy captive. Two years later, with the covert assistance of Queen Yolande and loyal members of the Valois administration, the Burgundians released him from prison, only to discover that he had since become acting head of the House of Orléans.

In 1423, after several successful field operations, the Dauphin appointed the Bastard Lieutenant General of the kingdom, and, in that capacity, he defeated the English in 1427 at Montargis. Just last year, as one of France's few recently successful field commanders, the Dauphin appointed the Bastard commander of all troops in Orléans.

Now, as his men marched northward past the city, the Bastard took note of the topography of the immediate area. The land was relatively flat.

"Don't tell me we've done it again!"

Beginning at the turn of the fifteenth century, the once-powerful French army began to suffer catastrophic losses at the hands of the English, who had begun to hold ground where they could easily and quickly dig in, planting long pikes, camouflaging them, and using their longbowmen to funnel the French into the hidden

41

spikes waiting to impale both man and horse.

The French well knew of this strategy, but on the morning of February 12, 1429, by the time the Bastard realized what had happened, it was too late. Fastolf's convoy had halted and circled their wagons into a round makeshift defensive fortification in the middle of the almost-featureless grassy plain.

Unaware of the situation in the dim morning light, the twenty-eight-year-old Duke of Bourbon, Count of Clermont, led a French column into position on the edge of a clearing and told this advance guard to halt. The Dauphin had initially ordered his forces to organize in Blois under Clermont's command, but had later commanded him to join with the Bastard's troops upon word of the English supply train. Clermont felt annoyed sharing command with the Bastard of Orléans, family ties to the Dauphin notwithstanding.

Realizing they had nearly marched into a trap, Clermont barked instructions to be scribbled down by a courier. "All troops will remain mounted except for gunners and crossbowmen. Forward forces will deploy small-caliber cannons and begin bombardment of the English wagons." He paused, waiting for the scratching upon parchment to cease. "Also," he continued, "under no condition are any troops to attack without specific written instructions from me!"

The Bastard carefully assessed the situation. "A direct counterattack by the English against our tight a formation would be suicidal," he said more to himself than La Hire or de Xaintrailles. "Besides, our cannons are well beyond the range of their longbows."

Reassessing Clermont's position, the Bastard couldn't help notice the growing impatience of the Scottish troops and shook his head. He knew Sir John Stewart of Darnley and his Scots cared more about maiming and butchering the English than defeating them. If it hadn't been for the desperate nature of the French military position—especially in Orléans—the Bastard would have recommended Charles send the Scots home months ago.

The Bastard saw that Stewart's troops wanted to break ranks. The discipline required to hold their positions in the unusually hot February sun while the English pummeled them again and again had become unbearable. They were itching for a fight.

"Come on!" a boisterous Scotsman shouted. "We clearly outnumber them at least two to one!"

"What's Clermont waiting for?" screeched another.

Stewart glared at the Bastard from across the field, arms shrugged as if to ask what the holdup was. Wary of the man's flammable personality—and his well-known distrust of young French field commanders—the Bastard called for a courier.

"Send this to my lord Stewart," he said. "My sincere thanks to you, my lord, for holding your position despite the extreme difficulties of your current situation."

Some minutes later, the courier returned with Stewart's response.

GO TO BLAZES!

"What do you think, my lord," La Hire wondered, "are these Scots going to hold?"

"They better," the Bastard replied.

"Some of my men have sent word that Stewart is under heavy pressure from within," de Xaintrailles added. "The Scots may ignore Clermont's orders."

No one spoke as a blast from another French cannon filled the late-morning air.

La Hire shook his head. "Clermont keeps hiding in those trees and sending out orders, apparently unaware of what's going on with Stewart's men!" he growled. "He should be out here talking to Stewart!"

The Bastard took a deep breath. "This will end badly unless we do something to stem the tide. **And quickly.**"

Within the past hour, barrels of herring had been reduced to splinters by French cannon and the dead fish lay all about on the frozen ground near the English supply detail. Surprisingly, the French and the Scots still held their positions.

"*Merde!* That smells terrible!" La Hire grunted, waving a hand in front of his nose.

De Xaintrailles chuckled, but the Bastard was scowling. From within the wreckage of the English fortifications, whole lines of troops streamed out.

"Archers!" the Bastard shouted. Untethered from behind their wagons, he could see that the English longbowmen could now easily reach the French positions. The Scots would probably charge and play right into Fastolf's hands.

The Bastard spurred his horse, riding hard to intercept Stewart.

"Commander, Commander!" he yelled, frantically waving both heavily armored arms. "Do not break ranks. They're baiting you. It's a trap. Hold your position!"

But the Bastard's warning had the exact opposite effect. Seeing him approach, Stewart galloped full speed at the English position. That was all the Scottish troops needed. With a colossal roar, they sprinted after their commander toward the English archers, screaming with a primal rage.

The bait taken, the English fell back inside their makeshift fortifications. Fresh bloodthirsty shouts of "Cowards!" and "Come on, you sons of whores!" bellowed forth from throats of the hard-charging Scots. Led by Stewart and howling like a pack of rabies-filled wolves, the Scots and several hundred inexperienced French volunteers ran straight into a blinding hail of English arrows.

The arrows immediately felled Stewart, tumbling him from his horse with a primal scream, dead as he hit the ground. Fixed pikes impaled the few soldiers on foot who actually made it to the English position.

"*Mon Dieu!*" said La Hire.

"Damn," Clermont shouted. "Damn! Damn Scotsman!" How could this have happened? He had given explicit orders to do nothing without a direct written command from him.

"Sir," said the courier, "what would you like me to say?"

"Tell them to obey their commanding officer!" Clermont spat. "Tell them to ignore their wounded and dead and get back into position. Tell them that!" His breath came in spurts, his men shifting uncomfortably around him. His head felt fuzzy, and he could see spots before his eyes. He pushed fingers into his eyes and shook himself.

"Sir?" Clermont looked up from his hand at the boy. "Is there no way to salvage the situation?"

Clermont wiped his nose with a gloved hand and looked out at the massacre of the forces he commanded, helpless as he saw the Bastard take an arrow in the foot and fall from his horse. He could only shake his head.

At last he said, "Give the order to charge."

Fastolf quickly ordered his archers onto their horses.

"Ride out and strike at their rear flanks," he barked. "Kill as many of those Frogs as you can, then ride hard for Orléans. Go!"

His troops moved out as he mounted his own horse. The officer he had spoken to the night before rode up. "Sir, we really should be going."

Fastolf looked around at the damage to his supply train, much of it destroyed or strewn on the ground. One of his men lay half-buried beneath one of the shattered wagons, leg bones exposed under a broken wheel and begging for help.

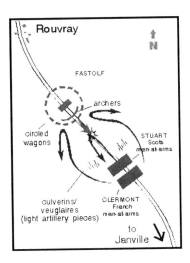

*Battle of Herrings final troop
movements of both French
and English forces*

Fastolf sighed. "Someone should really teach these imbeciles of ours how to use their damn cannons," he muttered. He pointed at the pinned soldier. "Do something to put that man out of his misery," he said to no one in particular.

"They were not too easy, then, sir?" said the officer, offering a nervous smile. "The Frogs, I mean."

Fastolf frowned and shrugged, eyeing the scattered herring. "I was rather looking forward to eating some of that fish. Pity that."

Despite the French's attempt at a rally, striking back at the scattered English and killing a few dozen, it was poor consolation. The new royal French army, organized to liberate Orléans, had been decimated by Fastolf's forces. The Bastard and Clermont were badly wounded and the French soldiers who had traveled with them had been delivered a terrible blow, their morale so fractured it would take a miracle to raise it again.

Several days later, when news of the battle reached Vaucouleurs, the governor could not ignore that Jehanne had accurately foretold the outcome at Rouvray. He had already received word from the Dauphin that if the governor became convinced of the girl's *bona fides*, Charles would see her.

Nonetheless, Baudricourt continued to worry himself: Into what dire state had France fallen that God should see fit to send a farm girl, of all people, to save the country? Why should she to be able to see the wounded French generals three hundred miles away?

With great ambivalence, the governor informed Jehanne of his decision, arranged for six trusted men to guide her through enemy territory en route to Chinon, and presented her with a new horse, warm clothing, and an outer covering of new chain mail.

On February 23, 1429, the detail left with strict instructions:

"Guard her with your life," he told them, "for she holds ours with her every breath."

In Orléans, the people blamed the young Count of Clermont for the disaster at Rouvray. They called him a coward through the streets and shouted for him to leave. They didn't care that he had suffered a serious wound. Poton de Xaintrailles couldn't blame them. He understood Clermont's anger with the Scots, but the man had proven himself a poor commander.

Six days after Rouvray, Clermont left Orléans with nearly two thousand demoralized men-at-arms and announced his intention to visit the Dauphin at Chinon. Regnault de Chartres, La Hire, and a dozen knights and squires went with him.

"I promise," Clermont shouted, "we will return with food, supplies, and more fresh troops. We will come back!"

But the people didn't listen. They didn't care. They even threw garbage at him.

"Waste of good lettuce, if you ask me," said La Hire.

De Xaintrailles chose to remain behind, keeping an eye on the Bastard for La Hire while his wounds healed.

"Awww, look," La Hire had teased, "the Bastard has a bug bite on his foot!"

But once they had taken their leave, de Xaintrailles had a hard time keeping a sense of humor. Morale within the city reached a new low. Heated exchanges broke out across the city, the possibility of surrender growing from a whisper to a grumble to a roar.

"The people want it," de Xaintrailles told the Bastard over a bowl of stew. "They don't care who's sitting on the damn throne. They want to eat."

"It's wrong!" the Bastard insisted.

"Listen, they don't want you to stab Charles in the back. They want to be left alone. Neutrality."

"You do it." The Bastard sipped down the last of his stew. "You're so keen on it, you talk to Burgundy."

"Come on, Jean, you know your name carries more weight than mine."

The Bastard winced as he stood, foot still not healed. He hated when people used his real name. "Here," he said, slamming something down on the table. "Stewart may have been an idiot on the battlefield, but he had a way with words."

As the Bastard of Orléans, limped away, Poton de Xaintrailles slid the piece of paper his friend had left on the table toward him.

"GO TO BLAZES!" in Stewart's hand.

In March 1429, Philip III, the Duke of Burgundy, listened with great interest to a proposal to take Orléans under his protective care as a neutral city. The idea so intrigued the young duke that he rode directly to Paris to propose the arrangement with the English regent, the Duke of Bedford, in person.

Bedford listened patiently, studying his knotted, bony fingers. "Are you done?" he asked finally, voice booming and resonant even at a low volume.

"Excuse me, Sire?" said Burgundy.

The old man leaned forward, aching to pounce. "The only way Orléans will be permitted to surrender is if they do so to me," he said with great emphasis, "personally. I have not toiled there for seven months for the sole benefit of the House of Burgundy."

"Sire, I—"

"You're excused."

Burgundy stood from the table, chair shrieking across the cold, stone floor.

"Thank you, my lord," he said with the barest nod.

Bedford's oily words echoed through the duke's head all the way back to his coach, all the way back from Paris, clacking through his head as the wheels clattered across the stone and the brick and through the mud and dirt.

When he finally arrived home, he called for a courier. "Take a note," Burgundy said when the boy finally arrived. "Inform my commanders at Orléans that they are to withdraw all fifteen hundred of our troops from that siege. We will no longer toil there for the benefit of the House of Bedford."

CHAPTER VI
Chinon, March 1429

The people of Orléans soon received word that a young woman had recently passed through the town of Gien, proclaiming, "My name is *Jehanne la Pucelle*," and that she was on her way to Chinon to see the Dauphin. "The kingdom of France is not the Dauphin's but my Lord's," said the girl. "But my Lord wills that the Dauphin shall be made king and have the kingdom in custody. The Dauphin shall be king despite his enemies, and I shall lead him to his anointing."

She further claimed that she had been sent by God to raise the siege of Orléans, and then escort Charles VII to his coronation in Reims.

These reports came from a credible French military courier who—along with dozens more—regularly delivered top-secret communications from the various war fronts to the Dauphin. This news that a teenage maid of lowly origin would soon bring divine help to Orléans made a huge impression on the morale of those drained by the horrors of the siege. Word of la Pucelle excited them with such a burning curiosity that the Bastard thought it a wise move to encourage this renewed hopefulness. The military situation in the city seemed bleak—a temporary diversion might buy time for him to further strengthen the city's defense readiness.

51

Accordingly, the Bastard dispatched two faithful knights to inquire at Chinon concerning the "special girl" from the Lorraine Valley. One was Sire Archambaud of Villars, governor of Montargis, whom the Bastard had already used to send a message to the Dauphin during the siege. He was an aged knight, once the intimate friend of Duke Louis of Orléans, and an Orléans citizen since childhood. Despite his age, he had vigorously defended the southernmost access bridge to Orléans (*Les Tourelles*) on the 21st of October 1428. The other, Messire Jamet du Tillay, a French nobleman, had recently won great honor by protecting the French retreat at Rouvray with his own men. These two trusted soldiers of distinction immediately began their journey, while the whole city anxiously awaited their report.

Had the visiting military courier to Orléans been more curious about what others had heard in Gien concerning "the Maid," he might have reported the surprising words Jehanne shouted when she rode away from the le Royer home: "I do not fear their soldiers, my way lies open. If there are soldiers on the road, I have my Lord with me, who will make a road for me to reach the Dauphin. I was born for this."

As she and her small military escort (including de Metz and de Poulengy) began their perilous trek across the muddy Burgundian-held territories with rain-swelled brooks and rivers, la Pucelle sought to reassure her six companions: "Fear not: What I do, I do by commandment. My brothers and sisters in Paradise tell me what I must do. It is four or five years since they first told me that I must go to war to restore the kingdom of France."

Later in their tension-filled 525-mile journey behind enemy lines to Chinon, one of her pages noted a shared confidence by Jehanne with those accompanying her on horseback: "I set out from Vaucouleurs in men's clothing. I carried a sword Robert de Baudricourt had given me, but no other arms. With me there were a knight, a squire, and four serving men. Robert de Baudricourt made those who went with me swear that they would guide me well and safely. To me in parting, he said, 'Go, and whatever may come of it, let it come.'"

However, no mere human could have known that Jehanne la Pucelle now traveled toward Chinon for one of the most important meetings in the history of all Europe. Certainly, the Dauphin and his court had no idea of its ultimate importance. To Charles, a meeting with a peasant girl from Domremy—although now personally recommended by the trusted Sir Robert de Baudricourt—would most probably prove to be nothing more than a waste of his time by another deluded opportunist, possibly even a witch.

———※———

By 1429, to say that the House of Valois had become an immoral and dysfunctional family barely clinging to power would grossly understate the situation. The unraveling had begun with Charles VI.

In 1392, Queen Isabeau realized that her husband faced a life of physical and emotional deterioration due to schizophrenia. As a spoiled and pampered former Bavarian beauty, the queen gave up hope for ever having a fully functional marriage and family. She made arrangements to be absent from her husband whenever he suffered periods of insanity, which, over the years, came more often and for longer periods of time.

For her own conscience and peace of mind, the queen arranged for the king's every physical need, including making sure he had access to sufficient mistresses as his needs required. However, during his infrequent periods of sanity, the queen often shared the king's bed, and they produced many children, only eight of whom survived infancy. Their two youngest surviving offspring, Catherine (born 1401) and Charles (born 1403), came into the nurturing care

of Jeanne du Masnil—the long-suffering Valois family governess. Catherine and Charles grew up together on the grounds of a
Parisian palace, the Hôtel Saint-Pol. One of the lesser buildings
inside that sprawling complex was the Hôtel du Petit-Musc, and it
was inside those walls that these two Valois youths received their
lessons and realized how little they were loved during their early
years.

King Charles VI de Valois had a younger brother named Louis
(aka the Duke of Orléans). In 1402, Louis sired a son out of wed-
lock with a married royal woman. Louis gave the infant the name
Jean d'Orléans, which—as soon as he was given the choice—the
boy asked to have changed to the Bastard of Orléans. (Bastard was
not a name of derision in those days.) During a rare lucid moment,
King Charles VI, along with Queen Isabeau, placed the boy in the
care of Jeanne du Masnil, who now operated a three-child boarding
center for the royal family.

No one had thoughts of the young Charles ever becoming king.
On the day of his birth, he stood third in the order of succession
behind older brothers Louis (Duke of Guyene, born in 1397) and
Jean (Duke of Touraine, born in 1398). Consequently, his mother
gave instructions that Charles was to be thoroughly schooled in
the arts, music, games, and comforts of French royalty.

From the beginning, Catherine, the eldest of the three, knew
she was the most pleasing to the eye and tried to impose her will
on Charles. The Bastard now assumed the role of big brother to
Charles—although only a year older, he was physically much bigger and stronger. Charles, on the other hand, from the moment
of birth, was mocked by his family because of his appearance. He
had a long, thick nose too big for his otherwise petite face. Through
large, trusting, greenish-gray eyes, the little French prince looked
out at a world he already knew found his face wanting.

Catherine loved to tease and make fun of her younger brother because he was so much smarter than she; he loved to read, write, paint, and play chess—a game at which he often defeated adults. Catherine seemed only interested in playing with her dolls and pestering her governess for newer clothes, the latest in hair fashions, and riding lessons.

Both Valois children came to hate visits with their father. They occurred infrequently and only by special appointment so his staff could make sure the king was coherent, bathed, and clean shaven—not an ordinary circumstance. On such visits, Catherine and Charles were accompanied by Jeanne du Masnil (Queen Isabeau made it a point to absent herself from such encounters). However, the king reserved the right to invite other members of his court.

The children knew their father suffered from an unnamed disease, that their visits were to be brief, and that they should only speak when spoken to. Both trembled with fear one day in the fall of 1409 as they crossed the marble floor of the king's private meeting room. Their governess remained behind at the doorway.

"Oh, my goodness," the king said from his raised chair. "My sweet little Catherine grows taller and prettier by the day." He extended both hands in her direction. "Come here, my child, so I can get a better look at you."

She did as her father requested, and he bent over from his royal perch, placing a light kiss on both her cheeks.

"I'm here, too," Charles said quietly.

His Majesty picked up his seven-year-old daughter and placed her on his lap. He gently ran chubby fingers over her beautifully coiffed blond hair, then began covering her head and brow with fatherly kisses. "You are such a little beauty."

"Your Majesty," Catherine began, "let me tell you about—"

"Don't forget about me," the boy interrupted loud enough for all to hear.

Several young knights in casual attire, amusing themselves

with a ball in front of a huge fireplace across the hall from where the king sat, stopped and looked in the direction of the loud child's voice.

The king squinted and looked at the knights by the fireplace. "Did either of you hear a strange noise?"

"It was I who spoke," Charles announced.

His father squinted in the direction of the youthful voice. "And who are you?"

"I am your son—your youngest—five years old. My name is Charles."

"Ah, yes," the monarch said, narrowing his eyes a bit more. "Come closer."

The boy followed the instructions.

"Now I recognize you," the king said. "You don't look a bit like me or your mother. You're that little gargoyle child—now I remember . . . one of her fiendish friends, no doubt. And why are you so small? Are you really five years old?"

"Yes, Your Majesty."

The man closed his eyes and placed Catherine on the floor. "I'm afraid I feel a headache coming." He waved at the governess to come take the children.

"But, Your Majesty," Catherine protested, "I have something to tell you."

"Tell me another time," the king said. "This is not a good time to tell me anything."

While Madame du Masnil hurried forward, the boy's father stared down at the child. "I don't envy you, young man, having to go through life with a face and body like that. I just hope you don't end up like me. I wouldn't wish that on anyone."

And as the governess and her two charges bustled away, they heard the king bellow, "Everyone thinks that my brain has stopped working. And the queen thinks I'm stupid and don't know what's been going on around here!"

Du Masnil and the children then heard the sound of running footsteps and a chorus of voices trying to reassure their monarch that everything was going to be just fine, and that he was the most important man in all France.

"Just because I'm sick doesn't mean I'm stupid!" he roared at the top of his lungs. "I'm still the king, and that sow queen of mine better keep that fact firmly fixed in her debauched little Bavarian brain!"

Both children trembled and tears streamed down the face of Charles as they and their governess scurried out of the king's quarters.

By the time Madame du Masnil had escorted her charges back to their private quarters within the Hôtel du Petit-Musc, Charles and Catherine were glaring at each other with such venom that the young Jean d'Orléans thought they would come to blows. It certainly wouldn't have been the first time; Catherine usually overpowered Charles unless Jean intervened. Catherine knew better than to physically challenge the Bastard—his size and strength could overcome boys much older, but he never went looking for trouble. His father, the Duke of Orléans, had always made it a point to remind Jean that physical strength should only be used as a last resort.

The Bastard had been waiting for their return. He put down his paintbrush and easel and wiped both hands. He and Charles loved to paint landscapes with watercolors when they were alone, and there was no one telling them what to do. "So, how was it?" their young cousin wondered, drawing a deep breath. "Did the king remember your names?"

"He remembered mine," Catherine sneered at Charles.

The youngest Valois male sat down by the fireplace and tried to collect his thoughts. Early success on the chessboard had trained him to keep his face blank and think carefully before acting or speaking. It wasn't that he disliked his sister, it was just that she treated him with such hatred.

"Are you going to sit there like a fool and say nothing—again?" Catherine said. "Or are you just a baby whose brain will never work?"

Charles stared into the leaping flames in the fireplace as they popped and crackled.

"Why are you acting like this, Catherine?" the Bastard asked.

"He interrupted me. The king had me in his lap, and I was going to explain to him about my new curls, but Charles kept whining."

Charles continued to study the fireplace.

"Whining?" the Bastard asked, trying to calm the situation. "Like what?"

"I don't know—ask him. It was just stupid and childish." With that she stomped off in the direction of her room.

As Catherine strutted away, Charles turned to observe his sister, then looked back at the fire once she disappeared into her own suite.

The two male Valois cousins became silent for a few moments before the Bastard asked, "Are you all right?"

Charles nodded—barely. "Yes." More silence. "Thank you for asking."

Early in 1413, John the Fearless's Burgundian régime in Paris was routed. During that slaughter, Charles VII barely escaped with his life. No one had any thoughts that he might one day become the Dauphin—since one of his two older brothers would assume that title based on seniority once Charles VI passed.

Toward the end of 1413, Charles became betrothed to Marie of Anjou, the nine-year-old and eldest daughter of Louis II of Anjou,

58

king of Naples, and his wife, Yolande of Aragon. However, Louis II devoted most of his energies to his kingdom of Naples and left the administration of Anjou—located in northwestern France—almost entirely in the hands of his wife. Charles went to live in Anjou, where Queen Yolande—beautiful, energetic, and accustomed to governance—established a lasting relationship with her new young male charge.

In 1417, Louis II died, leaving Queen Yolande as regent and governor of this French duchy. Because of young Charles's vulnerability, Yolande had already developed a great emotional attachment to the boy. In May 1418, he barely survived another round of deadly Parisian political riots. This attempt on his life and the one in 1413 left him emotionally scarred; he was rescued in 1418 by members of his household—placed there as a precaution by Queen Yolande. As the years passed, Charles left no doubt about his fondness for Yolande by often referring to her in private as his "real mother," which in fact, she had become.

———◆━◆———

As Jehanne slowly made her way westward across France in the winter of 1429 to meet the Dauphin, Charles was feeling abandoned and without sufficiently trustworthy allies, close family, or friends. His father had died from natural causes in 1422, and his two older brothers had died under suspicious circumstances while under the care of the House of Burgundy—leaving him highly distrustful of everyone except for his betrothed and her family. In 1422, he'd married Marie, and one year later she presented him with a son.

In the years leading up to Charles's marriage, his biological mother had been busy working feverishly against her son, forming an alliance of convenience in 1418 with the House of Burgundy in hopes of advancing her own political and financial fortunes. Two years later, in 1420, she brokered the Treaty of Troyes that, among other things, labeled Charles as an illegitimate heir to the French throne and effectively handed to the English king the future succession to the French crown.

Queen Yolande, on the other hand, recognized that her future son-in-law needed people in whom he could place his confidence and to whom he could turn for reliable political, military, and financial advice. In as much as she had been trained in the convoluted world of European politics, Yolande became a constant source of insight for the young man she hoped would soon become king of France.

Yolande had begun placing key household staff around the Dauphin before the death of his father. Robert le Maçon first became chancellor to Yolande, and then an advisor to Charles in 1416. Jean Jouvet cemented his connections with the court by the betrothal of his daughter Marie to the Bastard of Orléans. This took place mere days after Charles's betrothal to Marie of Anjou. Another close advisor was the lawyer Jean Dauvet, who would later become one of the young man's most invaluable and trusted associates.

Queen Yolande felt great affection for Charles—almost as if he were her son. In her eyes, Charles, though far from perfect, was a good, well-intentioned, pious, and loving young man who had been deeply wounded by the circumstances of his early life: an insane and distant father; a narcissistic and depraved mother; traumatizing brushes with death in the Paris riots of 1413 and 1418; two nightmarish murders that deeply affected the boy—one of which was his uncle, the other took place in his presence; the inexplicable collapse of an entire floor in which he was holding court at La Rochelle in October 1422 (he survived with severe bruises, while many for whom he cared deeply were killed).

As a young adult, Charles de La Valois remained short, frail, and unattractive. Despite an absence of physical charm, he could be a witty and engaging conversationalist when alone with trusted friends. He loved to read, listen to chamber music and poetry, watch lawn games, and often invited local artisans, artists, and actors to display their newest creations at whichever castle he'd chosen to occupy that season.

At age twenty-six, Charles had a timid public demeanor, hating war, attending daily Mass, and suffering from swollen knees that left him in constant pain. This illness presented a significant impediment for his leading troops into battle which he longed to do in order to gain the respect of his people. After all, that's what his grandfather, his father, his uncles, and most other respected men of royalty did—get on a horse and physically confront the enemy.

Ironically, the fact that he didn't expose himself to the bodily dangers of hand-to-hand combat presented serious problems for those who wished him dead or—at the very least—out of their way. How could you kill a man who seldom left a well-guarded castle? Whether by design or happenstance, Charles left the fighting of bloody battles in support of his claims to the French crown to the noblemen and professional soldiers of his court. The fact that the Dauphin had to fight for himself too often in the equally dangerous battles of his own court left him all the more withdrawn and suspicious. Despite the vigilant efforts of his wife, mother-in-law, and their Armagnac supporters such as the Bastard, several of his key advisors spent long days and nights secretly working against the best interests of the Valois cause.

The worst of these was Georges de la Trémoïlle. The irony is that this man had been recommended to the French prince by two people Charles trusted and who should have known better—Queen Yolande and Arthur de Richemont (at the time Richemont was grand chamberlain of France, but wanted to go out into the field and lead troops into battle on behalf of the Dauphin). As a young man, Trémoïlle had allied himself with the Burgundy faction, then switched sides in 1413 when the Armagnac Party came into power in Paris. At that time, he concluded that the House of Valois and the Armagnacs held all the power cards for the ongoing war with England.

Trémoïlle was of average height, barrel-chested, and possessed several large appetites. In 1416, he married the widow of Jean, Duke of Berry (the second brother to King Charles VI) which gained him immediate wealth and status within the Valois court; that wife mysteriously died in 1422. By 1429, he was forty-seven years old, obese, and even wealthier than before, thanks—in large measure—to his second wife, the duplicitous Catherine de Giac. She had been the wife of Pierre de Giac, one of Charles's apparent friends (it later became clear that de Giac was no friend, but rather, a Queen Isabeau operative) whose murder (unknown to the Dauphin) Trémoïlle arranged in 1427 for his own ends. Catherine de Giac was also a major player in the death of her husband.

At the urging of Queen Yolande and de Richemont, Charles convinced himself that Trémoïlle should be his new and most reliable political advisor. The fact that Trémoïlle made it easy for Charles to borrow vast sums of money—one of the many things in short supply following the death of Charles VI—undoubtedly figured prominently in the young man's decision. Soon after the death of de Giac, Charles appointed Trémoïlle grand chamberlain of France.

Queen Isabeau had a hard time not laughing herself sick when she heard the news. The inexperienced shepherd had now given a wolf in sheep's clothing a free hand as member of the herd. Making the situation all the more treacherous for the Dauphin was his other major endearing—but fatal—character flaw—stubborn loyalty to those he deemed trustworthy. Since he had complete confidence in Yolande, and she had enthusiastically recommended Trémoïlle, why would he ever think to question the loyalties of the latest grand chamberlain of France?

———————⋗✳⋖————————

Lent had already begun when Jehanne and her specially chosen escort left Vaucouleurs for Chinon in late February of 1429. Their destination required them to ride unnoticed around seven enemy-held population centers during northeastern France's severe cold and rainy season. Deep wooded gorges with slippery slopes and ice-covered streams kept everyone in a state of high anxiety. Five overflowing major rivers also had to be negotiated and crossed without drawing attention.

They traveled as much as possible under the cover of dim light or darkness and when they eventually reached exhaustion, they rested in groves or tall thickets. Like the men, Jehanne slept on the ground in her chain mail top, sword always at the ready. Baudricourt's orders had been that she was to sleep between de Metz and de Poulengey so they could protect her in the event of a sudden enemy attack.

At Saint-Urbain, Auxerre, and Sainte-Catherine-de-Fierbois, Jehanne convinced at least one of her escorts to attend Mass with her. Without knowing it, a few enemy soldiers caused her momentary fright after Mass when they teased her about how small she was compared to her large, burly companion. But each time, Jehanne said nothing and let her companion handle the situation—usually by ignoring the taunts.

The village of Chinon lies in midwestern France along the northern bank of the slow-moving Vienne River just before it joins the westward flowing Loire River, approximately seventy-five miles southwest of Orléans. Because the people in this village (population less than 5,000) had remained faithful to the Dauphin and that his military advisors considered the castle virtually impregnable, Charles VII sought refuge there in 1418 after his near-death experience in Paris at the hands of his mother and John the Fearless.

In the ensuing years, it had remained his favorite residence. In the spring of 1429, the Chinon castle still maintained its imposing presence over the village below as it had during its original construction in 954. From the massive edifice, the Dauphin could look northward at green, rolling hills dotted with wild snapdragons and yellow wallflowers, thick woods, and the many vineyards of the Touraine Region. To the south across the Vienne River valley, lush green farmlands and thick forests spread out in a 180-degree panorama as far as the young prince could see.

His fortress had been divided along its length into three enclosures, each separated by a deep moat. The easternmost was known as Fort Saint Georges, the central called the Château de Milieu, while the westernmost was named the Fort du Coudray. The architects of the castle had imbued their creation with "the full grandeur of its imposing bastions, deep fosses, and lordly towers, with formal gardens laid out inside the enceinte [inner fortification walls]."

Jehanne arrived on the outskirts of Chinon, Sunday, March 6, 1429. It was the fourth Sunday of Lent, known then as *Laetare* Sunday or "Rejoicing Sunday." Catholics across Europe celebrated the passing of the middle of Lent—a time of voluntary fasting to commemorate Christ's fasting for forty days and nights before beginning his three-year ministry. And now that she had finally traveled to within twenty miles of Chinon, Jehanne couldn't help but feel a deep sense of joy and humility. With God's help and against all logic, she and her six traveling partners had just successfully traversed hundreds of miles through enemy territory for eleven days and nights on horseback.

While outside Chinon, the girl dictated a note to the Dauphin's messenger, then later explained what she had done to the others: "When we came to Sainte-Catherine-de-Fierbois, I sent a letter to my king to ask if I might enter the town where he was. It said that I had traveled a hundred and fifty leagues to come to help him, and that I knew many things which would profit him."

Jehanne felt proud of her dangerous adventure, yet none of that success would matter, she quickly reminded herself, unless the Dauphin would believe she had been sent by God. Jehanne also well understood that she had little time to accomplish her mission.

———◆———

When la Pucelle arrived inside the village of Chinon, it was near lunchtime. She soon located lodging near the castle with a woman known to be respectable and of strong faith. In keeping with the tradition of Lent, Jehanne maintained the fast that she had begun before leaving Vaucouleurs; once settled in her Chinon quarters, the girl had little choice but to wait and pray.

"The Dauphin knows I'm here," she reminded herself. "Everything now rests in the hands of the Lord. I must wait with faithful patience."

But her waiting did not lack for excitement. Emissaries from Charles began coming and going and asking endless questions, and each time they left in more of a puzzlement than when they first came.

On the second day, a team of four bishops came to visit with no advance notice. Once again, the woman of the house arranged a semicircle of chairs facing away from her large fireplace toward Jehanne who sat by herself in a single chair facing them.

De Metz and de Poulengy kept a close watch on the visitors and within earshot at all times.

At first, the four men of the cloth simply stared at the girl without speaking. Finally, one of the prelates with the least hair and the most wrinkles wheezed, "We understand that you would like an audience with His Majesty. Is that true, Jehanne d'Arc?"

"That is true, Your Excellency," she said.

"Please tell us why you seek such a meeting."

"That I will not do, sir," she replied from between clenched teeth. "I have told all of your interrogators the same thing: I will tell that only to the Dauphin himself."

Thereupon, the bishops set to arguing with her that they had been sent by the Dauphin himself and that anything she said to them would be the same as if she had said it directly to the Dauphin.

With chin on chest, Jehanne kept shaking her head, and they kept insisting.

Finally, the most senior of the four said, "We are busy men, Jehanne. If you're not going to answer our question, then we might as well leave."

They started to rise from their chairs.

With that, the girl took a deep breath, still shaking her head. "We're getting nowhere," she said and raised her head, tears streaming down her face. "I have come with a message from my God in heaven. He bids me tell the Dauphin that I have been sent by God to raise the siege at Orléans, and after that is done, I am to accompany the Dauphin to Reims, where he shall be anointed and crowned."

The four bishops had returned to their chairs as Jehanne spoke, and now they stared back at her once again—no expression on their faces. Finally, the youngest of the four spoke in a deep, authoritative voice. "We have no more questions, Jehanne. We will, of course, convey your message to His Majesty."

With that, the four rose as one and silently paraded from the house.

Unknown to Jehanne, her presence in the village had caused quite a stir, not only among the common people, but among those who the Dauphin routinely turned to for advice. The truth was that military messengers, the clergy, and the merchants from around the Loire Valley were abuzz with Jehanne's journey to Vaucouleurs, and then on to Chinon. For most Frenchmen, it was a miracle beginning to come true. To others, it was news that interfered with their plans.

One group led by la Trémoïlle insisted, "She's no more than a bewitched peasant girl who can do nothing of any real value for a future king!"

Self-aggrandizing men and women claiming to be sent from God had never been in short supply in France. Furthermore, the Trémoïlle group argued vigorously, the only real hope for settling the ongoing war with the English-Burgundian alliance lay in continued secret discussions with the Burgundians. "Allowing this peasant farm girl to stumble into the middle of such a delicate dialogue," Trémoïlle contended, while always bowing and smiling toward Charles, "could only work to the detriment of Your Majesty." Somehow the fact that la Trémoïlle had an older brother named Jean who still served the House of Burgundy as its Grand Master and Grand Chamberlain had originally gone unnoticed by the House of Valois and Queen Yolande.

However, Yolande, her daughter Marie, and their many friends, led a group who asserted that the Dauphin would be well-advised to meet with la Pucelle. By now, Yolande and her close associates knew that Trémoïlle as a trusted advisor had been a mistake, and, therefore, she and her supporters considered Jehanne to be the one ray of hope in an otherwise rapidly deteriorating situation for the Valois cause and all France.

Yolande now understood that the Battle of Herrings had almost cost her son-in-law the city of Orléans. Had Fastolf pursued the defeated French forces immediately following that battle, the city would have fallen under enemy control in February. She also knew that young Charles had made contingency plans to flee to Scotland or Spain on short notice should Orléans fall into English hands. Still, Yolande couldn't overplay her hand—Charles had to fully believe that his decision about Jehanne would be his own.

After much private prayer and meditation, the young prince decided to meet with Jehanne. Besides, the oily Trémoïlle was beginning to annoy the young man—more than just a little—and as long as the city of Orléans remained loyal and under Valois military control, all good things were possible with God.

The single fact that made the major difference in the Dauphin's final decision (a full thirty hours after Jehanne arrived) relied heavily on the note he'd received from Sir Robert de Baudricourt. Charles knew personally that this fierce soldier of France was loyal to a fault and unusually levelheaded in the face of deadly provocation—his courageous and successful defense of Vaucouleurs last year had proved that beyond any doubt. The Dauphin also knew of Baudricourt's high intelligence and ambitions for his future, which meant that the governor of Vaucouleurs would never have recommended Jehanne to the man ultimately responsible for his future without first being absolutely certain of her *bona fides*.

Chapter VII

Jehanne Meets With the Dauphin

Tuesday, March 8, 1429

Jehanne received a formal notice that Charles VII of France would receive her that evening at his residence in the castle. He would send a military detail to escort her.

Darkness had fallen as Louis I, Count Vendôme, and his military entourage—torches held high—slowly made their way down the long cobblestone hill from the Chinon castle into the village, to escort Jehanne to the Dauphin. This grand military detail had come to ensure that Jehanne and her party of two (de Metz and de Poulengy) arrived safely at the apartments of Charles VII.

During the many hours her two faithful nobles had done her bidding for this meeting, many Chinon townspeople—knowledgeable about and sympathetic to her mission—had offered elegant dresses and accessories suitable for such a meeting. But Jehanne decided to wear only the newly washed attire the people of Vaucouleurs had gifted her—a black tunic and leggings, black boots, and a hooded dark leather doublet.

The teenager felt overwhelmed with the excitement, joy, and wonder at the power of the Lord. Just over six weeks ago she had

left Domremy with her uncle—no more than an illiterate farm girl—
and yet, at this very moment, she was on her way to meet the
crown prince of all France.

God is so good.

Nonetheless, she still felt ashamed of how she had left home
without properly saying good-bye to her parents—without telling
them of her intentions. She decided to dictate a letter to them once
she'd met with the Dauphin. She hadn't intended to show disre-
spect or cause worry, but her mother had told Jehanne that her
father was against her taking any trip with soldiers. He informed
their sons he would sooner kill her than allow her to become part
of any military force—Burgundian or Dauphinists.

Jacques d'Arc had had a nightmare that Jehanne, wearing
battle attire, was leaving home with a company of soldiers. To the
"tough-loving" head of Jehanne's household, that could only mean
one thing: she had become a prostitute. He loved Jehanne more
than he knew words to express, but for her to become a prostitute for any reason, and especially to the soulless warriors of this
brutal and senseless war, was something he could not permit. The
possibility that she might have had an entirely honorable and innocent reason for being in the company of French soldiers never
occurred to Jacques—the father, farmer, Catholic, and respectable
God-fearing citizen of Domremy.

Jehanne knew she had to put all that out of her head. She had
to focus her entire energies on the immediate task. She must convince her gentle Dauphin that the Lord had sent her to help raise
the siege of Orléans, and then escort him to Reims for a proper
coronation.

By now, she assumed Uncle Durand had told her family all
he knew—that she had set out from Vaucouleurs for Chinon on a
donated white horse in the company of six soldiers under direct orders from Governor Robert de Baudricourt. If she failed to convince

the Dauphin, the question of what she had been doing the last forty-five days would amount to just that—an interesting tale to share with those who might still desire the meaningless details.

But she had no intention of failing.

———✦———

Approaching the castle, Count Vendôme led his small but smartly attired military detail up the steep stoned roadway through the darkness. A late-winter wind swept across the Vienne and buffeted both horses and riders. With one hand, Jehanne held her black chapeau in place under her leather hood. As the gusts swirled, Jehanne knew that she could expect little or no kindness from members of the Chinon court once she stepped onto the castle grounds.

As a result of their several meetings with the Dauphin and his counselors, de Metz and de Poulengy had vigorously emphasized that essential point to the girl. The growing excitement now felt by citizens of Vaucouleurs, Gien, Chinon, and even Orléans about la Pucelle and her mission made no difference to the courtiers to the House of Valois. The ordinary people of France were no more than pawns to a handful of the cynical men around Charles, many of whom had an agenda known only to themselves.

Within minutes, the Vendôme detail approached the long drawbridge that would lead them under the tall clock tower en route to the Château de Milieu where the Dauphin had agreed to receive la Pucelle. However, as she followed the count and his men toward the drawbridge and was about to cross, one of the castle guards galloped hard toward them.

"Isn't that the Maid?" he shouted. "I deny God. If I had her for a night, she wouldn't remain a maid."

The words had barely crossed his lips when Jehanne flung

them back at him. "Ha! In God's name you deny Him," she shouted, "when you are so near to death."

Within the hour, that guard would be dead, the victim of a chance accident whereby he lost his balance and fell to his death in the moat below.

The military detail then proceeded inside the castle walls without further incident. In silence, Count Vendôme formally escorted Jehanne by the hand up the steps to the grande salle which connected to the Dauphin's well-appointed living quarters on the upper floor.

Jehanne had never been in a building so beautiful in all her life. Its elegance, ornate furnishings, and luxurious appointments left her breathless, but she kept reminding herself to stay focused.

Dinner had already been served and consumed long before the count formally announced Jehanne, la Pucelle, to the assembled nobility. By now, the expensively dressed French aristocrats had packed the room. Some felt surly and angry at the decision by Charles to permit such a public effrontery by a country peasant girl. Others looked forward to an evening of mindless frivolity at the farm girl's expense, but all longed to view this latest uncouth curiosity. In their minds, Jehanne held the same level of interest as a troupe of acrobats, a company of actors, a magician, or even a juggler—low expectations for someone they hoped would take their minds from the defective nature of the Valois court and the perilous state of the war against the English.

As she entered the large dining room, Jehanne could scarcely believe its enormity, nor did she expect the hundreds of people packed elbow-to-elbow to observe her. Overhead more than fifty torches lined the richly tapestried walls and blazed like small suns. A large hooded fireplace supplied more than enough warmth to offset the late winter cold the girl and her royal escort had just ridden through.

A sudden pall filled the room as all eyes stared in dismay at the small, young peasant woman, dressed like a boy. Before Count Vendôme could escort her toward the young gentleman dressed in royal attire, now assuming a disdainful pose in the king's elevated chair, Jehanne pushed back her hood, and removed her hat. Her closely cropped dark hair had matted against her head and her attire was that of a young French male. She was about to curtsey when she stopped herself and carefully studied the man currently occupying the chair of prominence. He didn't look anything like what she'd been told in Vaucouleurs. She bowed respectfully in his direction, then cast her eyes about the room.

Murmurs and gasps of disbelief buzzed through the hall. Men and women of all ages had assembled: some were clean-shaven nobles—thin and narrow shouldered of slender build, lean legs in tight hose, and feet in long, pointed shoes; some were bearded and dressed in robes and furs; and there were numerous fully armed barons—pushing, crowding, and elbowing for a better view while the royal usher flitted everywhere, trying to maintain a semblance of decorum.

They had come from near and far to see the Maid from Domremy, about whom they had heard so much. The two special emissaries from the city of Orléans were there, as were the Count of Clermont, Sir de Gaucourt, La Hire, and Sir de la Trémoïlle, and the Lord Archbishop of Reims, chancellor of the kingdom.

But Jehanne had little interest in making any of their acquaintance at this particular moment. She hadn't come all this way in the freezing cold and rain through the dangers of enemy-held territories to meet with a gaggle of self-indulgent, strutting peacocks.

The room buzzed with a secret amusement, and Jehanne sensed that some game was afoot. Slowly she scanned the room for a distinctive male in his twenties whom she hoped her "visitors" would help her recognize. Finally, she bowed once again in the direction of the young man playing his role on the Dauphin's throne, and then turned toward one of the thick, wooden support beams that ran from floor-to-ceiling. Behind the massive post stood a short, frail young man, dressed like a page, trying desperately to go unnoticed.

What kind of game is he playing with me? she whispered to herself and walked straight toward the undersized male.

The girl stopped a few feet from the young man, curtsied deeply without rushing, and said, "Gentle Dauphin, I am Jehanne the Maid. The King of heaven sends me to you with the message that you shall be anointed and crowned in the city of Reims, and that you shall be the lieutenant of the King of heaven, who is the King of France."

Muffled gasps and whispers filled the room.

The man dressed as a page replied, "It is not I who am the king, Jehanne. There is the king," he said and pointed in the direction of the young man sitting on the throne.

He wants to see if I can really pick him out of this crowd.

"In God's name, noble prince, it is you and none other," she said gently.

The Dauphin blushed and quickly conceded to his clumsy ruse. He then took Jehanne aside toward a corner of the room and instructed his guests, aides, and advisors to stay away—completely out of earshot.

Jehanne's heart beat so fast she thought her chest might explode. Sweat beaded up on her forehead and small droplets ran down her spine. She was about to have a conversation with the crown prince of France. This is what she had been working for with every fiber of her being for the past three years.

"Jehanne the Maid," he said, so only she could hear, "what would you like to tell me?"

Please, dear Blessed Virgin Mary, help me find the words.

The girl forced herself to swallow, then whispered, "I bring you news from God, that our Lord will give you back your kingdom, bringing you to be crowned at Reims and driving out your enemies. In this I am God's messenger. Do you set me bravely to work, and I will raise the siege of Orléans."

The Dauphin squinted hard and looked directly into her large blue eyes.

He wants to believe me, Lord. What will convince him?

"Sire," she said, "if I tell you things so secret that you and God alone are privy to them, will you believe that I am sent by God?"

"I cannot say what I will do, but I am interested in what you have to say."

She swallowed again.

"Sire," she said, "do you remember that on last All Saints' Day, being alone in your oratory in the chapel of the castle of Loches, you requested three things of God?"

The prince took a step back. How could she know this? Staring intently at her he answered, "Yes, I recall."

Thank you, dear Jesus. He's beginning to really listen.

"The first request," she began, "was that it should be God's pleasure to remove your courage in the matter of recovering France, if you were not the true heir, so that you should no longer be the cause of prolonging a war bringing so much suffering in its train.

"The second request was that you alone should be punished either through death or any other circumstance, if the adversities and tribulations which the poor people of France had endured for so long were due to your own sins.

"The third request was that people should be forgiven and God's anger appeased if the sins of the people were the cause of their troubles."

Please, dear Father in heaven, help me. Right now.

The Dauphin's face turned ashen, and he again scrutinized her for several moments.

What should I do if he says he still doesn't believe me?

"Jehanne the Maid from Domremy," he whispered, "indeed, you have spoken the truth."

Charles then cleared his throat and addressed his guests, face still ashen. "Until further notice," he announced, "Jehanne la Pucelle will make her residence within the Chinon castle walls as my guest, and she should be treated accordingly. Any mistreatment of her would be construed as a direct affront to me and the House of Valois."

Furthermore, he told her, he planned to see to it that she would immediately have her own household staff and that she was free to come and go as she saw fit.

Jehanne's mind reeled out of control. She wanted to jump up and down for joy, but knew better.

Thank you, my dear Lord. Thank you, sweet and glorious Mary.

The fact was that Dauphin had found Jehanne so intriguing he went to great pains to have her watched around the clock under the guise of calling her an honored guest, housed in the royal apartment of Fort du Coudray. He longed to believe that she'd been sent by God, but dared not without concrete and independent confirmation. Lord knows he'd been misled before—the Battle of Herrings being only the most recent example.

Against his will, Charles had been impressed by Jehanne beyond any words he tried later to express with his wife, mother-in-law, and the most dependable members of his Council. La Pucelle was like no one he had ever encountered—a sense of God's perfect love invisibly radiated from her being.

Also, this simple farm girl had inexplicably known—according to the note Charles had already received from Baudricourt—the outcome of the Battle of Herrings almost exactly the moment it took place, and she had accurately predicted the death of one of his armed guards while en route to her first meeting with him: Already he had been informed of the foul-mouthed guard at the drawbridge who had stumbled and fallen to a watery death.

But those incidents aside, Charles still found himself unable to adequately explain what made Jehanne so special.

More mysteriously, by the next morning, word of his meeting with la Pucelle had spread across the country and touched off a wildfire of hope and elation that raced unchecked—especially in the minds and hearts of the French peasants and men-at-arms in and around the city of Orléans.

CHAPTER VIII
Is She or Isn't she?

Once the Dauphin announced that Jehanne would be his houseguest for the foreseeable future, confusion filled her thoughts. She had no idea why her host referred to her as "an honored guest." If the Dauphin thought her so "honored," why couldn't she simply get on a horse and ride to Orléans and start fighting the English that very day? Her divine visitors had told her many times that she had less than a year to complete the major parts of her mission.

Jehanne felt better when the Dauphin motioned for Jean de Metz and Bertrand de Poulengy to come over from where they had been standing and watching the evening's festivities. Jehanne had no idea what Charles had in mind once her two friends arrived, but she liked having them close. At least *they* were her friends.

An instant later, an older man and woman came over and briefly conferred in private with the Dauphin. He then introduced his majordomo Guillaume Bellier and his wife to Jehanne. "They will do everything they can to make you feel at home; they stand ready to meet your every need—day or night—or answer any questions. You'll find them to be most kind and thoughtful; Madame Bellier is also known to spend a lot of time in prayer. You both should have much to talk about."

Jehanne smiled graciously and said, "How do you do?"

Monsieur and Madame Bellier nodded.

Not knowing what else to do, Jehanne curtsied in response to their nod.

"No, no, my dear," said Madame Bellier. "That's not necessary. You're the guest—*we* serve *you*."

She then led the girl and her two male companions outside into the blustery night toward Jehanne's new residence in the Tour du Coudray section of the castle. De Metz and de Poulengy posted themselves at its entrance. For the moment, Jehanne didn't know what else they should be doing.

Essentially, a tall masonry tower that connected to the Dauphin's residence via a large drawbridge, Jehanne's new residence had a huge circular stairway, but only one room per floor in addition to an attached chapel to which only she had access. Originally built as a place for professional archers to conceal themselves as they rained down arrows onto outside attackers, it had since been converted to a residence for special guests.

Having shown Jehanne her new quarters on the top floor, Madame Bellier then introduced fourteen-year-old Louis de Contes who had just arrived with an armful of blankets and clean sleeping clothes for Jehanne. "He will serve as your personal page," she said. "You understand that he is your personal servant while you are here, don't you?"

Jehanne nodded graciously at the boy and smiled. "Yes, madame, I do now. Thank you."

Madame Bellier continued: "Louis will be here with you each day from dawn to dusk at which time several older women from our staff will keep you company downstairs in separate bedrooms until dawn. If you feel the need to bathe or for warmer fires, or the like, just let one of us know. Feel free to take your meals here or with

His Majesty. As his honored guest you have unlimited access to him and a standing invitation to take your meals when and where he does."

The older woman took the blankets and bedclothes from the boy and began making up the bed for Jehanne.

Louis sprang into action to assist Madame Bellier.

"Also," the woman continued, "in case you're wondering about your two male companions, Louis will show them where they can find comfortable quarters just outside this apartment. They can billet in with the palace guard, but they're not to stand guard for you. We take care of that, but they're more than welcome to accompany you as your guests wherever you wish to take them."

"Thank you, madame. You're most kind."

Madame Bellier studied Jehanne for a moment. "What happened to your neck? Is that an old injury?"

Jehanne blushed and placed a hand over the right side of her neck. "No, madame, it's a birthmark. My mother says they run in her family."

"I see," said the older woman, still inspecting the girl with her eyes—head to toe. "Are the clothes you have on the only ones you brought?"

"Yes, madame," Jehanne said while observing the older woman's expert touch while preparing the girl's bed. Already she felt sleepy. "I have others where I was staying, but I'm used to washing my own clothes each day," she continued, "just before going to bed."

"That won't be necessary while you're here," Madame Bellier said matter-of-factly. "Give whatever clothes you need washed to the women when they come each night, and they'll have them back to you before you rise each morning. Also, if you wish additional clothes, simply make those needs known to the overnight women as well. His Majesty wants you to feel completely comfortable while you're his guest."

Once again, Jehanne bowed. "Thank you so very much, Madame Bellier. You are so very kind."

"Just doing my job, Jehanne." The older woman took a deep breath and looked around Jehanne's bedroom. "I believe we're done here. Do you have any questions?"

Louis stood to one side out of the way.

"No, madame. Thank you."

Madame Bellier continued to study the girl. "When was the last time you ate a full meal?"

Jehanne shrugged. "I don't eat that much these days. It's Lent."

"While you're a guest of His Majesty, you need to eat regularly. He would take great offense if you refused his food. He employs some of the best chefs in all Europe and takes great pride in the meals we serve."

"Madame Bellier, I wish no offense, but—"

The older woman put her hand up to signal that she expected Jehanne to stop speaking and listen. "Not to worry, my dear. I'm going to the kitchen now and will have the chef make you a light snack—some hot tea, warm biscuits, cheese, and stew."

She looked around to make sure she hadn't overlooked anything.

"Louis, when the clock strikes at the quarter hour, come to the kitchen and bring Jehanne her tray of food." She paused to look Jehanne directly in the eye. "I suggest you eat some of what he brings—it will make a good impression on His Majesty."

Jehanne took a deep breath as Madame Bellier disappeared down the stairway.

The girl and the young man stared at each other. "Louis," she said finally, "would you please go down and introduce yourself to my friends and show them where they are to spend the night. I'm going to the oratory now to give thanks to our Father in heaven."

Louis remained silent for a moment, then spoke quietly. "I

prefer if you would call me Minguet. That's what my friends call me."

Jehanne studied the boy. "Are we friends?"

"I would like that to be so."

"Why?"

"Because you're on a mission to serve our Lord God. That's a much different situation from what I've been doing lately. I very much want to serve the Lord too."

Jehanne sat down on her bed and closed her eyes. "And who have you been serving lately?"

"His Excellency, Sir Raoul de Gaucourt, governor of Orléans."

The girl frowned. "And why have you been now assigned to me?"

"It's mostly about my age—only three years younger than you. They're hoping that you won't suspect that I'm watching you. I'm supposed to make daily verbal reports on everything you do and who comes to see you and who you go to visit or spend time with. I'm even supposed to try and overhear your prayers."

"Indeed?" Jehanne blessed herself and knelt on the floor. "And who gave you these instructions?"

"The governor himself."

"And who do you report to?"

"His wife. She stays here when he goes on business to Orléans."

"Has he already left for Orléans?"

"Yes. He left soon after His Majesty introduced you to the Belliers."

"I see."

Jehanne closed her eyes in silent prayer, slowly shaking her head side to side. Finally, she stood and faced the boy. "Minguet, are you in the state of grace?" she asked, looking him in the eye. "Did you receive Holy Communion this morning?"

"Yes, and I plan to stay in the state of grace and attend daily

Mass. I have dedicated my life to the Lord since I became a page. Needless to say, I'm hoping to one day become a knight, but that's years in the future. Right now, I want to serve the Lord by serving you."

Jehanne nodded slowly. "All right then . . . all right. Henceforth, we are friends." She shook his hand. "Thank you for sharing that information about Governor de Gaucourt and being so straightforward about his instructions to you. I want you to always tell me the truth of what you hear and what you report, but I don't want you to do anything that would jeopardize your job. Do we have an understanding?"

"Yes, Jehanne, we do."

She smiled ear to ear and gave the boy a quick sisterly hug.

"Now, go get me that tray of food from the kitchen so I can make a good impression on the Dauphin and his chef. And maybe you can help me eat some of the food too. When I'm fasting, my appetite for food goes away, but not my need for sleep. Tonight, I think I will sleep well for the first time in many days. In fact, I'm looking forward to at least three or four hours of deep rest."

While the residents of Chinon slept soundly that night, the Dauphin and Jehanne had no idea of the firestorm of yearning, expectations, and hope they had unwittingly unleashed across the rolling hills and valleys of France inside the minds and hearts of millions of their fellow countrymen.

By dawn the next day, news of their dramatic meeting reached the ears of Duke Jean II d'Alençon, twenty-three-year-old handsome and married son-in-law of Duke Charles d'Orléans. Alençon had originally learned the news of Jehanne's arrival in Chinon on March 6th. He then learned of her new honored guest status while en route to Chinon from his home in Saint Florent, prompting the young duke to rush the rest of the way to visit his longtime dear friend Charles to see firsthand what all the commotion was about. Just who was this seventeen-year-old girl from Domremy?

Alençon was only too aware that he had a lot of catching up to do regarding the French military situation versus the English—especially at Orléans. He had been captured by the invaders in 1424 at the Battle of Verneuil and held for an extraordinarily high ransom ever since. While in captivity, he received little current news of the war and was finally released less than a month ago—once his family and wife raised the necessary funds. He couldn't help but wonder if the French military had so deteriorated that they were now going to enlist females into the ranks of professional men-at-arms.

As Duke Jean d'Alençon rode through the breaking dawn toward Chinon, life in the Dauphin's castle on this new day had already begun with a trumpet blast at sunrise; some of the castle's long-term servants had already begun fires in the kitchen and great hall while also preparing a small breakfast for the lower-class servants. Soon they would all begin the daily task of sweeping the common area floors of any debris, and washing out basins. Laundresses would then begin the day's wash.

Once the Dauphin, his wife, and family got up and dressed, chambermaids would enter their bed chambers, sweep their floors, empty their chamber pots, and wash basins. The first of the two main meals of the day for the Dauphin and his guests would be served between 10 am and noon. And before that, Mass would be said in the family chapel. The Dauphin made it a point to attend Mass three times every day.

Going back to his childhood, Charles had received religious instruction so he would have better understanding of his faith and the critical role it might play in his life as a man, a husband, a father, and a possible heir to the throne. Queen Yolande took on this assignment once the boy came to live with her in 1413; she made it a personal priority to explain about their shared Catholic faith and how Jesus had died on the cross on Good Friday so that all people would have a chance to live forever in the presence of a God who loved all humankind equally.

When the trumpet announced the beginning of this new day— the first day that Jehanne would spend as a special guest of the Dauphin—she was already awake and on her knees, deep in prayer in her own small chapel. The older women hadn't left yet, but it didn't matter what they did; she had nothing to hide. The girl knew they had been watching her every move all night, hoping to unearth something they could take to the Dauphin to discredit her mission for God.

Dear God in heaven. Thank you so very much for bringing me safely to Chinon. Thank you for blessing me with the brave and loyal men who made sure I was secure at all times. Please forgive me for causing them so much concern as I sought to attend daily Mass, despite the risks. But most of all, dear Lord, thank you for my most blessed meeting with your dear, gentle Dauphin. Remembering it all still fills me with so much joy and wonder I can scarcely think about it—the Dauphin actually believed me!

While Jehanne prayed, Minguet came back on duty and the older women left—still in a dither about how much time the girl spent in the oratory. "All she does is pray," they complained to Madame Bellier. "It's just not natural for a girl her age to be doing so much praying. She barely slept a wink."

At the proper time, Minguet interrupted Jehanne and informed her that Mass for the Dauphin and his family would begin in a few minutes. As she left the Coudray Tower building, de Metz and de Poulengy awaited her and together with Minguet, the four made their way to the Dauphin's chapel.

As soon as they walked in, Jehanne noticed that this place of worship was bigger than the church of her village. As the Mass continued, she couldn't help but notice the graceful arches, the high ceilings, and bright stained glass windows. At the end of Mass, she remained in prayer for a few moments but eventually left the handsomely appointed place of worship. Her old friends were waiting across the hallway. Charles had stopped in the foyer to the chapel to join an animated conversation with some of the people she recognized from last night.

Stunned by the elegance in which the Dauphin lived, Jehanne glanced down the long ornate hallways with their marble floors and walls decorated with vivid tapestries. She suddenly noticed a tall, good-looking, and muscular young man walking toward where she stood. He had a slight smile on his face, but she knew she had never seen this man before—she would certainly have remembered his handsome face.

Just then Charles walked up beside her and whispered, "The gentleman approaching is Jean, Duke of Alençon, my cousin. Walk with me so I may introduce you."

After the appropriate preliminaries, the Dauphin presented Jehanne who greeted the duke with a wide, delighted smile, saying, "I am so happy to meet you. The more who are gathered together of the royal blood of France, the better."

Charles chuckled. "Well said, Jehanne."

D'Alençon returned the girl's cherry smile. "I, too, am most grateful to meet you, Jehanne," he said. "My wife and I have heard astounding things about you."

"What things?" she asked.

"How you and a few good men traveled more than 150 leagues on horseback through flooded enemy territories without injury, mishap, or capture. That was truly an amazing accomplishment."

Charles nodded his agreement.

Jehanne blushed. "God rode with us day and night. He's the

reason we made it."

Charles continued to nod while he took her full measure. "You mostly stay in the presence of the Lord, don't you, Jehanne?"

She shrugged. "I try to, my gentle Dauphin. Sometimes I forget—especially when I don't know what to say."

D'Alençon smiled approvingly. "I'd like to have a chance to talk further with you about your mission," he said. "How would you feel about that?"

"I would welcome it," she said. "I want to make sure that all men and women of French royal blood understand that God has sent me as their friend and helper. That is my only mission. And I have less than a year to get it done."

"Why don't we discuss it in more detail right now?" Charles said.

"Who?" Jehanne asked.

"Myself, Jean, you, and one of my advisors," Charles said.

"And who that might be, dear cousin?" d'Alençon wondered sarcastically.

"Monsieur Georges de la Trémoïlle, Lord Chamberlain of all France," said the Dauphin. "He often has interesting points to add to our discussions."

D'Alençon shook his head and rolled his eyes.

"I think a discussion would be very helpful," Jehanne said. "I'm ready to meet and discuss at your convenience, Your Majesty."

Within minutes, the Dauphin had a meeting room near the chapel prepared and the four gathered around a huge oak table.

Charles introduced Jehanne to Trémoïlle who merely nodded dismissively in her direction and plopped into his seat with a snort. Despite his great wealth, power, and expensive clothes, Jehanne couldn't help but notice that he smelled as if he hadn't taken a bath in weeks.

"Since I'm the least knowledgeable about your mission,

Jehanne, would you be so kind as to start from the beginning," d'Alençon said.

"Of course."

Jehanne then launched into a complete history of her relationship with her divine visitors and how they began coming to her in her twelfth year. She pointed out that at first they asked her to lead a good and holy life, but in her fifteenth year they started talking to her about her leading military forces into battle. In 1428, they told her that she needed to go to Orléans and help defeat the English. After that, her visitors wanted her to escort the Dauphin to Reims and arrange for his coronation.

"And when these visitors come, do you actually see them?" asked d'Alençon.

"Sometimes," Jehanne answered. "In the beginning, I always saw them, but now I mostly just hear them talking to me."

"Really?" said Trémoïlle. "What do they look like?"

"That's not really important," she said. "What matters is what they say. The first time Saint Michael visited me, he told me that everything was going to be fine, and I shouldn't worry. At that meeting, he stood at least two and a half meters tall. It took several more visits from him before I felt at ease."

Charles had been studying her. "So what are these visitors telling you today?"

"Just what I've been telling you, Your Majesty; that I need to hurry to Orléans and help defeat the English before it's too late."

D'Alençon looked puzzled. "What does that mean?"

"It's the same thing I've been telling everyone," she said. "I have less than a year to complete my mission—defeat the English at Orléans and lead my gentle Dauphin to Reims. These are the only things the Father has told me to do."

"This is ridiculous," snorted Trémoïlle. "Here we are listening to a farm girl prattle on about how she's going to defeat the English military at Orléans. I don't think I've ever heard anything more ab-surd, and the fact that we're taking what she says seriously makes us all appear to be fools."

"Calm down, Trémoïlle," Charles said sternly. "You're losing sight of some important facts. In the first place, she's already been vetted by some of the brightest theological minds in the realm, and I'm not nearly through with that process. Believe me when I tell you that the vetting process will be thorough with no detail overlooked.

"Secondly, her farming background has nothing to do with her mission. If God has chosen her to carry out His mission, that's consistent with what has He done throughout history. Look at the Virgin Mary and Joseph and Moses and Samson and David and Noah and Paul—the list is endless. God knows exactly who He wants to carry out His missions and why. That's one of the core beliefs of our faith.

"The most important question we have to decide is . . . is Jehanne really from God or is she from somewhere else? Our pre-liminary indications are that she is from God, but I intend to make sure that we have explored this subject in every aspect. Until that question is answered to my satisfaction, she is to be treated with complete respect by all of us.

"To sum up, Trémoïlle," the Dauphin said, "I think we need to be more open-minded in our assessment of the situation. None of us here are fools—especially Jehanne."

Trémoïlle nodded and smiled patronizingly. "But Your Majesty, so much more is at stake here than if an obscure farm girl is from God. As you know, we have ongoing in-depth negotiations concern-ing other more delicate aspects of this whole matter."

Charles took a deep breath, then exhaled slowly. "My dear Lord Chamberlain, there is no reason to speak here in euphemisms concerning our discussions with the House of Burgundy. It's no secret that if we could partner with them, the English invasion would be over in short order. So, of course, we're going to keep the lines of communication open with them. We would be fools to do otherwise."

Trémoïlle squirmed and recrossed his legs. "But if it appears to Burgundy that we intend to commit more troops and supplies to Orléans with or without him, what incentive does he have to join with us? What's in it for him?"

D'Alençon shook his head slowly, puzzled. "Monsieur Trémoïlle, why are you so concerned about the feelings of the House of Burgundy? They withdrew their troops from the siege in a huff because they couldn't get their way with Bedford so as to gain control of Orléans. With that blunder, they have now relegated themselves to spectators in what will probably prove to be the most important battle of the war. If they really wanted a place at the table, they'd come join with us now."

Trémoïlle stood, hands on hips, glaring at d'Alençon. "With all due respect, Duke, a naïve statement like that does you and your service to our country a great disservice. All of us here know perfectly well Burgundy is never going to join us without an apology from His Majesty."

The room became quiet as the large man paced.

Jehanne scowled. "Why is Monsieur Burgundy expecting an apology from our good Dauphin?" she said. "He's done nothing to him. Besides, we don't need the House of Burgundy to defeat the English. Send me to Orléans, and it won't make any difference what he does. God has told me that we will win, and I believe Him."

Charles watched Trémoïlle striding back and forth, took another deep breath, then yawned. "We seem to be talking in circles. I suggest we adjourn and table this discussion to a later date—when we have more information."

D'Alençon smiled. "I agree, my liege. A little food and spring sunlight will give us all a chance to give this matter some quiet and careful thought."

Jehanne's face clearly indicated her disappointment, but she forced a smile and said, "That sounds like a good idea, Your Majesty, but every day I'm not in Orléans is another day the English could defeat us. We're running out of time."

Charles nodded. "Yes, yes, Jehanne. I understand about your mission. For now, let's take a break and have dinner. Surely after all this talk, you must be hungry."

The girl had not been feeling hungry at all, but chose not to argue the point. She was his guest and, therefore, pretended to have a mild interest in the biggest meal of the day—one she seldom ever observed, especially during Lent.

Just before dinner began, Charles arranged for Jehanne to sit alongside d'Alençon. By now, there could be no doubt she enjoyed talking with the duke and that the feeling was mutual. Maybe this turn of events would prove a better way for Charles to learn more about his "honored guest" without having more "learned men of the cloth" ask her endlessly insulting questions.

Beyond his wildest hopes, Jehanne and the duke spent dinner laughing and sharing endless stories from their earlier lives. Right after dinner, Charles fully intended to ask his cousin what he had discussed with the girl and what was so funny, but they disappeared before he had a chance. Next thing he knew both of them were on horseback in the fields of the castle racing toward each other at breakneck speeds, lances at the ready while both joked and laughed as if they'd known each other since childhood. Their lessons of horsemanship—filled with laughter—lasted for several hours.

Later that afternoon, when Jehanne and the duke had assured themselves that their horses were being properly groomed and fed, she walked to her quarters to pray and d'Alençon sought out the Dauphin in his office.

Having a difficult time concealing a smile, Charles leaned back in his chair. "Well, my handsome cousin, you and Jehanne seem to have enjoyed yourselves at dinner and in the fields. She appears to have a penchant for humor and horsemanship."

"As always, my liege," the duke said with a smirk, "your powers of observation are beyond compare." He nodded silently for a moment, gathering his thoughts. "From all I'd heard before meeting her, I would never have expected her to have such a cutting wit and clever sense of humor. Not only that, but she tells me she had never ridden a horse until she arrived in Vaucouleurs, but between there and here she has become a horseman of high skill and command. She needs a little more practice in defending herself with sword under battle conditions, but I'll have her well prepared in a few days. If you had any concerns about her ability to handle a horse or herself in combat, you can put those thoughts to rest. She's one tough warrior and unbelievably strong! She would never embarrass herself or France."

Charles scowled and scratched his forehead. "Really? . . . . Before today, I had heard reports from her Vaucouleurs detail to that effect as well, but thought they might be exaggerating. But your report fully corroborates them, which is a most pleasant surprise. I now have strong evidence to answer those who wish to marginalize her because of her gender. You've done me a great service, Jean!"

The duke shrugged and bowed in jest. "Glad I could help, *Cousin.* Anytime!"

"She seems too perfect," Charles continued, slowly shaking his head. "From other reports I'm getting, all she does is pray, eat like a bird, and practice for combat. She's a seventeen-year-old farm girl. How can she be so dedicated—she never plays?"

D'Alençon took a deep breath. "You know what, Cousin? Sometimes you think too much. Why can't you just accept the fact that she's been sent by God? Don't you believe that God answers prayers?"

"Of course I do!"

"Well, then, what's your problem? Give her a horse and armor and let her go do what God sent her for. If you think she's a liar, send her home. It's that simple."

"No, it's not!" Charles stood up from his chair and began pacing. "It's much more complicated than that. There're what my Royal Counsel thinks and what my generals think. And don't forget what my wife and Queen Yolande think. Then there's—"

"But what do *you* think?" d'Alençon interrupted.

"You know . . . ." Charles sighed and stared out a window. "I have no idea what I think. That's why I pray night and day. I just don't know."

"Is Trémoïlle the one you're really worried about?"

"There can be no doubt—he's a *large* problem," Charles said, smirking.

D'Alençon covered his mouth to keep from laughing. "So, do you believe her?"

"Yes, but I need others to believe. Trémoïlle will never believe— he's too busy with his own agenda. That's why I need to make sure everyone else understands how careful I've been to establish that she's not a witch—beyond any doubt."

"And how are you going to do that?"

"Make sure all the ranking clergy in Chinon have had a chance to interview her."

"And then what?"

"Send her to Poitiers for a few weeks and have our good church doctors cross-examine her until they run out of stupid questions. She's already endured numerous interrogations by local clergy both in Vaucouleurs and in the Chinon village even before I sent for her. She seems to revel in leaving her examiners speechless."

D'Alençon closed his eyes and ran both hands through his thick dark locks. "Jehanne is frustrated by the endless questions. She's ready for battle right now, but you seem most interested in watching her parry and thrust with arrogant church academics. What do they know of battle? They're useless old men, Cousin."

"That's true. But I still must observe all the traditional protocols for them to see their way clear to write a favorable report about this girl. Also, I need to buy a little time for my investigators to journey to Domremy and question her family and neighbors. You know that Trémoïlle will use his vicious operatives to unearth something he can use to discredit her—anything at all!"

D'Alençon nodded, deep in thought. "So, assuming that you have the bishops' favorable report in hand and your investigators' favorable report from Domremy, then what?"

Charles scrunched up his lips and shrugged. "Then she will have to pass her most difficult test. It won't take very long, but it will be the most meaningful."

"What are you talking about?"

"I'm afraid that's all I can tell you for now . . . maybe later."

During the ensuing days, d'Alençon and Jehanne continued to practice on horseback the art of one-on-one combat—as time and opportunity allowed. Often they practiced and discussed military strategy for hours at a time, but always mixed with a combination of laughter and growing mutual respect.

But after the committee of bishops from his own Chinon Court reported that they could find no fault with Jehanne, on March 11th, Charles accompanied his "honored guest" on a fifty-mile journey to Poitiers. Since the fall of Paris to the English in 1418, Poitiers had served as a substitute court or parliament for those who wished to receive a non-Anglo-Burgundian interpretation of French law because the enemy still controlled France's capital city and all its governmental bureaucracy.

The trip took two days. Charles provided lodging for the girl in Poitiers with Jean Rabateau and his wife—a couple the Dauphin knew he could count on to keep a close eye on Jehanne. The couple had an oratory where she spent most of her spare time, which her hosts dutifully reported. Privately, Jehanne told the Rabateaus, "I know that I shall have much to do in Poitiers. But my Lord will help me."

Meanwhile, d'Alençon returned home to his wife and family, and, as Charles had predicted, Jehanne came through the Poitiers interrogations by recognized theologians and academics with a strong endorsement. One of their members wrote: *"Finally, after long examinations by the clergy of several faculties, they all deliberated and concluded that the king could legitimately receive her, and allow her to take a company of soldiers to the siege of Orléans, because they had found nothing in her that was not of the Catholic faith and entirely consistent with reason. Her incontestable victory in the argument with the masters of theology makes her like another Saint Catherine come down to earth."* For his own reasons, Charles decided to keep Jehanne in the dark about what the learned men of Poitiers had reported.

Chapter IX
Why?

onetheless, by now, the **girl's temper** had begun to bubble up, and she found it **more and more** difficult to maintain the fiction of a gracious exterior. She knew she lacked experience in these matters and tried her **best to accept** God's will, but so many of the questions by the **clergy and professors** were ones she'd answered many times before in **Vaucouleurs**, in Chinon, and now in Poitiers. By now they must **know she's not** a witch.

Jehanne stared up at the **crucifix in the** small chapel in Poitiers. "Please forgive me, dear Lord," **she whispered.** Tears ran down her cheeks. "I know I should be **doing something** about these endless questions, but I don't know what. **Please help me!"**

On March 22nd, to relieve **her frustration** from the barrage of inquiries and loss of valuable **time, Jehanne** sat down in private with her page and dictated a **letter to the** English, giving them notice that she would soon be **coming to Orléans**, and that they would be well-advised—for the safety **of their troops**—to remove their men from the siege. Afterward, she **told her page** to hold onto the letter for the time being.

By March 24th, Charles had **what he needed** in writing from the theologians of Poitiers, so he sent **the girl back** to Chinon with word that her testing to date had gone **well. "But I still haven't heard the** final reports from my emissaries to Domremy and Vaucouleurs," he informed her just as she was about to climb into the royal carriage for the return trip to Chinon. "However," he continued with an impish grin, "you may begin fittings for a new suit of battle armor and a sword for self-defense."

Jehanne's heart leaped for joy, and she began kissing his hand. "Thank you, Your Majesty. Thank you. Thank you. You have no idea how happy you've made me!"

Charles blushed. "You're most welcome, Jehanne, but I had nothing to do with it. You did it."

She stopped kissing his hand, studied him for a moment, then bowed.

"No, Your Majesty, I did not do it," she said quietly, moved by the love she felt for the Lord. "God did it all, and He'll keep on bringing you excellent reports until you finally decide it's time for me to go to Orléans and do what He has sent me to do."

She whirled, pulled herself up into the carriage, and slowly shut the door.

Please help me, dear Lord. I'm having trouble with my temper.

From inside the carriage, she said to him, "Every day, my gentle Dauphin, that goes by without me being in that beleaguered city is another day the English could attack with their superior forces and newly arrived food and ammunition stores. Are you comfortable with that possibility?"

The Dauphin blushed with anger. "Of course not!"

He took a deep breath. "Jehanne, I wish you a safe journey back to Chinon; I'll catch up with you in a few days. I think I'm going to have some more good news for you when next we meet. God bless and keep you safe, Jehanne."

He nodded to the coachmen and guard, and they galloped away with the young "honored guest" still trying to say something to her host—something he never heard.

On April 2nd, Jehanne sent a single messenger to the church of Saint Catherine at Fierbois to look for a sword she claimed was "buried in the ground behind the altar." Back in February, Jehanne and her escort had briefly stopped there en route to Chinon, but no one of that Fierbois church knew or had ever heard of such a sword.

Nonetheless, when Jehanne's messenger dug into the ground exactly where she told him, he did find an old rusted sword. And, as soon as he and the others began cleaning it, the rust fell off and the sword revealed itself to be battle-ready with the same five crosses Jehanne had described to her messenger.

News of Jehanne's second "miracle" raced across France like a rogue windstorm.

Meanwhile, on April 5th, the Dauphin received the long-awaited reports from Vaucouleurs and Domremy. Again, his loyal agents could find not a single person to speak against the seventeen-year-old girl. In fact, when her family in Domremy heard that she was the guest of Charles VII, her mother broke down and sobbed until she fell asleep.

When Lassois had originally told the woman that her daughter had left from Vaucouleurs "in the company of soldiers," so deep had been her grief that she wept nonstop for days. Yet now, Jacques d'Arc, learning of his daughter's Christian safety, gladly allowed two of his sons—Jean and Pierre—to make the journey back to Chinon with the royal investigators as a loving surprise to his astounding daughter.

What no one there except the Dauphin knew was that Jehanne had been moved to Tours for her final test. The girl had no idea what test would come next. Charles simply told her before she left in the royal carriage that the test she would now face would be the most important one of all. "None of the positive reports from

Domremy, Vaucouleurs, Chinon, or Poitiers will matter if you don't pass this final one."

"What is the test?" she asked.

"When you arrive in Tours," he said, "Queen Yolande will host you. She'll explain everything. She likes you, and you can trust her."

As the Dauphin's carriage made its one-day journey to Tours, Jehanne prayed to know what to do about her upcoming test. It occurred to her that it might be about her virginity since that subject seemed the basis for many of the questions she'd been asked.

Jehanne understood the popular myth about Satan and young women: if they were a virgin, they could not be a witch. However, if she were not a virgin, then it was believed that her virginity could have been lost to Satan. But since Jehanne knew she was still a virgin, she foresaw no problems. In her mind, she expected that a group of older women would ask her questions about her virginity and try to trick her into answering their questions in ways that would leave some doubt as to her current virgin status.

When Jehanne arrived in Tours, Queen Yolande greeted her and escorted her guest into the older woman's own private living quarters. There she introduced the girl to Madame de Gaucourt, wife of the governor of Orléans, and Lady de Trèves, wife of Robert le Maçon. "These ladies and I have been asked to thoroughly investigate you concerning the issue of your virginity."

"I understand," Jehanne said. "Thank you for your kind and generous hospitality."

The beautiful older woman smiled. "And thank you for your generous agreement to our test procedures. Have they been explained to you?"

Jehanne frowned. "No . . . .What test procedures? Do you mean that you're going to ask me personal questions, and I'm supposed to provide truthful answers?"

The three older women exchanged a quick glance. "No," Queen Yolande said matter-of-factly, taking a slow, deep breath, "that's not what we mean."

She knew her son-in-law meant well, but for him not to have explained what she and her committee had been instructed to do surprised the queen. She and her associates fully understood that Jehanne would be discredited immediately if the examination showed or claimed that she was not a virgin. As a proven liar, she would then be sent home, her mission with its claims of authority and integrity ended.

These royal women also knew that in the eyes of most French nobility, the test of virginity was, above all, a proof of sincerity. In the Europe of the early fifteenth century, men and women who consecrated themselves completely to God showed their acceptance of the divine call by remaining virgin and hence autonomous, totally at the Lord's service in heart and body, without division of responsibility.

Queen Yolande carefully explained how she and her assistants would be conducting the physical examination, then tried to reassure her. "It's going to be all right, Jehanne. You have nothing to worry about."

The girl began to cry. The fact that she must completely undress in front of three virtual strangers made her sick to her stomach. And then they would do unthinkable things. She wept at the thought of complete strangers putting their hands all over her naked body and violating her. Yes, they were women, but so what?

Why is God allowing this to happen?

On her knees, she begged Queen Yolande to deliver her from this horrible violation of her privacy and gender.

But the three women led Jehanne in silence to one of the empty royal bedrooms and quietly asked her to remove all her clothes, then wrap herself in a bathrobe.

100

Jehanne tried to steel her thoughts and think of something joyful like when the Dauphin told her that she had passed all her tests, but she couldn't stop crying.

Queen Yolande then asked the girl to sit down on the bed. "Jehanne," she said gently, "we completely understand how upset you are about this, and we don't blame you. I don't know if I would allow this to happen to me, if our roles were reversed. So you are going to have to make a choice: you can either let us proceed with what we have to do, or you can refuse the test and go home. But I'm not going to force you to go through with this. You can agree to let me proceed or you can tell me to stop."

Jehanne closed her eyes.

Why are you doing this to me, God? Everything I do is for you!

"Yes, I want you to proceed," she told Queen Yolande. "I didn't come all this way to be sent home. I won't betray my Lord or my gentle Dauphin." She braced her mind for this ugly moment to be over and sent her thoughts to God and her visitors.

Lord, how can you allow this to happen to me? Why won't you protect me?

Queen Yolande kept repeating softly, "It's going to be all right, Jehanne. We're so sorry to have to do this. You understand why we must, don't you?"

Jehanne nodded, tears running down her face.

Why is this necessary? Why have you left me all alone? Where are your visitors? Why aren't they helping me? I wish I'd never agreed to do any of this. I could be home with my mother and father and brothers, helping with the chores!

After a few moments, the royal elder women completed their assigned tasks and two of them left the room in silence.

Queen Yolande remained. "It's all over now, Jehanne," she whispered. "It's just as I said—everything is all right. We found exactly what I knew we would. His Majesty had to have proof, and now he does. You'll be going into battle soon, my dear. May God go with you always."

She gently squeezed Jehanne's small hand and left.

Jehanne slowly put her clothes back on and lay down on the bed, curling herself into a fetal position. She didn't care that she couldn't stop her weeping.

Why did you do this to me, dear Lord? I don't understand! I'm so sorry for losing my temper. Please help me with my temper, Father. I love you with all my heart, but my temper is like the snake in the Garden of Eden.

⊷≫✳︎≪⊷

With the news from Queen Yolande that Jehanne had passed the virginity test, Charles pronounced her a full-fledged field commander. In accordance with her new station, he kept his word and assigned Jehanne a full-time household retinue that reported only to her: Louis de Contes (nicknamed Minguet), her old page, and Raymond, a new page; Jean d'Aulon, a thirty-nine-year-old squire and steward, formerly in the employ of the Dauphin; two young heralds named Ambleville and Guyenne; two servants; and her two brothers, Pierre and Jean; and finally, her own priest and confessor, Jean Pasquerel.

Sires Alençon, de Metz and de Poulengy would not be a part of her immediate household per se, but Alençon had been appointed to serve Jehanne as a military tactics consultant. Moreover, de Metz and de Poulengy had already pledged themselves to her service back in Vaucouleurs with the tacit approval of Sir Robert de Baudricourt as well as his ultimate superior, Charles de la Valois.

Jehanne reluctantly accepted these tokens of generosity from "her gentle Dauphin" with as much grace as she knew how. In private, she told Jean d'Aulon, "I've come to realize that everything

I do reflects on the Dauphin. If he desires that I maintain the outward appearances of noble birth, then I will try to do as he asks. "I can see how it might benefit us both: he in his dealings with Trémoïlle and the rest of his difficult advisors, and I in my future dealings with fellow field commanders, as well as the political leaders of Orléans.

"However," she sighed in confidence to d'Aulon, "the ordinary families of France have little patience with such hollow matters. What they care about is for me to hurry to Orléans and send those ruthless *Goddons* back to where they came from."

D'Aulon nodded agreement and added, "All in God's time, my dear Jehanne. All in God's time."

Without consulting her, Charles had a second set of armor made for the girl. He also decided she had insufficient horses to complete her mission, so he ordered five coursers (battle horses) and seven trotters for the everyday "coming and going of your entourage," he said. He further authorized Jehanne to order her own field banners.

Unable to read or write, she dictated an unusual design: a white twelve-foot standard fringed with golden silk. Against that background, her artists painted a picture of the world supported by two angels along with a portrait of Our Lord and the words "*Jhesus Maria*," set to one side. One of the angels in her design held a fleur-de-lis, symbol of France being blessed by God.

Jehanne fully understood that all these outward symbols of nobility and rank would mean nothing if she couldn't regain her focus on what God sent her to do. But something strange had happened to her during her examination by Queen Yolande.

"I don't know how to explain it," she told Jean Pasquerel the next day in chapel, "but I feel as if I want to scream and jump out of my skin—like I've done something wrong and can't get it out of my mind! And then there're those horrible nightmares every night."

"Do you think going to confession would help?" he asked.

"Yes. Can we do it now?"

"Of course."

She knelt in front of him. "Bless me, Father, for I have sinned. It's been one day since my last confession."

"And what sins would you like to confess?"

"That's just it. I don't know what sin I've committed. I don't know what it's called, but I feel as though I've done something against God."

"Like what?"

Tears began to flow down her cheeks. "Maybe God wanted me to refuse to let those women in Poitiers examine me to see if I was female or in Tours to let Queen Yolande and her friends put their hands on me and in me to see if I was a virgin."

Father Pasquerel sighed and considered his next words. "Jehanne," he began, "you and I both know you had no choice but to allow those tests—you did not ask for them. But without them, your mission had no chance."

The girl openly sobbed and rolled down onto the floor.

Pasquerel bent over and handed her his cloth handkerchief.

Gradually, she brought self under control. "You're right, Father. I know."

He sat quietly, waiting for her to look him in the eye. "Doing God's will is often the most painful choice, but if we offer it up and submit to His will, He can use our suffering for good.

"No one ever said doing God's work was easy. Look at the Blessed Virgin Mary. Look what she had to endure. And look at what Jesus had to endure—both He and His mother fully obedient to the Father's perfect and loving will. And what about Saint Joseph? Think about all he had to go through to do God's will."

"But they were all adults. I'm just an unschooled farm girl— barely seventeen years old."

"You think our Father in heaven doesn't know how old you are? Besides, Mary was only fourteen when she conceived Jesus. Age has nothing to do with God's work. He chooses us all for a reason. We don't have to understand, just obey. That's what free will is all about. Each of us can choose to turn our back on God or answer His call."

He paused while she pushed herself up onto her knees.

"Is that what you want to do now?" he asked. "Say 'No' to God?"

She scowled and blew her nose. "No! I want no such thing! I want to do His work, but don't understand what I'm feeling and what to do about it."

"You realize, Jehanne, that Satan and his army of helpers are trying to distract you from doing God's will. All these crazy feelings you're telling me about is Lucifer lying to you so he can distract you from your mission. You need to pray to the Blessed Virgin Mary, Saint Michael, and Saints Catherine and Margaret to inter- cede with Jesus to protect you from Satan and to help you keep focused."

Jehanne nodded and looked up at the crucifix. "You're right, Father. I'm such an unholy sinner!"

I'm so sorry, dear Lord, for having doubted you and offended you. Please forgive me for feeling angry at you, dear God. Blessed Virgin, Mary, please help me!

Pasquerel remained silent for a time. "Listen, we're all sinners, Jehanne. We're all sinful humans, and God knows that. Jesus died on the cross for us anyway. We have bad feelings from time to time. We get angry at God sometimes. God doesn't mind our having bad feelings. What He does care about is what we do about our bad feelings.

"Do we turn our back on Him, or do we sincerely ask forgiveness?

Remember, *everyone* has bad feelings. It's what we *do* that matters!"

"So what should I do," Jehanne asked, "about my anger at God at having allowed me to feel so badly about what those powerful women did to me?"

Pasquerel took her by the shoulders. "Look at me, Jehanne."

She moved her eyes from the crucifix to the priest.

"Here's what I think," he began, "you need to throw your feelings on the back of an imaginary horse and put the horse in your imaginary stable, with the promise that you're going to come back to it one day soon.

"Meanwhile, you ask forgiveness of our dear Father in heaven and His guidance and courage to help you get on with what He sent you to do." He studied her eyes. "Can you do that, Jehanne?"

Tears kept seeping from the corners of her eyes. She wiped them with his handkerchief and began to nod. "Yes, Father, I can do that. But first I have to stop crying. We need to pray for me to stop my crying, Father, right now!"

Word quickly spread throughout the French people that Jehanne would be soon leading troops against the English. In Orléans, women, children, shopkeepers, and old men ran cheering into the streets. Able-bodied men left their homes and traveled from all over France to be a part of Jehanne's new army now gathering at Blois. They and their ancestors had been praying for a "maiden" for as long as anyone could remember.

The English had also received news that this unusual teenage girl would be soon coming to do battle in Orléans. In late April, they received a dictated letter dated March 22, 1429, of proposed truce terms from Jehanne in which she promised no further loss of life for the English army if they would abandon their siege. The English hierarchy—those who thought of themselves as kind and Christian—considered her terms impertinent and insulting in the extreme; for those less concerned with kindness and the teachings of their Catholic faith, they considered her letter the ranting of a deranged, ignorant French witch and teenage whore. What other explanation could there be?

CHAPTER X

Time Running Out for Orléans

During this same time frame, the Duke of Alençon often rode by the home of Madame Jean duPuy where the Dauphin had made arrangements for Jehanne to stay while in Tours. It was here that she had met her new household staff, and it was here that she had taken her first bath in over a month after learning that she had just been appointed the newest field commander in the French army. Since that day, Jehanne and her staff had been working long hours, preparing the details for her move to Blois where her new troops had already begun to assemble.

Seeing all the feverish activity, Alençon withheld the news he needed to share with Jehanne for a few days, but finally couldn't wait any longer. One day toward the end of April 1429, he paid a visit at the home of her host and asked one of her staff if he could see Jehanne in private. When she learned that Alençon had come to see her, Jehanne let out a small squeal and bounded down the stairs of the large home, grinning ear to ear.

They exchanged a brief hug, and she led him to the oratory where she knew they would not be disturbed and closed the door. She was dressed in new riding clothes because she still practiced

108

her riding every day under battle conditions simulated by her staff; she insisted that they force her to use both sword and shield.

Arms akimbo and still smiling at being in the unexpected presence of her dear friend, she said, "Well, my dear Duke, to what do we owe the honor?" There was a twinkle in her eye. "A little birdie told me that you've been seen riding by this house, but clearly you were too busy to stop and say 'hello.'"

Alençon took a deep breath and sat in one of the pews. "Clearly."

Jehanne sat in a pew behind him, forcing him to turn around to see her face.

An awkward silence filled the small place of worship, and Jehanne could see in his eyes that something troubled him.

"Seriously, Jean, what would you like to talk about?" she said.

Alençon stood and began pacing. "I wanted to share something with you in person so you wouldn't misunderstand."

"Misunderstand what?"

He stopped and looked her in the eye. "Charles has asked me to take personal responsibility for organizing the new troops assembling in Blois."

Jehanne scowled. "You bring wonderful news. I can now rest easy that the men there will be well-ordered and disciplined. Why tell me this in private?"

"Because I have unpleasant news."

"What?"

"I probably will not accompany you to Orléans."

Visibly stunned, the girl stood and walked toward the altar, looking up at the cross. After a few moments of silence, she quietly said, "Why not?"

"Because there's too much to do in Blois. Even after you leave for Orléans, much will remain to be done and approved by His Majesty and Queen Yolande."

"What's she got to do with it?"

"She's the one who has put up most of the money for all these new troops; in case you didn't know, she's always been one of your strongest supporters."

Jehanne turned, face ashen, and came toward Alençon. "Really, Jean? Queen Yolande is one of my biggest supporters? How is that possible?"

Alençon nodded. "She always has been—from even before your first meeting with His Majesty."

Jehanne shook her head in disbelief while tears suddenly welled up and the girl began to cry.

"What's the matter, Jehanne?" he said, greatly puzzled. "What's wrong?"

She knelt in one of the pews and blessed herself, body quivering as she tried to stem the tide of tears. "I'm sorry, Jean," she mumbled, "I need to be alone to pray right now. . . I beg you to just leave . . . I'm so sorry, Jean."

Still puzzled, Alençon started for the door. As he was about to open the door, he turned and said, "You won't be seeing much of me in Blois—there's too much to do."

Jehanne nodded, unable to stop her weeping.

———◆⋗✳⋖◆———

On April 21st, Jehanne received official written word from the Dauphin to proceed to meet her new troops at Blois. The journey would require three days. It was the first time the girl had worn her new silver suit of armor; it was heavy, hot, and a poor fit despite the fact that it had been custom made.

Nonetheless, she decided not to take it off until it was time to rest that night. She had to get accustomed to wearing the clumsy mechanism, she reminded herself, without allowing it to distract from her meeting her new troops and their field commanders.

Her stomach whirled and ached, yet she could hardly wait for the meeting to take place. The Bastard of Orléans and La Hire were to meet her there. She'd heard great things about each man and held them in high esteem; but before she could meet them, she faced the daunting task of mounting a horse, dressed in her armor, and then completing the thirty-three-mile journey to Blois on horseback. She'd never thought to practice for that.

Young Minguet wrote in his journal: *"I saw her mount one of the great black chargers from the Dauphin, a little (battle) ax in her hand, armed entirely in the silver armor, but for her head. The horse, which was making a great fuss before the door of her lodging, would not allow her to mount, so she asked one of the men from her staff for help. From astride her horse, she then organized the rest of her household retinue, the priests, and the other contingents who would accompany her to Blois."*

On April 24, 1429, Jehanne and those who rode with her arrived in Blois. During the three-day journey from Tours, the girl and Father Pasquerel gave the upcoming meeting with her new troops considerable thought and prayer. They agreed that the fighting men had to know from the beginning that each of them would be going into battle for God and that He would want them to stay in the state of grace. That meant daily Mass, confession, and communion. That meant no foul language. That meant prostitutes would no longer be welcome around Jehanne's new army.

The girl fully understood that she would be taking a huge chance—one that might result in many of the men who wanted to fight for France changing their minds. "With God," she said to Father Pasquerel, "we can't say that we want to follow Him, if we're not going to match our words with deeds. Mostly, God cares what we do."

Later, Jehanne and her spiritual advisor also decided that she needed to begin her relationship with the men by meeting with her good friend, the Duke of Alençon. What better person to introduce her to her fellow French field captains?

Thus agreed, Jehanne asked Pasquerel to have a new banner made in addition to the standard and pennon she'd already had made. However, this new banner instead of floating backward from the pole, would act as a religious, rather than a military rallying point and hang from a crosspiece and look like one of the banners carried in religious processions. The image on this banner would be that of the crucified Christ.

On the day Jehanne and her party arrived in Blois, she soon proceeded with de Metz, de Poulengy, and Father Pasquerel, to the tent of the Duke of Alençon who, in short order, arranged a meeting with several of the field captains who had already reported for duty: Gilles de Rais, Charles de Bourbon (the Count of Clermont), Admiral de Culan (commander of the king's navy), Ambroise de Loré, and the maréchal de Sainte-Sévère. "Many others are on the way, Jehanne," Alençon told her. "You're the talk of France."

At the meeting, her staff stood aside and after appropriate introductions, Jehanne asked Alençon and those present for their permission to address some of the assembled troops in small groups. "My prayer," she explained, "is that these introductory talks will be nothing more than an informal exchange with the long-suffering fighting men of our country. My intention is to present an opportunity for them to meet me in a relaxed atmosphere and to understand that they'll be fighting for God and France."

With these words, she quickly glanced in the direction of Alençon, who was by now scowling. "'Fighting for God and France?' What does that mean?"

Jehanne swallowed a smile. This is what she and Father Pasquerel had expected.

"It means," she said, her face turning slightly red, "staying in the state of grace; no more swearing and no more prostitutes in camp."

Alençon looked incredulous. "You think that the fighting men of France are going to agree to that?" He shook his head and smirked as if he were about to lecture a young child. "Jehanne, you're free to talk with any of the men here as you see fit, but don't be surprised if they laugh in your face."

"Hear, hear," chimed a few of the other commanders.

Jehanne now took a deep breath and cleared her throat. "Does that mean all of you are going to laugh in my face too?" She peered into the eyes of each man.

No one spoke.

"These rules are for everyone," she said, raising her voice slightly. "No exceptions!"

Alençon looked at the ground still shaking his head. "When did you get this idea, Jehanne?" he said. "I don't ever remember you mentioning it before."

"Mentioning it before?" she said, her voice quivering higher with emotion. "From the beginning, I've told everyone, including you and His Majesty, that I've been sent on a mission for God. If I'm on a mission for God, what else would you expect from me but to insist that everyone who wants to join in my mission also be committed to doing God's will? How can any of this be a surprise?"

The maréchal de Sainte-Sévère began nodding his head. He was one of the veteran French field commanders of many campaigns; in 1426, had been appointed marshal of France. Sainte-Sévère also enjoyed universal respect throughout the French military.

"I agree with Jehanne," he said in a deep baritone voice. "I came to Blois fully prepared to comply with whatever requests she made. If Jehanne wants me to stay in the state of grace, stop swearing, and throw all the prostitutes out of camp, that's fine with me. I'm interested in only one thing—stomping the *Goddons* and sending them back where they came from!"

Alençon blushed. "I'm sorry, Jehanne. I misspoke. Of course, if you want me to refrain from swearing, stay in the state of grace, and banish prostitutes from the French army, then be assured of my full support. But that's a long way from getting our fighting men to agree with your rules."

"Thank you, Duke and Seigneur de Sainte-Sévère, for your support." She glanced into eyes of the three other commanders. "May I assume that I have the full support of all present?"

Everyone nodded.

Jehanne flashed a wide smile. "Thank you once again, kind sirs. Now if you will excuse me, I would like to start talking with the troops."

⸺►⸙⚹⸙◄⸺

As soon as Jehanne returned to her tent, she went to confession with Father Pasquerel, asking him for forgiveness of her loss of temper in the meeting with Alençon and the others. She then waited until dusk to seek out the largest campfire.

Still dressed in her suit of armor, and accompanied by her brothers, d'Aulon, de Metz, and de Poulengy, she spotted a fire beside a large tree stump that looked to be some two meters in diameter. She made her way to it, climbed up, and stood there. About thirty soldiers had already gathered around the crackling fire, eating, drinking, and laughing, but when they caught sight of Jehanne standing on the huge stump, the cracking of the fire became the only sound.

The men stared while the girl—who to most of them looked like a young boy in battle attire—took a moment to cast her large blue eyes upon each of them, smiling graciously all the while.

"Fellow Frenchmen," she began in a voice loud enough to be

heard, but not shrill or threatening, "my name is Jehanne the Maid, and I'm from the village of Domremy in the Loraine Valley, south of Vaucouleurs."

The words had barely crossed her lips when each of the men around the fire stood and began clapping and shouting and chanting, "Jehanne the Maid, Jehanne the Maid, Jehanne the Maid!"

A stunned smile lit up Jehanne's face.

"Praise the Lord for His many blessings," she said waiting for their acclamation to end. Slowly, the girl in armor slightly raised her hand and waited for the quiet.

Finally, they let her continue.

"I want to thank each of you for this heartwarming welcome," she said, "but we need to speak about why we're all here. You and your families have been fighting in this war since before I was born. Many of you have lost loved ones and many here have been wounded—some more than once. And yet, here you are ready once again to risk your lives . . . Your courage and that of your loving families are an inspiration to families across our beautiful country, and yet, we all know that unless we defeat the enemy at Orléans, France will be no more."

The men remained quiet.

"Noble and brave solders of France, I have come here tonight to bring you news of hope and victory. After all these years of pain and suffering, God is going to help us."

An eruption of cheers and joy filled the air and forced her to stop, and when their eruption finally ebbed, she continued.

"He has sent me to tell you that now is the time for us to defeat the English, and He has promised to help us in that fight. Those of you who ride with me to Orléans and fight with me will do so with all of God's might and love behind us, and victory will be ours, provided . . ."

They didn't let her finish. A roar of joy burst forth from the men's lungs, and they began chanting her name, "*La Pucelle, la Pucelle*" over and over.

Once again Jehanne raised her armor-covered arm to be heard.

"God will assist us, provided . . ." She paused to make sure they would hear her words, "provided we are willing to be obedient to His will . . . provided we will keep ourselves in a state of grace . . . provided we go to daily confession, Mass, and communion—especially before we go into battle."

The men turned silent. They all knew the teachings of their Catholic faith—that anyone who died with a mortal sin on their soul would go to hell for the rest of eternity unless they made a sincere confession before dying or received last rites. But they were hard men. Soldiers. And they had been fighting this brutal war for a long time without anyone telling them they had to go to confession or to attend Mass.

"That means no swearing," Jehanne said. "That also means no getting drunk . . . That means no more gambling or looting or asking ransoms . . . That means no more prostitutes . . ."

Now the men started booing at the top of their lungs.

"We don't want to become priests," one of them yelled, "just fight for France with Jehanne the Maid!"

The men then started to clap and shout, "Jehanne the Maid, Jehanne the Maid!"

This time the girl held up both arms so she could continue.

A large brute of a man stepped forward. His scarred face and gnarled hands testified to the fact that he was a man who had seen many battles.

"Jehanne the Maid," he began in a deeply accented voice, "my name is Basque, and I was born in Spain, but have been lately living in Paris. When I heard of you and the Dauphin, I came to Blois to join your army and do whatever you ask. If you say God wants me to be in a constant state of grace, then that's what I'll do. No country has a right to invade another, and that's why I want to help you fight these rotten English butchers and their Burgundian swine."

The crowd once again started to clap and shout. "Jehanne the Maid, Jehanne the Maid, Jehanne the Maid!"

Again, the girl held up her hands until there was quiet.

"I have brought many priests with me so each of you can go to confession, and Mass, and receive communion every day. That is the only way God will allow *me* to fight for Him, and I ask that each of you do the same."

She looked around at all of them once again.

Several soldiers began to mutter among themselves.

"Are you with me?" she shouted. "Will you fight the enemies of God and France?"

Men from nearby campfires had heard the commotion and now gathered around the fire to see what was going on.

"I'm with you!" Basque shouted with emphasis. "Whatever it takes, I will do it."

A weak chorus of agreement followed from the others.

"Make up your minds, men of France. It's the only way we can fight for the Lord." The girl flashed another of her charming smiles and started to climb off the stump, then stopped. "Trust in God," she added. "Go to confession, receive communion, and lead righteous lives, and God will help all of us. Become righteous and we shall have the victory, by God's help."

She climbed down from the stump.

"Now go tell all the others," she said. "We must be united in God if we are to succeed. Everything we do together is for our Father in heaven—everything!"

For a moment, no one spoke.

Jehanne started to walk away, but changed her mind and returned to the stump to address everyone again.

117

"At dawn tomorrow everyone in this camp is going to start the day with confession, Mass and communion—myself included. No exceptions."

As Jehanne walked away this time, her retinue right behind her, Basque began to shout his support. Immediately, large numbers of others joined in, and by the time she had reached the tent of the Duke of Alençon, she could hear the loud shouts of, "Jehanne the Maid, Jehanne the Maid!" echoing up down the roadways of their tents.

Alençon was waiting for her with a big smile. "There can be no doubt you have their support," he said pointing in the direction of the tents.

She gave him a faint triumphant grin, and then said, "Would you please send out word that everyone is to report at dawn tomorrow to a central gathering for confession, Mass, and communion? They'll be plenty of priests to hear everyone's confession, and Mass will follow. Anyone who refuses should be sent home."

Alençon smiled and nodded slowly. "Yes, Jehanne," he said. "It will be done as you have requested."

The French advance on Orléans, with Jehanne as one of its field commanders, began in Blois on April 26, 1429. None of her fellow commanders would yet admit that the military force they headed had now become a religious crusade. Before leaving Blois, the other field generals met in private. Many of the captains—especially the late arrivals—seemed to think that the Dauphin had taken leave of his senses. "What else could we expect from the son of Charles VI?" they asked each other.

CHAPTER XI
The Wrong Side of the Loire

At an early age, Jean d'Orléans asked to be called the Bastard of Orléans. In fifteenth-century France, "Bastard" was a term of respect since it publicly acknowledged Jean as a first cousin to the Dauphin. The Bastard's father died in 1407. His legitimate half brother, Charles, became an English prisoner at the Battle of Agincourt in 1415. This left Jean the only free adult male of the House of Orléans.

The Bastard and his jailed brother—the Duke of Orléans—maintained close communications with each other about the administration of their city. Orléans was on their land, and they looked upon its residents as members of their extended family. And the defense of their city and its people was their sacred responsibility.

Blessed with a nearby rock quarry, the rectangular perimeter of the city's stone masonry walls measured almost 10,000 feet in length. Built into these impregnable walls were circular masonry guard towers at roughly 100-yard intervals—approximately the average range of an arrow—giving the fortress unparalleled firing range. In addition, five heavily guarded gates (including a bridge gate) controlled all ingress and egress to the city's interior via a well designed use of deepwater moats and drawbridges.

Sitting on the northern bank of the Loire River and eighty-one

miles southwest of Paris, the city designers had long ago constructed a 1,100-foot bridge to accommodate all traffic across the river.
At the point where this overpass connected to land on the south
side of the Loire, the city architects ordered two giant guard towers
and a fort built to protect the nineteen-arch overpass from attack
and unwelcome visitors. They named it Les Tourelles.

After the French took heavy losses at the Battle of Vernueil in
August 1424, it seemed to most Frenchmen that it was only a matter of time before the English moved south to capture Orléans, the
remaining obstacle to a successful English invasion. Consequently,
the city had the benefit of three full years of preparation to install
and reinforce its defenses, store food and supplies, and train a
disciplined militia in coordination with its essential support infra-
structure—citizen noncombatant men, women, and children.

There was never any doubt about the allegiance of the Bastard
and the people of Orléans—they were Armagnac/Valois supporters. Their mutual and strong dislike of the English and their
Burgundian allies had become blind hatred after the murder of
Louis I, then Duke of Orléans (brother to King Charles VI), in 1407.

And after the Battle of Agincourt in October 1415, when the
English seized the badly wounded and beloved new young Duke of
Orléans for ransom, the good citizens of Orléans developed an open
animus of the English and their allies. But that turned to unbridled fury when the city paid an expensive ransom for Charles, only
to have the English take the money, but keep their duke prisoner.

In an attempt to demonstrate his solidarity with the people of
Orléans, in 1427, the Dauphin appointed a fifty-eight-year-old veteran warrior, Lord Raul de Gaucourt, governor of the city—at the
strong suggestion of Georges de la Trémoïlle. Gaucourt understood
that his job depended on making Trémoïlle look good in the eyes
of the Dauphin. Immediately following his appointment, the new
governor supervised an in-depth review of the city's defenses, and

then ordered major improvements and upgrades for the Orléans armaments months before the English began their siege in the fall of 1428.

However, by the last week of April 1429, six months after the siege began, the leaders and citizens of this once-beautiful and cosmopolitan city thought defeat by the crush of the English iron boot seemed inevitable. They had almost no food, ammunition, or hope, but they vowed to fight to the last man, woman, and child.

On the afternoon of April 28th, the Bastard believed his only hope of correcting that situation was through Jehanne d'Arc and her supply train currently traveling from Blois. He had just received word that she had arrived on the outskirts of Orléans on the southern bank; he decided to go greet her and personally make her feel welcome.

The English, on the other hand, had convinced themselves that victory at Orléans would be theirs in a matter of days. Their morale had begun to rise after their defeat of the French in February 1429 at the Battle of Herrings. As a direct result, they now had plenty of ammunition, weapons, and, most importantly, fresh food supplies, including considerable amounts of dried fish for Lent. Their soldiers could now devote most of their time repairing and resupplying their forts which encircled the city.

Their autumn strategy placed heavy defenses on land west of the city to prevent fresh provisions being brought into Orléans along the northern bank. However, Lord Talbot, Lord Scales, the Earl of Suffolk, and Sir William Gladsdale—the English brain trust for the siege of Orléans—now took note of unusually vigorous preparations by the French, despite shortages of food, troops, and ammunition. This activity led the English to assume that a new French offensive would begin any day, but felt comforted by news of additional English troops due any day. Lord Talbot decided that in light of that fact, the English should keep a low profile until those fresh troops arrived.

———— >✻< ————

Jehanne and her detail of 500 soldiers had left Blois for Orléans on Wednesday, April 27, 1429, with Father Pasquerel and the priests leading the procession while flying their new banner and singing *Veni Creator Spiritus* (Come Holy Spirit). Behind the clergy rode a handful of Dauphinist captains and Jehanne, flanked by her household fighting team, including her two brothers. Once again, she dressed herself in the new silver-colored armor and carried her embroidered standard. After these came the men-at-arms and archers.

Each understood the essential role the 600 wagons of foodstuffs and ammunition, 400 head of cattle, and 435 pack animals would play in the upcoming battles for the city. Without them, there could be no victory against the English at Orléans and, therefore, they had to be protected at all costs.

The first day out Jehanne and her entourage covered about twenty miles of rutty roads and dust. Then, at curfew, they halted and made camp to the sounds of priests singing "Gabriel Angelus." That night the entire detail, including Jehanne, slept in the fields on the cold spring ground. Despite the best efforts of La Hire, Jean d'Aulon, and her staff, no one could persuade the girl to remove her armor. "I want to show our fighting men and captains that I can withstand the pain and discomfort," she said. "I don't want them to think that I'm going to wilt like some dainty flower."

Before sleep, Jehanne sought complete privacy to pray for patience about the upsetting news she'd received just before leaving Blois. The Duke of Alençon had explained that the new troops would arrive at Orléans in two groups. The first contingent of fresh soldiers—500 in number—were to accompany her, but with two "life-and-death" responsibilities: a fierce defense of the food train against any attack by the English, and "by whatever means necessary," to escort the desperately needed livestock and food supplies to within the city walls.

The remaining 3,000 troops from Blois would arrive in Orléans within a "couple of days" because all the necessary supplies and armaments for the second contingent had not yet arrived in Blois.

Alençon was beside himself with frustration and apologies as he delivered this news to the Dauphin's newest field commander.

Dear Lord in heaven, please grant me strength and patience. These endless delays continue to block your mission. My visitors tell me that I have little time, and so I don't know what else to do but to try to keep calm, no matter what. I need your help, dear Lord, because I am such an impatient sinner. Thank you, dear God.

At the dawn of April 28th, Jehanne had awakened on dew-dampened ground that had left her sleep-deprived and aching from tossing and turning in the poorly fitted suit of armor. She'd had the good sense to remove her helmet before trying to sleep, and her helmet underhood had kept her head warm through the night. But right after morning confessions, Mass, and communion—a seasonal downpour blew in from the west.

The storm brought sheets of water pounding down on the supply train and the girl with such ferocity she could barely see beyond ten meters. By the time her household staff managed to get her rain surcoat on over her armor, the rain had splattered inside and drenched her undergarments clear down to her boots.

Meanwhile, the animals balked and bellowed at being driven through the muddy and gusty conditions, but their handlers knew what was at stake and would not be deterred. Fortunately, those in charge—La Hire, the maréchal de Sainte-Sévère, plus five other well trusted Dauphinist generals—also understood the importance of the supply train and insisted that the animals be kept moving, no matter their loud objections.

The air filled with the splattering sounds of rain, punctuated by men yelling, whips snapping, and the cries of angry animals braying and bellowing into the cold morning. Jehanne strongly disagreed with harsh treatment of the animals and welcomed how the rain washed away her tears.

The supply train was making progress, she reminded herself, as they inched closer to Orléans. Besides, there was nothing she could do to speed things up, so she fell into silent prayer. As she thought back on all that had happened to her since her first meeting with the Dauphin, she felt overwhelmed by God's great love.

Father God, please forgive my impatience and lack of appreciation of all your many blessings as I try to do your will. And how you have kept me safe during all the times I've had to answer personal questions about my faith—thank you. I guess you were keeping me safe also when I had to take that virginity test with Queen Yolande and those two other royal women, but I didn't feel safe.

I still cry when I think back to when I had to go through that, but humbly ask your forgiveness, dear Lord, for my anger. You know best. So much of this journey has been new to me and my years on our family farm, and I have no idea what I'm supposed to do most of the time. Thank you for helping me, Lord. With all my heart, I really want to do your will. I love you, dear Lord.

By late in the day, the French supply detail could finally see the city of Orléans above the roiling Loire River, through the floating mist and driving rain. The raging storm protected them from view by the English, so the French captains decided to pitch camp opposite the most eastern English fort—Ile Saint Loup Bastille—little more than a mile away from the city walls. They reasoned that even if the English could see the new troops and supplies, in these conditions, it would be impossible for them to mount an effective attack to prevent them setting camp. The French did not know that the English were under orders to "hold in place" until their new troops arrived from Paris.

Due to the lack visibility all that day, Jehanne now realized for the first time that she and her troops had been purposely led on the south side of the Loire—across the river from Orléans.

Who did this? Why?

Her staff tried to convince Jehanne to retire into a tent they'd quickly erected for her so she could change into dry clothes.

"I'm not the slightest bit interested in my comfort!" she yelled.

The girl dismounted her horse—with assistance—and began to pace along the riverbank in the driving rain, still dressed in her muddy and rain-filled armor, helmet tucked under one armored arm to see better through the rain. She began kicking at the mud and shallow water as she walked back and forth.

The rest of her household and military staff stood about ten meters directly south of her, not sure what to do next.

"Where is the Bastard of Orléans?" she said in a loud voice but addressed to no one in particular. "I want to talk to him right now." She peered over the heaving water.

No one spoke.

Out on the river itself, rough swells pitched and rolled under a thick, misty cloud cover. The girl now saw a small vessel bob into view, tossed by the heavy water and currents. Burly soldiers at the oars pulled against the waves, slowly propelling their single passenger toward shore. Jehanne thought she recognized the tall powerful man in his early twenties from descriptions she'd been given.

She continued to pace at water's edge until the craft finally came close. Her brothers, d'Aulon, de Metz, and de Poulengy, rushed down into the shallow water and helped pull the small vessel out of the water.

The man in the boat stepped down into the water and, seeing Jehanne, bowed.

His crew quickly picked the boat up out of the water, lifted it high above their heads onto their shoulders, and marched in the direction of where the newly arrived troops and generals had already begun the task of erecting waterproof tents in which they could all change their wet clothes and get warm.

"Are you the Bastard of Orléans?" Jehanne said, voice quivering with emotion.

He nodded.

"I am Jehanne the Maid, sent to this city by our Lord God in heaven."

"You are most welcome," the Bastard said in a deep baritone voice.

Although the storm continued to swirl and pour down in sheets of rain, the girl could see that the Bastard possessed a well-built body, a handsome face with water-soaked blond hair, a high powerful forehead, and dark brown eyes filled with kindness.

It took Jehanne a moment to choose her words. "Was it you," she began, "who counseled that we should be on this side of the river, and not march straight to where Talbot and the English are hiding?"

"Yes," he said politely, "I, and others wiser than I, believing it safer and surer."

"In God's name!" Jehanne blurted and slammed her helmet onto the muddy ground as hard as she could.

"Our Lord God's counsel is surer and wiser than yours or any of your associates. You and the others sought to deceive me, but it is yourself that you deceive. For I bring you better assistance than ever came to captain or town, which is from the King of heaven. Nor is it granted for love of me; God has taken pity on this town of Orléans. *That's* why I'm here—to do God's work for this city and its people!"

While Jehanne spoke, the Bastard went to where her helmet lay in the mud, squatted, and began to wash it in the river tide.

When she finished talking, he looked up at her and spoke with quiet confidence, still washing away the mud. "Jehanne, I'm sorry we have upset you. It certainly was not our intention. We have information that the English plan to attack and kill anyone bringing supplies to this city. They also plan to capture and hold you for ransom."

He stood and handed Jehanne her now-clean helmet, which she promptly placed on her head as protection from the continuing downpour, but with the visor up.

"Also, by having you and the others follow the southern route, we believed that strategy would give us the best hope of the supply train arriving safely. We cannot defeat the English here without the help of the people of Orléans; they have been on the verge of starvation for weeks."

The girl still paced along the shore, arms now akimbo. "Why didn't anyone tell me of this?"

"I don't know, but you know now, and you're still clearly upset."

"Upset? Now *why* do you suppose I might be upset?" She began waving both arms as she spoke. "Let's see. At first they told me I was a guest of the royal family at Chinon, and then they spent weeks having me examined by the local 'learned' clergy; then it was off to Poitiers. There, I was cross-examined again by a different group of 'learned' academics, and they too concluded that theologically, I'm not going to embarrass the House of Valois. But that still wasn't good enough. So back I went to Chinon to wait for reports from Domremy about my childhood, and if I was ever a liar. But they find nothing.

"Next, I was told I have to go to Tours to pass the virgin test. And guess what? I passed, but am I now allowed to do the job God sent me to do? No! First, I have to go to Blois and deal with the

insults of French field generals who still don't believe that our God
in heaven sent me or if He really knows what He's doing. 'After all,'
these generals say behind my back, 'she's only a child, and an illiterate one at that!' As if the Blessed Virgin Mary was an older and
learned woman when she conceived and bore Jesus. As if David
was such an old, learned man when he defeated Goliath.

"Then, after all that, it's finally time to leave from Blois and
march to Orléans, but only 500 troops are ready. The other 3,000
will come later, they tell me—in a 'few' days, whatever that means.
So I've now been a 'guest' of the House of Valois since early March.
It's not as if my mission can be a big surprise to anyone.

"But now—finally—I'm on my way to do battle, I tell myself—
to do God's work. So for two days I remain ready for any battle,
keeping dressed in armor, despite the cold and a sudden torrential
downpour that's lasted this whole day. And then what happens
when we finally arrive in Orléans?"

Jehanne stopped pacing by the water and looked the Bastard
straight in the eye and stared at him for a long moment, then began shaking her head.

"Our own French generals decide to keep secrets from Jehanne
the Maid who has been sent here by God. They don't ask me what
God wants to do. They don't tell me they're worried for my safety.
Instead, they treat me like a frightened child who might run at
the first sign of trouble. How soon they forget that I just rode 150
leagues through icy valleys and rivers in the middle of winter with
howling winds all around and Burgundian soldiers searching for
us night and day.

"And as this beautiful city finally comes into full view through
the pouring rain, are we now in a position to join in a new attack against the English just as God has instructed me since I
was fifteen? Have our 'learned' generals organized a surprise attack
against the English while the enemy remains weak and hiding from

the rains in dry quarters? Has anyone in the French high command asked me for what strategy God has in mind at this time? The answers are NO, NO, and NO!!"

She stopped speaking and looked around at those from her household as well as the troops who had overheard her loud words and drawn closer.

"And why is the answer 'No' to all my questions, Monsieur Bastard of Orléans?"

She waited for the Bastard to respond, but he said nothing. He did continue to study Jehanne, but no words passed his lips. She thought she saw kindness, compassion, and understanding in his eyes, but he said no words. The only sounds were those of more sheets of rain blasting into her face and into those watching.

"Because . . ." she began to raise her voice and remove her helmet. "Because you, monsieur, and your associates want to be 'SAFE AND SURE!'" she yelled at the top of her lungs, and then slung the armored helmet as far as she could into the roiling Loire. "But I didn't come here to be 'safe'! I came here to do God's work . . . RIGHT NOW!"

A short while later the Bastard and several of her household staff escorted Jehanne into a dry tent, where they helped her out of her water-soaked armor. She asked to be alone so she could shed her wet undergarments, dry herself, and get dressed in some warm, dry clothes. The Bastard left word that when Jehanne felt ready he would like to meet with her in private.

Later when they did meet in her tent, he acknowledged her frustration and in quiet tones explained his own disappointment at not being able to resupply the city the way he had originally planned. With great patience, he succeeded in calming the overwrought girl. He further explained in detail his plan to cross the river at Checy—five miles further east—so the badly needed stores could arrive in the city through the poorly guarded eastern side. But he also shared that they could not cross today; the wind remained in a westerly direction and was too strong for the supplies, horses, and men to be ferried across.

While he spoke, an intense expression crossed Jehanne's face, and she wiped tears from both cheeks. "Would you kindly wait a short while outside before making a final decision about how you transport the new provisions into the city?" she asked.

He scratched his head and studied Jehanne for a moment. "Of course," he said. "I will wait, as you have asked."

Jehanne blessed herself and promptly sank to her knees in prayer.

Loving Saint Michael, Saint Catherine, Saint Margaret, I need your assistance. Please. It's become clear that those leading the fight for our beloved Dauphin are trying to keep me safe and away from any battle. They think I'm a fool and a great danger to myself and the entire military effort. Please, my kind and divine visitors, help me show them that I can be useful—wholly according to His will.

Sometime later, Jehanne could hear that the wind and rain had stopped, and she sent for the Bastard. Once he entered her tent, he reached out his hand and helped raise her to her feet. With a simple bow, he said, "Thank you. And thank you, dear God in heaven. The weather has changed and the wind will now help us bring the supplies to the city."

Jehanne smiled with elation and nodded. "You see now that God is with us?"

The Bastard returned her nod. "Yes, I really do see."

"I'm glad," she said. "I'm glad you really understand."

He smiled. "While you were alone, I made arrangements for you to sleep in a house—not a tent—with people I know who will welcome you and keep you safe."

This time, Jehanne smiled and blushed.

Jehanne spent the night of April 28th outside Orléans in the home of Gui de Cailly, a good friend of the Bastard. The girl slept well for the first time in days—the discomfort, bruises, and pain of her armor forgotten once she'd taken a hot bath and washed the mud from her person. During the night, Jehanne prayed for guidance from her divine visitors.

Unknown to her, the Bastard's plan for delivering the provisions to the city had already begun. The Orléans militia organized a diversionary assault on the Bastille Saint Loup while the citizens began sailing the precious supplies and livestock across the Loire, making their way into the eastern gate of the city without interference.

Next morning, Jehanne learned more of the Bastard's plans.

Jehanne's new 500-man army contingent, too numerous to risk an extended crossing, would return instead to Blois to join forces with the troops there. They would be led by most of the same French captains who had just brought them to Orléans, including de Metz, de Poulengey, and d'Aulon.

Jehanne felt anguished that her fresh troops had to leave Orléans, lest they lose the manifest presence of the Holy Spirit from their daily sacraments. Understanding her fears, Father Pasquerel said, "Jehanne, I promise to you and to our Lord to make sure the men keep their promises and receive the sacraments each and every day."

Jehanne took a deep breath and sighed. "Many thanks to you, my dear Father Pasquerel. You are truly doing God's work."

Jehanne would remain behind. The Bastard and La Hire decided to stay with her. Despite her misgivings about sending her troops back to Blois, Jehanne realized she had no authority to change the Bastard's plans. So she spent most of April 29th assisting with the successful transport of the livestock and provisions.

She also spent a good deal of that day helping refocus her troops before they left—mingling with and greeting as many as she could. In her heart she feared that these same soldiers might lose their enthusiasm for fighting the English. After all, the fact remained that the English had at least 4,000–5,000 troops still surrounding Orléans, and the French knew the ferocity of the English in battle.

The ruthlessness of the English didn't scare Jehanne because she knew she had God on her side, but she also realized that in the recent past—such as at the Battle of Herrings, the minds and hearts of French men-at-arms had proven flighty and easily manipulated. Right now, her troops backed her mission for the Lord in heaven, but she had no way of knowing what might happen along the journey between Orléans and Blois.

She also worried what the English might do now that she had reached Orléans. There could be no doubt that her letter of March 22nd had alerted them to the fact that more fresh troops would be arriving soon. That being the case, what else might the English plan? The possibility of an English attack was all the more reason why the French should go on the offensive as soon as possible, but she reassured herself that the Bastard and his collection of generals most probably had a plan for such an attack. She didn't know that for sure, but drew the conclusion on her own. It certainly wasn't because any of the generals had bothered to include her in any of their planning sessions. Nonetheless, Jehanne reasoned, once she proved herself in battle, maybe a few of them would welcome her presence.

As this spring day began its final stages, the time for the 500 troops to begin their return to Blois presented itself. Jehanne took her time in saying good-bye. She wanted these men-at-arms—for whom she had developed a personal fondness—to know and remember how much she appreciated their commitment to God's work. She knew from her divine visitors that as part of her mission she needed to vigorously encourage her men in their fight against the English invaders. She needed to talk to as many of them as possible and remind them how they and she were all on a mission for God. She would not abandon her post; she would do her very best to wait patiently for their return.

In her heart, she knew she would miss being in their presence and the calming presence of Father Pasquerel. In the relatively short time he had been a member of her household, the sweet and wise little man had become precious to her. She would need to locate a temporary replacement church or chapel in Orléans where she could pray and receive the daily sacraments in private until his return.

Lack of solitude for prayer reminded Jehanne of what it had been like in Vaucouleurs—people staking out where she went or where they thought she might go, even to where she prayed. She appreciated how the people had supported her with such enthusiasm. Their belief in her mission had certainly been a major factor in Sir Robert's willingness to give her a second chance to show she had been sent by God, but it still made her ill at ease. She deserved none of their adoration—God was whom they should be thanking and giving honor and glory.

And today on the outskirts of Orléans—just like in Vaucouleurs—the people of the city quickly spread the news of her being the "savior virgin from Lorraine," only this time it was about a "miraculous" changed wind direction. She had tried to remind everyone—in Vaucouleurs, Chinon, Poitiers, Tours, and here—that she hadn't performed any miracles—God had.

Without God's help—she reminded herself—she would remain merely what she had always been—a farmer's daughter. Jehanne the Maid was not important—He was. Everything she had done since Vaucouleurs was about God and His incredible goodness and love—especially for the people of France and Orléans. She wanted to make sure everyone understood that—everyone . . . But how?

As the Bastard and Jehanne watched the troops and their captains recede into the dusk along the southern route back toward Blois, he turned to her and said, "Are you worried about what to do with yourself for the next few days?"

She returned his gaze. "That's true; I'm already missing my friends."

"I think I understand," he said. "I too look forward to their return, but for the next few days we—you and I and La Hire—have a job to do: Keeping up morale."

"And how do you suggest we do that?"

He thought for a moment. "Are you aware of all the rumors about you?"

"Some."

"You want to stop them?"

"And how would I do that?" she said.

"By coming into the city with me."

She sighed and shrugged.

"It's so simple, Jehanne," he said. "Let the people see and get to know you. They've existed minute-to minute, hour-to-hour, and day-by-day for six months while friends and neighbors died or became diseased before their eyes, but now you've come with food, ammunition, and hope. They want to embrace you and make you part of their family and tell you how much they appreciate you. What's wrong with that?"

She studied the darkening cloud formations. "There's nothing wrong with that by itself, I guess," she said. "I just don't want them believing that I'm personally responsible for making their dreams come true. Our dear Lord in heaven is who brought me here with the supplies and food and troops. And God will bring the rest of the new troops in a few days. I don't really matter—I'm just an illiterate farm girl on a pretty horse, dressed in a shiny suit of armor, trying to do God's will."

He smiled. "Jehanne, they know who you are, and they want you to come pay them a visit today—they've waited long enough."

She nodded and kept looking up at the dark rain clouds gathering on the horizon. "I think you're probably right. I just hope they remember that God's in charge."

Chapter XII
La Pucelle Enters Orléans

Friday, April 29, 1429

The Bastard now had to find a way to get Jehanne across the Loire River and into Orléans safely. He'd already discarded his original plan of placing Jehanne and her retinue on barges and gliding them past the Saint Loup fortifications—too many things could go wrong.

After more discussions with his fellow captains, the Bastard hit upon a safer plan: cross the river where they were, then lead Jehanne and her staff directly north from Checy for about a mile into the Orléans forest, and then toward the city at a southwesterly angle, eventually crossing through the open space (about three-quarters of a mile between the Bastilles Saint Loup and Saint Pouair) under cover of darkness.

The English sentries at both fortifications might overhear them as the Bastard and his escort detail entered the city through the Porte Bourgogne gate, but there wouldn't be enough time for the English to mount an effective attack.

Jehanne and the Bastard stood beside their horses just outside the home of Gui de Cailly, ready to mount as he finished explaining this new plan.

"So, what do you think?" he asked.

The girl scowled for a moment. "That's a terrible idea," she said, trying to remain calm. "It's cowardly and unchivalrous; I won't be party to such a thing."

He took a deep breath and paused.

"But it will ensure your safety," the Bastard said, his voice reassuring, "as well as that of your household and brothers. Your safe arrival and theirs within the city walls are my highest priorities."

"I didn't come to Orléans to be safe," she said, voice rising with emotion. "That's not my mission. I'm here to defeat the English and install the Dauphin as king. I'll have no part of slinking into Orléans like an escaped murderer!"

He shook his head with puzzlement. "But you cannot beat the English and install Charles unless you're alive," he noted gently. "I'm on your side, Jehanne."

She looked directly in his eyes and pursed her lips, looking up into the late-afternoon mist. "Would you give me minute?" she said after a short silence.

Jehanne then walked a few feet away, knelt under a young oak tree, and crossed herself.

Instead of doing nothing while she prayed, the Bastard decided to tighten the cinch of her horse. In this wet weather, he could take nothing for granted.

When Jehanne finally returned, he could see that she'd been crying.

"Sire, you are right," she said. "Your plan has the best chance."

━━◆━━

Earlier that day, the soldiers inside the Saint Loup Bastille had been caught off guard by the Orléans militia. The ragtag group of amateurs launched a direct charge at their position in the darkness of early morning, and the English took heavy casualties.

137

But then, inexplicably, the French withdrew mere hours later and surprised the English once again by withdrawing and rushing back inside the city walls.

Greatly relieved, the English soldiers at Saint Loup could now tend to their dead and wounded still lying where they had fallen. These men had been briefed several days earlier to expect a new French offensive when the "Armagnac whore from Domremy" arrived with "green" troops. But later that same day, another briefing detailed how 500 new French troops en route to the city were only an escort for the safe transport of livestock and food, and that the French would not launch a new attack with these men.

This same garrison then received a third briefing from Sir John Talbot and his associates that Jehanne would soon return to Blois with her new troops, and then join with the main body of French reinforcements. Talbot advised that the new troops would then march on Orléans several days later—all 3,500 of them—including Jehanne.

But that same day, Saint Loup received yet another change to the rules of engagement. They were now on 24-hour alert and to return all fire, but only if attacked first "in numbers." The men of this bastille were to interdict and disorganize any substantial French troop movement to or from Orléans via la Porte de Bourgogne, and to operate as a sentinel and response detachment in the event the bastilles Saint Jean le Blanc or Saint Augustins came under attack.

Despite these confusing orders, the entire Saint Loup garrison, including their most experienced captains, could not bring themselves to take seriously the possibility of a renewed French attack. The moment these men mentioned the Battle of Herrings among themselves, chuckles broke out all around.

"The French know they're going to lose and will try anything," one crusty veteran shouted out.

"Yeah," another chimed in. "You know they're desperate when

they send a teenage farm girl from Lorraine to lead their troops. What a bunch of cowards."

Catcalls and whistles all around.

"The French are a laughingstock," yelled a third. "Always have been, going back to Charles VI. He was nutty as a fruitcake, and now his son is just as bad. Imagine, sending an illiterate shepherd girl to lead men into battle!"

More laughter.

The old crusty veteran spoke again. "I hope the Frenchies do attack us in the next few days. It'll be like Agincourt and the Battle of Herrings all over again—only much easier—like taking candy from a baby!"

Hearty laughter filled the bastille and echoed out into the rainy darkness.

———✦———

The Bastard and Jehanne began their dangerous journey at dusk. Once across the river, using the fading daylight and the darkened forest to conceal their movements, the Bastard and his well armed detail guided the girl and her household slowly and quietly through the thick forest foliage. All rode in a state of high anxiety—half-expecting English swordsmen to jump out from behind the closely grown trees any moment.

Aware of the real possibility of attack, Jehanne had once again worn her armor—helmet visor down, sword at the ready.

Because of the morning downpour and afternoon drizzle, with each stride the French soldiers and their wards dislodged rain droplets from low-hanging branches, soaking both riders and horses. Men and mounts had to step with unusual care to avoid losing traction through the fresh mud. The air hung heavy, pungent with the smell of wet bark and spring blossoms. High above, bright stars

Jehanne's heartwarming entry into Orleans April 29, 1429

sparkled in a cloudless sky.

Out of respect and admiration, the Bastard had given Jehanne a fresh, beautiful white stallion before they left Checy for Orléans. At first, the girl thought she shouldn't accept such generosity, but when she learned her original mount had come up lame that morning, she graciously accepted.

To guard against a possible English attack, the Bastard had insisted that thick plates of specially pressed metal cover the main body of Jehanne's horse and chain mail protect its mane and upper forehead. But by the time they had traversed the thick forest, both horse and Jehanne were spattered with mud.

When Jehanne and her escort finally reached the western edge of the Forest of Orléans, the light above the city was so bright and close to the mammoth masonry walls, it might have been from a huge fire, except for the absence of smoke.

Jehanne, the Bastard, and the others could hear a loud hum from inside the city—almost like bees circling a giant hive.

"That sound, Jehanne," the Bastard explained, "is the people of the city preparing to welcome you. For them, you are what they have been hoping and praying for during these last six months. Having to wait this late is almost more than they can bear."

The girl shook her head, clearly overwhelmed by the volume of the people's excitement within the city walls.

Dear God in heaven, please help me do your will.

The Bastard studied her. "Are you all right?"

Jehanne nodded. "I think I'm ready."

The city bells tolled 8 o'clock, Friday night, April 30, 1429, when Jehanne, the Bastard, and his detachment of about 200 men-at-arms approached la Porte de Bourgogne and the battle-ready knights guarding its huge gate. While their horses pawed at the mud, several guards held blue and red banners of the still-imprisoned duke, Charles d'Orléans. All knew how much that meant to the Bastard and Jehanne, and all shared the sting they felt from the hateful and cruel treatment the English had dealt the family patron.

Immediately recognizing the Bastard and his detail, the paladins lowered their swords and bellowed that the cross-hatched metal portcullis should open. The monster machinery then yawned wide and shot out a ray of blazing light from the thousands of burning torches.

Jehanne gratefully removed the rain-splattered helmet and tied it to the saddle. Her short dark hair glistened in the light, and she shook her head to stop the sweat and rain from further sliding down her neck.

One of her squires, Minguet, removed its protective sheath and unfurled Jehanne's white standard, and then maneuvered himself in front of her. In silence, several of the other soldiers who had accompanied her to this point formed an escort to lead the entire contingent into the city.

When Jehanne finally did ride into full view of the packed crowds, a momentary hush fell over the city, followed quickly by a building crescendo of cheers and shouts. A mass of humanity swarmed at the girl, roaring with jubilation. To them, their *Pucelle* had finally come—a blessed angel on a horse had now appeared before their very eyes—and they shouted out *l'Angéligue, l'Angéligue* as loud as they could.

Jehanne realized she could not proceed because she was surrounded on all sides by people howling with joy. The noise almost deafened her; the air reeked of tobacco, filth, alcohol, and fresh cold rain. Still, she managed to collect her senses, flashed a winning smile, and waved back at the pushing throngs while they cheered all the louder.

Jehanne began to seriously fear for the safety of her beautiful new horse and cast a worried look in the direction of the Bastard. Nothing like this had ever happened to her in Vaucouleurs or Tours or any of the other places where the French crowds cheered her presence.

Fearing that this throng was on the verge of getting out of control, the Bastard urged his mount forward, taking care not to trod upon any of the people pressing in on the procession; Jehanne followed—both of them smiling and waving as best they could. Shouts of "Jehanne la Pucelle!" reverberated and echoed over and over into the night while Minguet and the advance guard moved slowly forward, making sure none of the crowd suffered injury.

Cheering with elation along the narrow cobblestone streets, men and women eight deep from all walks of life waved hats and scarves; most held blazing torches to light Jehanne's path. Some adults lifted children onto their shoulders, jumping up and down with delight while tears ran down their faces.

High above from windows and rooftops, the damp standards of France and Orléans undulated slowly in a slight breeze while men and women threw flowers and garlands down toward Jehanne. Near many of the flags stood members of the French defense force, gaunt from sleep and food deprivation, but flashing wide grins of thanksgiving across their unshaven faces. They waved swords and maces in salute as Jehanne and her escorts slowly rode by.

Down below on the street, men, women, and children struggled to touch any part of Jehanne or her horse; some kissed her armored feet. A few brave children picked up a thrown flower and tucked it into the armor of her horse.

Suddenly, Jehanne's standard caught fire from a careless torch in the crowd. Minguet didn't notice, but she did. Jehanne spurred her horse into action and deftly wheeled the animal about so she could crush the fire with her armored hands.

Little damage was done to her banner and none to the pressing crowd. An earsplitting roar of delight filled the night for her quick action and skill.

Jehanne waved back, her joyous smile bringing tears of happiness to the countless multitudes. They loved their Pucelle—nothing would ever change that. The rest of the world best take notice.

It took Jehanne about an hour to reach her destination adjacent to Porte Renard. Once there, she—still in muddy armor and exhausted beyond words—asked to be heard. When the people finally calmed, she addressed them in a quiet but firm voice from her saddle.

"Thank you all for such a warm and loving welcome. My Lord has sent me to help the good city of Orléans. Keep hoping in God. If you have good hope and faith in Him, you shall be delivered from your enemies. Thank you. I need to get some rest now. It's been a long day."

The Bastard had made arrangements for Jehanne and her household staff to stay with the family of Jacques Boucher, treasurer of the Duke of Orléans. Once dismounted, Jehanne entered the home of her hosts, led by the Bastard, who introduced them to the head of the house, his wife, François, and their eight-year-old daughter, Charlotte.

Jehanne noticed the great anxiety on the faces of Monsieur and Madame Boucher and shot a questioning glance at the Bastard.

Grasping her concern, he said, "Jehanne, your hosts are concerned about the sleeping arrangements. Since you and your staff require more rooms than they have bedrooms, they wondered if you would mind sharing a bed with their daughter Charlotte."

Jehanne flashed a smile at her hosts and their child who had long blond curly locks. To the girl from Domremy, she looked small for her age. "When I was younger," Jehanne said, "I had to share a bed with my sister for a number of years. I would be most honored to share a bed with you, Charlotte, and I promise not to snore!"

Everyone chuckled.

The Bouchers had prepared a sumptuous meal, but Jehanne had only two things on her mind: removing her armor and taking a bath. Later, she joined the Bastard and the others as they ate; she wore the same clothes she wore when she met Charles, and would only—with polite and heartfelt apologies—consume small pieces of bread dipped in weak wine. After dinner, Jehanne asked to speak with the Bastard. Madame Boucher showed them to the family's small chapel and left the two knights alone.

They sat sideways in a pew, facing each other.

"First of all," she began and folded her hands on her lap, "I want to thank you for getting me here in safety. I know it's been a difficult day for you, and I want to apologize for making your job even more difficult."

He smiled. "Thank you, Jehanne. I accept your apology, but it's unnecessary. I understand that you've been under a lot of stress as well. Believe me, I want to help your mission as much as I possibly can. I truly believe you have been sent by God."

She stared at him and covered her mouth, eyes wide. For a moment she couldn't speak while tears welled up in her pupils, eyelids blinking.

Finally, she got herself under control enough to say. "I don't want to cry, but I can't seem to stop. I wanted to thank you for everything, but I think I'd better be alone for now—if you don't mind."

He stood and slowly bowed. "I don't mind at all, Jehanne. I'll talk to you tomorrow. I pray that you can get a good night's sleep."

With that he withdrew.

Jehanne blessed herself and knelt in the pew.

Dear God, why do I keep wanting to cry at the strangest times? I shouldn't be crying so much, dear Lord. Please help me stop. And please know how thankful I am to be here in Orléans at long last without having sustained any injuries or attack. The Bastard is really such a great gift to us all. And thank you for his being able to find warm shelter for me and all of my staff. I feel as though things are finally beginning to come together—it's just going to take a few more days. I've waited this long. A few more days until the rest of the troops arrive shouldn't make that much difference—I hope not, anyway. And please God, help me with my patience—it's such a problem for me.

About an hour later, Jehanne finished her prayers, and then retired into Charlotte's bedroom. Much to her surprise, there was plenty of room for her beside the little girl in the bed they were to share.

CHAPTER XIII
Ugly Words

When originally built, the Saint Loup complex served as a church and abbey for the Brothers of Saint Loup who abandoned it just a few years before the Anglo-Burgundian forces marched on Orléans in the fall of 1428. Shortly after his troops arrived at the outskirts of the city, the Earl of Suffolk decided to convert the abbey's old buildings into a battle-ready bastille.

The 400-man English garrison that now occupied the Saint Loup Bastille could not believe that Jehanne and her escort had slipped past them during the rainy night. That the French had out-thought the English seemed inconceivable. Each man fully expected severe disciplinary reprisals at any moment from the English high command now headquartered in the Fort Laurent bastille.

Due west of Saint Loup, on the far side of the city, stood Lord Talbot's headquarters. He now paced the floor; he, too, couldn't believe the French had slipped Jehanne past Saint Loup, but he didn't hold those men responsible.

When the Duke of Burgundy and his 1,500 men left in anger last month, Talbot had immediately requested reinforcements from Lord Bedford in Paris. Talbot knew that the English siege against Orléans had been severely weakened by the withdrawal

147

of Burgundy's troops, but there was nothing he could do to correct the situation for the moment. Up until March, his siege had controlled traffic in and out of Orléans—especially large deliveries of food and munitions. Now, not only had vital supplies been delivered, but the Maid herself had slipped into the city under their very noses.

Ironically, Talbot had received word earlier that morning that Sir John Fastolf had left Paris with more than enough men, ammunition, artillery, and supplies to turn the tide in Orléans against the French. But Talbot doubted those troops could arrive in time to offset the large number of French reinforcements now en route from Blois. He would try to stall the French until Fastolf arrived.

Eleven hundred feet south of the Saint Laurent bastille and across the Loire on its southern bank stood Les Tourelles, the most defensible fortification for the English outside the city. Sir William Glasdale commanded its 700-man garrison; that morning, he had received word from Talbot that Jehanne d'Arc had made her way into the city under cover of darkness.

He showed the message to his most trusted junior field commander, Sir William de Moleyns. Although only twenty-four, de Moleyns had distinguished himself against the French over the past five years under Glasdale.

"I don't care what that ignorant farm girl does," the older man said, hands clasped behind his back while he paced around his private quarters inside Les Tourelles, "she's nothing more than a witch and whore. Anyone who pays the slightest attention to what she says or does is either a fool or under one of her spells."

De Moleyns nodded and stared absently through window across the Loire at the high walls of Orléans, then added, "The people of the city certainly seemed excited at her arrival. Did you notice all the cheering and bright lights late last night? For a while I thought it was a huge fire."

"If Orléans caught fire from all those torches, that would be something worth talking about," Glasdale observed, still studying the floor and pacing. "Talbot keeps distracting us with useless intelligence—the farmer's daughter has arrived in Orléans, Fastolf is on his way from Paris with troops and food stuffs, French reinforcements are on their way from Blois with their own fresh supplies and reinforcements. None of it is worth talking about or even giving a second thought."

The younger knight looked at Glasdale. "So what should we be talking about?"

"Talbot should be calling all our field commanders together and developing a plan that anticipates how the French are most likely to attack. If I were the French, I'd attack Saint Loup, then Saint Blanc, Saint Augustins, and finally Les Tourelles. But the French aren't that daring or smart."

"What do you mean?"

"Well, look what happened at Rouvray—charging our fixed positions on foot? Anyone with half a brain knows you don't charge an enemy on foot who has a fixed position surrounded by long-pikes. You would think the French would have learned that lesson at Agincourt."

De Moleyns cleared his throat and sighed.

Glasdale stopped pacing. "What?"

The young knight shrugged. "Clermont was in charge at Rouvray, but the Bastard is in charge here. He's a lot smarter than Clermont will ever be."

Glasdale nodded. "That's true, he is smarter . . . but not enough smarter," he said after several moments of pacing. "The simple fact is that the French—as a nation—do not produce much in the way of tough-minded and disciplined soldiers or field commanders. The Bastard is the rare exception. Other than him and a few others like

La Hire, none of the French seems to really care, and I don't see that changing in my lifetime. Besides, the only reason the Bastard is in charge of the defense of this city is because his older brother is currently a paying guest in one of our Paris prisons. The Dauphin and the Bastard are trusted friends and cousins. They grew up together in Paris."

"So, what does all that mean for us?"

Glasdale chuckled. "What that means, *mon cher*, is that no matter how hard the Bastard tries, the French will still remain the 'ugly Frogs' they are on the battlefield—especially with that peasant whore from Lorraine prancing about and getting in the way. There's no excuse for stupid—military or otherwise!"

For the Bastard of Orléans, the situation in his city seemed on the verge of a nightmare scenario; he had to do something quickly. Ever since Jehanne had arrived, the people had teetered on the brink of morphing into a vicious mob, searching for the slightest excuse to vent their hatred of the English. Many of the boys and girls who had witnessed the militia's successful surprise attack on Saint Loup had now taken to the streets, urging them to do it again. In the twelve short hours since Jehanne's arrival, many citizens had convinced themselves that their local volunteers, together with the French professional soldiers, would be invincible on any field of battle against the English.

The Bastard knew he had to find a way to prevent these long-suffering men and women from talking themselves into a foolhardy attack before the new troops arrived. Or better yet, establish for certain that the 3,500 troops had left Blois. He worried that the long hand of Trémoïlle might disturb their departure by whatever means necessary.

From the time Jehanne arrived in the village of Chinon, the Bastard had obtained reliable reports that the advisor the Dauphin trusted most—Trémoïlle—worked night and day against the girl. According to the same reports, Trémoïlle and his coconspirators realized they could not control her—money or power held no interest for her. And without any influence over Jehanne, the Bastard worried that Trémoïlle might try to shake the confidence of the soldiers destined for Orléans—to make them believe that the war against the English would be lost any day.

With no other apparent viable options at hand, the Bastard decided he had to leave his city for a few days. He informed Jehanne of his decision at the first war council meeting at which she was an invited guest. It took place in the large meeting room on the second floor of the Boucher home.

"What do you mean?" she began. "You're going to Blois today and leaving La Hire and de Gaucourt in charge? Why? It makes no sense. There're others you could send."

The Bastard shrugged. "That's true, but I don't want to send someone else. Mine is not a mission I choose to delegate."

"What if the English decide to attack while you're gone? What if rogue elements of the militia decide to launch an attack of their own?"

The Bastard smiled. "Believe me, Jehanne, La Hire and Gaucourt know exactly what to do in the unlikely event the English decide to attack in my absence."

"This is crazy. Just when we're about to win this war, you decide to ride off and leave this city and its people to fend for themselves!"

"I'm not abandoning anyone. I'm simply going on a reconnaissance mission."

"Well, I believe you're making a huge mistake; I wish you would reconsider."

The Bastard took a deep breath. "Thank you for your kind suggestion."

"You're welcome, but I fear you've already made up your mind."

The others in the room remained quiet.

Sire de Gamaches chuckled and shook his head in disbelief at what he had just heard. He was a short, balding veteran of many campaigns and abruptly rose from his chair. Addressing the Bastard he said, "Since you give more weight to the advice of a little saucebox of low birth than to a knight such as myself, I will no longer protest her presence here; when the time and place come, my good sword will speak; I may meet my end in the doing, but the king and my honor demand it.

"Henceforth I lower my banner and am no longer anything more than a simple squire. I prefer to have a nobleman as my master rather than a hussy who may once have been God knows what."

The knight rolled up his banner and handed it to the Bastard.

Before de Gamaches could exit the room, the other knights around the table rushed to block his path, but Jehanne remained seated.

"Stand aside," de Gamaches said. "I have no interest in challenging any of you. This is simply a matter of honor—I feel greatly dishonored by the presence of this inexperienced child in the midst of such vital war discussions."

The Bastard had not moved, but did narrow his steel-blue eyes and clench his jaw. "Sire de Gamaches," he whispered, "so, you feel dishonored?"

He paused, arose, and walked to face his fellow knight.

"Do you think the Dauphin felt dishonored when he ordered 3,500 new troops to join Jehanne in defense of this city? Do you think any of those new men-of-war feel dishonored as they prepare to join us here in a coordinated attack on the English?"

He paused and looked about the room, catching the eye of La Hire. "Do you think La Hire feels dishonored?"

"The Maid could never dishonor La Hire," the man with the deeply scarred face blurted. "It is an honor to serve with her."

The others now joined in a mumbled chorus of support.

De Gamaches looked around at the others, trying to find the right words.

The Bastard knew he had to speak and quickly. "Sire, I fully realize how this whole situation has spiraled outside the bounds of usual behavior. But history has shown that we must sometimes strike a contract with opportunity—like how we've joined forces with the Scots. They don't care who wins our war; they just want Englishmen dead and lots of them. Their blind hatred cost us the Battle of Herrings, but they're still here, ready to kill the English anytime we ask; that's something we still badly need.

"And so it is with Jehanne: her entire mission is to defeat the English and to crown Charles king of all France. Sire de Gamaches, I fully appreciate your grave reservations about Jehanne's unproven fitness as a soldier and especially her sudden presence at our war council meetings.

"Nonetheless, our Dauphin has conducted a long and vigorous investigation into her background and satisfied himself and his council that she has been sent by God to help us defeat the English. Simply because she lacks noble birth, should we send her away—even if all the signs are that she really has been sent by God?"

Jehanne's eyes began to blink, but she fought off the tears.

De Gamaches shook his head slightly and looked up at the Bastard straight in the eye. "Perhaps I've been a bit hasty."

He reached for his banner still held by the Bastard.

The man from Orléans smiled, bowed graciously, and then handed the banner back to its owner. De Gamaches turned and headed back to his place at the map table as silence filled the room.

Jehanne crossed her arms over her chest. "I have nothing but the highest respect for the esteemed Lord de Gamaches and his great dedication to France and the crown," she said in a soft voice.

"It would be an honor to serve our Lord in heaven and the Dauphin alongside such a brave and noble knight of France."

"Well said, well said," the others chorused.

Jehanne walked over to an astonished Lord de Gamaches, hand extended.

The knight stood, took her small hand, and gently kissed it.

Later that afternoon, when the council meeting had ended, the Bastard asked Jehanne to stay behind for a few moments. After everyone left, he closed the door and sat back down at the map table, where she joined him.

"The problem for you, Jehanne," the man from Orléans began, "is that the church and the Dauphin have determined that you're not crazy, that you're not a woman who sells her body, and that you're not a witch. As a result, most everyone of noble birth is scared of you and has no idea how to deal with you, unless they get to know you or already believe in you and your mission."

Jehanne thought for a moment in silence. "And which one are you, Sire?"

The Bastard smiled. "I already know you and firmly believe in you and your mission. I've believed in you from almost the first moment I heard of you."

The girl grinned and nodded. "I am glad, Sire. You are most kind."

"That may or may not be true, but you should expect—for the moment—no kindness from your fellow French captains unless they volunteer it. They'll come around but only after they've seen you in action on the field of battle. And you should expect nothing but crude vitriol from the English captains and their soldiers whenever you are within earshot. It's safe to say that they hate you with every fiber of their being and would move heaven and hell to kill you."

"But I don't hate them," Jehanne said. "I just want them to go away and leave France; I don't want them to die. God loves all of us. He sent me to raise the siege here, and then lead the Dauphin to Reims for a proper coronation and Mass. That is all."

The Bastard studied her for a moment. "I know, Jehanne, but the English don't believe you've been sent by God. They think you are a witch and have bewitched us all. They see all of us who fight alongside you as a horde of demons with you as our leader. And as such, you are someone they very much want to kill—any way they can, and they believe it would be a good and noble thing to end your life."

He stopped and studied her across the table for a moment.

"While I'm away, please try very hard to bear that fact in mind at all times."

By the end of Saturday, Jehanne was at peace as to why the Bastard had to leave for Blois early the next day. But just because she understood it didn't mean she liked it or felt comfortable with it. Her divine visitors had remained unusually silent as to the step-by-step details of how God's plan should be put into action in Orléans. The teenager knew to place herself in the hands of the Lord so He could silently guide her as she improvised her way through each new challenge.

As always, she had only one plan—the immediate implementation of God's will. But since she realized that she had no experience as how best to get God's work done in a world of royals and knights and French nobility, she found herself acting on feelings and hunches. Her feelings told her that the days and nights until the reinforcements arrived from Blois would be filled both with dangers for her mission and endless ridicule. She would indeed keep constant prayers for patience and guidance on her lips.

Since her conversation with the Bastard, Jehanne felt certain the troops from Blois could arrive any day. She also concluded that God would want her to give the English more fair warnings. She dictated a second letter, and this time addressed it to Lord Talbot. Her letter stated that the English still had a choice—they could abandon their siege of Orléans and leave with no casualties. But, if they stayed, Jehanne's note continued, she and the French army would deliver such an assault upon them that she could not guarantee their safety.

She sent this letter via her two teenage heralds Ambleville and Guyenne, but only after they calmed her fears.

"We'll be fine," Ambleville told her. "We've both brought messages before during battle. Everyone knows we're just messengers and to be treated as if we were members of the diplomatic corps."

"That may be true," Jehanne said, "but the English have been known to break the rules of war whenever it suits them."

"We'll be just fine," added Guyenne with an impish smirk. "They may threaten to do us harm, but in the end, they'd have to get permission from Paris before they can do us any serious harm. That could take weeks, but we'll have driven them back to Paris by then," he said with a wink.

When Talbot received Jehanne's message, he took great umbrage at yet another effrontery from the girl and allowed only Ambleville to return. He threw Guyenne immediately into irons.

The message he sent back with Ambleville included every foul and rude word Talbot and his captains could dream up, including the promise that if they ever caught Jehanne they would burn her at the stake, and that, as a preview of that event, they would now burn her herald as an example and warning to her.

However, after Talbot sent that message, he immediately deployed his own herald to the University of Paris for permission to set the boy on fire.

Horrified at Talbot's message, Jehanne sent Ambleville back again with a message that if the English didn't immediately release her other herald, the French army would begin executing English prisoners currently held in Orléans.

The English returned Ambleville with still another foul message that also included the English offer to allow the girl safe travel back to her farm in Domremy.

At dusk, a mounted military escort, a few impassioned citizens of Orléans, and Jehanne left the protection of the city walls through the Port du Pont and rode south along Boulevard de la Belle-Croix Bridge past the Ile Saint Antone fort and stopped at the end of a ruptured structure, facing Les Tourelles. Because the French had destroyed two arches at the end of the bridge when the English began their siege, the girl now had to shout her message over the water into the English garrison inside the twin-spired bastille.

She called out to Sir William Glasdale. "I am Jehanne the Maid, sent by the King of heaven to command that you surrender this place and return to your own country. In the name of God, if you do not give up yourself and your men, you will face your destruction, for God has given me the power to drive you from this city!"

"Sheep-wench! Farm whore," came the immediate reply. "When we catch you, we shall burn you! Has Charles no real men to send against us such that all he has left is a silly and pathetic court jester?"

Jehanne glared through the dim light where these words had originated.

"You respond in peril of your lives and your souls! For God has promised that you shall be driven from this kingdom of France, and He will give us the means to do it."

"Do you expect us to surrender to a peasant girl, and a cheap harlot at that? Someone please take this milk hand back to where she belongs, back to your barracks for the night where she can do the kind of good God created her for."

"She's got to be good at something!" another added.

Loud laughter erupted out of Les Tourelles.

Jehanne's ears turned blush red. "You are all liars!" she shouted, "You will pay the price for your blasphemy!"

She turned her big white horse and began back along the Boulevard de la Belle-Croix Bridge. The sound of men's voices shouting insults at her echoed through the dusk as the girl fought her urge to tears.

Jehanne needed to compose her thoughts. She rode back across the bridge, noticed the church of Saint-Croix, dismounted, and asked the others to go on their way and let her be alone. Inside, she prayed, saw that a priest was hearing confession, and entered.

She told him who she was and explained that she had grave misgivings about her ability to carry out her mission.

"Jehanne, you need to trust in the Lord," he said. "He sent you here for a reason."

"I know, Father, but I didn't expect the people to be so wild and out of control."

She stopped talking, trying to maintain her composure.

"I don't know what to do when they follow me everywhere, cheering and yelling at the top of their lungs. They should be thanking God and praising His holy name. I am nobody—just a little farm girl from Domremy. I don't know what to say when they shout my name as if I were something special. I'm not special—God is."

The priest remained silent for a moment.

"Jehanne, you need to remember that you are his handmaiden—his faithful servant. Your being here is His will." He paused, deep in thought.

"Do you have any idea how much you mean to the people of Orléans? How you have given them hope? How they now believe they might live to see tomorrow? How their children and grandchildren and neighbors may live to see their tomorrows?"

Jehanne considered his words. "Well, I know what you say is true, but I can't say I understand it. I'm just a young girl and have only witnessed a small amount of suffering where I grew up. So, I don't really know what it's like to have huge boulders and flaming tar raining down on my home and those I love nearly every day for six months. But I can imagine that it's horrible . . . beyond words . . . a living nightmare."

"Well, that's a good start," he said.

Neither spoke.

"All right, Jehanne, make a good act of contrition and keep in mind what the people of this city have been through, and how much God loves and trusts you to do His will in order to help them *and* this country."

Chapter XIV
Rumors and Lies

Sunday, May 1, 1429

While Jehanne had attempted to deliver her personal warning to the English at Les Tourelles in the sincere hope they would accept that she had—in truth—been sent by God, the Bastard was carefully considering his own next moves. He understood how nervous and confused Jehanne felt because of his decision to leave her in Orléans while he rushed off to Blois. To offset some of her anxiety, he decided to take her steward Jean d'Aulon with him. He hoped that with d'Aulon at his side in Blois, Jehanne would later learn through the eyes of one of her most trusted associates how much the situation there teetered on the verge of collapse.

On Sunday morning, Jehanne and La Hire, together with a small detail of fifty soldiers, arose before dawn and quietly rode east across the city. After that they escorted the Bastard and d'Aulon out the Porte de Bourgogne and made a wide path around the Bastille Saint Loup—they fully expected the English to give chase any moment.

When they finally reached the Loire, a small barge awaited the Bastard and d'Aulon to take them across—they hoped it would be well out of sight of the English. Once on the south bank, the two men and a handful of soldiers retraced the path Jehanne had followed when she first came to Orléans from Blois—only this time it wasn't raining and the Bastard and his detail could travel at full gallop.

Jehanne and La Hire still thought an English attack likely as their small escort accompanied them back to Orléans through the same gate—they hoped to outrun them. But once safely back inside the city walls, La Hire turned to Jehanne.

"Well, that was certainly strange. Why didn't the English charge us? There're at least 300–400 men in Saint Loup. They could easily have overwhelmed us, if they had the mind to. It makes me nervous when the English pass up a chance to fight—a fight they might easily have won. Something most unusual is going on here."

"I feel it too," Jehanne said. "It's as if they're trying to set a trap for us—waiting for us to let down our guard. The whole city seems completely determined to keep celebrating—not paying any attention to the danger that could come at any moment."

Later, Jehanne and La Hire would recall this brief conversation—glad they did not know what was about to happen.

For the moment, the whole city seemed ready to renew the celebration they had begun Friday night—especially the soldiers. To their great delight, the Bastard had made arrangements for the troops to receive their pay that day. And by the time the girl reached the Boucher home, crowds thronged through the streets.

The ringleaders knocked so hard on the Boucher front door, Jehanne feared they might break it down. And they kept shouting *L'Angélique! L'Angélique!* over and over, which upset Jehanne so much she wanted to scream at them to be quiet and stop using that name.

I am most definitely not an angel!

Yet their exuberance signaled their belief in her mission, it occurred to her as the cries continued. The people wanted to see their *L'Angélique*, so why not let them see her all about the city? Why not just ride slowly through the streets most of the day and reassure the people how much she appreciated their countless sacrifices of time, treasure, and their very lives. Why not smile and be pleasant and ask them to pray for military success against the English in the name of the King of heaven?

The majority of her household had gone back to Blois with the Bastard, except her two pages and Ambleville. She could have them take turns holding her banner so she would be free to shake hands with the thousands who already filled the streets. Dozens of knights and squires would gladly accompany her along the city streets and at its holy places. The presence of military men with her would assure that things stayed under control. Her biggest worry: Citizens of the city getting hurt during their celebration.

So down the streets of Orléans she rode, banners held high, accompanied by a small detail of La Hire's most trusted men. And then out of their homes poured more people—the old and young, the rich and poor, men, women, and children; they crowded and gently pushed against each other to glimpse her.

Since it was Sunday and an unspoken truce should have existed, Jehanne decided to depart from the protection of the city walls on its western side. She left the city through the Renard Gate and rode toward the English fortifications along the Blois Road, through a village outside Orléans whose walls had been burned to the ground by the invaders. Surrounded by a double moat, a bastille stood on a slope at its crossroads called la Croix Boissée—so named because the townsfolk had erected a cross there, which every Palm Sunday they would dress with branches blessed by a priest.

Jehanne fully intended to reach this bastille, and then onto the camp of Saint-Laurent-des-Orgerils situated between la Croix Boissée and the Loire where she mistakenly thought Talbot and the English had established their headquarters. She still hoped to gain a hearing from them. But at the foot of the hill, at a place called la Croix-Morin, she met a group of enemy soldiers on watch duty.

As always, Jehanne worried about their spiritual health. "Surrender and your souls shall be spared," she said to them. "In God's name go back to England. If you do not, you will suffer for it," she continued.

They answered her with much the same insults as those at Les Tourelles. One of them, the Bastard of Granville, cried out mockingly, "Would you have us surrender to a mere child? We're soldiers of England. We're not going to surrender to some ignorant farm girl on horseback."

"If you did, you might save your immortal soul," she said.

The English laughed. "Go away, sheep-witch, before we put you to flame!"

Not only did these men direct their vile language at Jehanne, but at the soldiers with her. They called them pimps and tried to shame them for being in the company of a witch and whore, but they did not attack. Whether they thought her power rendered her invulnerable, or because they held that it would be too dishonorable to strike a female, as had been the case on several other occasions since Jehanne left Vaucouleurs, the English elected not to fire upon the girl or attempt to take her prisoner.

Later that night, exhausted and frustrated, Jehanne returned to the church of Saint-Croix where she found the same kind priest hearing confessions. He listened, and then gave her absolution and communion. She remained in the empty church on her knees in deep prayer for several hours until she remembered that the Boucher household may be worried about her. She led her horse through the darkness with a hood covering her head so no one would recognize her. She'd had enough of cheering crowds.

At the Boucher home, they welcomed her and offered food. As

before, she partook only of bread and watered wine, prayed again in their chapel, and retired.

———— >✳< ————

On Monday, May 2nd, when the Bastard and his small detail arrived back in Blois during the early morning hours, he first made sure those who came with him had proper accommodations. Next, he proceeded directly to the tent of Duke Jean d'Alençon.

They exchanged hugs. "Am I glad to see you," said d'Alençon, hurriedly waving the Bastard inside his tent. He instructed his guards to allow no interruptions.

Once both men were seated, d'Alençon began. "Sire Regnault de Chartres and his agents have been spreading misinformation among the troops about the situation in Orléans—especially among the veteran fighting men. He's telling them we have no hope of success in Orléans, and that the city is about to fall to the English siege."

The Bastard sighed. "I suspected something like that from Trémoïlle. That obese snake is scared he'll lose his power if we win in Orléans. The only reason Charles keeps him around is because he's the only one who will lend him money, and right now, the House of Valois is basically broke. If it weren't for Queen Yolande and her money, the battle for Orléans would be over."

D'Alençon nodded his agreement.

"Not only that, but if we were to win in Orléans, Trémoïlle and his friends would lose vast amounts of money invested in land and influence—not only in France, but across Europe—especially if Jehanne should also succeed."

The Bastard smiled. "Looks like my hunch to come here was right."

Later that morning, de Chartres et al. skulked out of town.

Meanwhile, Charles VII didn't know what to believe about the situation in Orléans. Having decided to remain in Chinon—ninety miles from the action and safe—it was impossible to obtain up-to-date intelligence; it took two to three days for information to arrive by special messenger on horseback.

Worse yet, Trémoïlle kept pushing the young prince to make preparations for a worst-case scenario. "After all," he repeated ad nauseum, "if you plan your next moves in light of a possible defeat in Orléans, you can rest assured that all alternatives will have been considered and that whatever the outcome, the best of your vital interests will have been given full weight."

And, as usual, Trémoïlle continued to argue for a possible healing of relations with the House of Burgundy since its duke had squabbled with Bedford and pulled his essential troops from Orléans. "Perhaps the time has arrived for a new understanding?" Trémoïlle proposed to Charles in private, never mentioning his older brother.

If it hadn't been for the Dauphin's wife, Queen Yolande, and their family's well-established intelligence sources, Charles might have been led astray by his closest advisor. God and his close staff knew that the young prince prayed for guidance, but Trémoïlle remained relentless. Much was at stake, and both men knew it. The English-Burgundian forces controlled most territory north and east of the Loire River and south to Lyon, plus the Bordeau territory on the southwestern border. If Orléans fell, the enemy would control the rest of the country. The people knew it too—especially inside the city.

The latest royal messengers from Orléans bore news of Jehanne's uproarious entry into the city, followed closely by the Bastard's quiet departure for Blois.

On the night of May 2nd, as the Dauphin paced anxiously in his Chinon Castle apartment, Jehanne attended the sunset daily prayer service called vespers at the Saint Croix cathedral, and then went back to confession.

"Bless me, Father, for I have sinned," she began, wiping away tears.

"What sins would you like to confess tonight, Jehanne?"

"I have come to realize that sooner or later fighting men are going to be dying in battle—with me being responsible. I don't want to be the reason men die or become disfigured. I didn't agree to that with my divine visitors."

The priest didn't say anything for a moment. Finally, he said, "Jehanne, surely you've always known that when men go to battle, some are going to be wounded or killed. That shouldn't come as a surprise."

"Yes, I know," she said, "but I thought since God sent me, He would make sure that when the enemy heard He sent me, they would realize they could never win. The English are Catholics the same as we. They know about God and His power."

"But," said the priest whose face she'd never been able to see in the darkened confessional, "just because you say God sent you doesn't mean a thing to the English. They say you're a witch, and that you've cast a spell on the Dauphin and anyone in the French army who has pledged to support you."

"But I've made my troops go to daily confession and Mass and communion. A witch wouldn't do that—and God wouldn't let her."

"They think it's all a trick to deliver both countries to the Evil One."

"A trick?" Her voice cracked as she began to sob quietly. "After all the priests and bishops and cardinals and learned men of the church put me through who cross-examined me for weeks and weeks down to the smallest detail of my life, and now the English think I'm helping Satan? They're liars!"

Lord, please help me get myself under control.

She wiped both eyes on her sleeves. "Dear Lord, I don't want to be the cause of French and Englishmen dying. Father God, please help me know what to do and forgive me for not knowing your will—for not listening correctly. And please, God, forgive me for my bad temper. I'm so very sorry. Please forgive me . . . For these and all the sins of my life, I am sincerely sorry."

The priest then granted her absolution and assigned her a penance—to kneel in silence until she felt sure she knew God's will for her in Orléans.

Jehanne did exactly what the priest requested, and then began new petitions. She prayed that if there was a way to avoid bloodshed, that the Lord and His visitors would give her guidance toward that path. She wondered if the two upcoming holy days—the Feast of the Finding of the True Cross tomorrow and the Feast of the Ascension on Thursday—might galvanize public prayer toward mercy for the English if they could be convinced to immediately withdraw.

When she finally arrived back at the Boucher home, she dictated another letter to Talbot proposing that the English immediately withdraw and that they would spare their lives and those of their men.

Glasdale saw Jehanne's proposal as an opportunity to firm up morale amongst his men and erase any traces of concern about her entry into the war. He called a meeting of his entire garrison—except those on guard duty—and invited each man to help himself to the many barrels of rum he'd requisitioned for just such an occasion.

After an hour had passed and with mug in hand, Glasdale announced, "I would like to propose a toast to the whore from Lorraine and Charles, the Bastard of Chinon, for their invaluable assistance in helping us prevail in the battle that will occur here in the next few days. Who but a whore and a bastard could have done such an incredible job of ensuring our victory?"

The men cheered wildly in agreement.

De Moleyns suddenly raised his mug. "And to think she had the unmitigated cheek to suggest we surrender to her. Those Frenchies must be wearing that poor girl out at night. No wonder she's taken leave of her senses!"

Glasdale stifled a smirk.

The garrison continued their bingeing well into the night until most of them fell asleep in a drunken stupor.

Before retiring, Glasdale and de Moleyns exchanged a quick wink.

On Tuesday, May 3rd, the Cathedral of Saint Croix celebrated the Feast of the Finding of the Holy Cross. According to tradition, Saint Helena, mother of Roman Emperor Constantine, discovered the sacred wood of Christ's cross. At age eighty, Helena had led a group to the Holy Land to search for the True Cross. There, she unearthed three crosses in the year 326. At the suggestion of Saint Macarius of Jerusalem, Helena took the crosses to a woman afflicted with an incurable disease, and had her touch each one.

Once her hand held the third cross, she was immediately cured. Helena built a church on the spot where she had found the cross and sent pieces to Rome and Constantinople.

In Orléans, on the morning of this feast day, Jehanne decided to ride her white horse and join the cathedral's procession, along with the city's magistrates and townspeople. While dressing for the parade, she told Madame Boucher, "I want to show the people of this beautiful city how important they are to me, and how much the Feast of the Holy Cross means to us all. It's such a miraculous symbol of hope for all Catholics—of Christ's eventual triumph over death."

"Why do you think it so important that the people understand that?" Madame Boucher asked. "They love you and believe you are their miracle come to save them from the English. They want you to defeat this vicious enemy who has brought them so much misery and death these many months and years. When they see you on your horse in the parade, they'll start to believe that you are more than a symbol—someone who will take action. They've had enough talk and symbols."

"You have no idea how much I want to take action today, but those who are more experienced in these matters say that we should wait until all the troops from Blois arrive. I have to admit that waiting is not one of my favorite gifts from God."

Tensions were running higher throughout Orléans with each passing hour; rumors spiraled out of control. The citizens would never forget Count Clermont and his cowardice at the Battle of Herrings, and they now had heard the rumors that the Dauphin's advisors were trying to betray Orléans in Blois. Another rumor held that the Marshal de Boussac, who had started with the Bastard to escort the second convoy of supplies, and who had been scheduled to arrive on May 3rd, decided not to come at all. A third rumor held that Regnault de Chartres, chancellor of France, might disband the entire French army.

Despite these rumors, Jehanne forced herself to show only warm and friendly smiles as she rode through the city during the day's feast day processions, waving and graciously acknowledging the people's applause and shouts of joy at seeing her.

"Rest assured," she told all in the crowds who would listen, "the fresh troops from Blois are safe and well on their way."

No one bothered to ask how she knew.

That same day, armed garrisons from the towns of Gien, Château-Regnard, Montargis, and Châteaudun arrived in Orléans.

Their presence quieted much of the gossip and raised morale. Toward dusk, word came from the late-arriving garrisons that the Bastard and the army from Blois had already begun their journey to Orléans.

Worried about what the English might be planning, La Hire posted around-the-clock sentries that afternoon in church towers: they were to ring the bells if the English gave any indication of preparing for an attack. The lookouts were also instructed to send immediate messages to La Hire, Jehanne, and the other captains within the city, once they spotted the torches, banners, and lances of the fresh troops from Blois.

Excitement filled the city much as it had in the days leading up to the arrival of the Jehanne the Maid. Only this time, there could be no doubt that the time of waiting was about to end. The battles with the hated English would begin in a matter of days.

Before going to bed that night, in the privacy of the Boucher chapel, Jehanne prayed about her failures and tried to banish the mind-numbing fear that she might let the people down. She had no idea what to do about their wild expectations and had no specific plan for how to defeat the English in battle.

And the idea of having to witness nonconfessed men hacked and maimed in combat made her sick to her stomach. She had tried to talk the English into leaving with honor, but they wouldn't listen. In the hours of greatest need for those men, she had fallen short in her attempts to do God's work through reason and logical negotiation. She felt great disappointment in herself.

Bloodshed would soon be unavoidable.

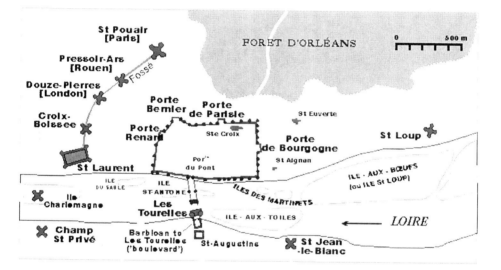

City of Orleans geographical map showing placement of English forts

CHAPTER XV
The Battle of Saint Loup

WEDNESDAY, MAY 4, 1429

At daybreak, Jehanne and La Hire rode out through Porte Renard between the English fortifications of Saint Laurent and la Croix-Boissee to meet the advancing troops from Blois, now known to have camped on the northern bank of the Loire. Jehanne wore her armor and full-battle gear. Alongside her rode Lord de Villars, monsignors Florent d'Illiers, Alan Giron, Jamet de Tilloy, several other squires, and men-of-war totaling approximately 500.

Like Jehanne, each soldier expected an English attack before they left the walls of Orléans. But the La Hire-led escort detail passed within bowshot range of Saint Laurent and la Croix-Boissee without incident or even a loud English "Hurrah!" Not even the usual vile insults for Jehanne came from inside the English fortifications—just an inexplicable silence.

Jehanne made it a point to have one of her pages hold her banner high for the English to see. She wanted to make sure they could never truthfully say she hadn't followed chivalric protocol at all times. The fact that the English had no immediate reaction to the French detail riding past their heavily fortified bastilles made La Hire believe that the enemy was planning an attack for when they returned.

172

And because the Bastard and the reinforcement troops had camped barely three miles west of Orléans, Jehanne and La Hire came upon them shortly. Leading the way was Father Pasquerel and his twenty priests singing "Veni Creator Spiritus" with their special banner held high.

"I kept my promise, Jehanne," Pasquerel announced in a loud voice. "All the men have gone to confession and received communion. Every day!"

Jehanne clasped both armored hands together over her head and shook them in vigorous delight and flashed her infectious smile. "Father, you are a man of your word. The angels in heaven are rejoicing this day for you and your incredible work!"

She turned her horse toward the rear of the column of foot soldiers, waving one arm. "We need to talk once we get back to the city."

Pasquerel waved back. "But of course."

Jehanne then cantered toward the rear of the column, searching for the Bastard. Seeing her approach, he quickly maneuvered his mount to a place where they could have a quick verbal exchange out of earshot of the marching troops and the other French captains. He dismounted and waited while she did the same.

When they were finally face-to-face, she raised her visor and said, "Greetings, my lord. I trust you had a successful mission."

He smiled and raised his eyebrows. "You might say that," he said, nodding in the direction of the marching troops. "We don't have time right now for all the details, but I suggest you consult with d'Aulon. He's been at my side since we left."

"Thank you, Sire. On our way here, we marched right past the English west side fortifications, but heard nothing. La Hire and the others think they might be planning an attack when we return."

"I doubt that," the Bastard said. "More likely their plan is to avoid confrontation until reinforcements arrive from Paris. I think

Talbot has ordered them to let us come and go as we please until Fastolf arrives with new troops."

Jehanne's face turned flush with excitement. "That's wonderful!" she exclaimed. "That means we can attack and overrun them right now while they're trying to avoid a fight. We'll catch them off guard and endure but few casualties."

The Bastard rubbed his forehead, deep in thought. "Jehanne, I know you think that would be a smart strategy, and I agree—in part. But, before we can do anything like that, we must first get all these new troops inside the city, settled, and coordinate an attack planned with the complete agreement of all field captains. Any attack before that would risk immediate defeat similar to what happened at Rouvray."

He paused, his thoughts interrupted by the grimace that stole across her face.

"Surely, Jehanne, you can appreciate the serious danger to your mission if we try to act before we have all the troops safely inside Orléans?"

The girl pulled off her steel helmet and shook her head. "No no no! I will not agree to any such thing," she said. "I have been more than patient. Two months have come and gone since I met with the Dauphin and told him that I had been sent by our Father in heaven to defeat the English right here. I've had to wait and wait and wait all this time, and for what? Now, we're not going to attack?"

The Bastard slowly removed his helmet and carefully placed it on his saddle.

Jehanne glared at him in silence, arms crossed in anger.

He pursed his lips and spoke almost in a whisper. "Jehanne, what would you like me to say?"

"That you've changed your mind and we're going to attack right now."

He took a deep breath and nodded agreement. "You have had

to wait a long time," the knight began. "And you have been incredibly understanding, especially having had no previous experience in such matters. I don't blame you for feeling frustrated and at the end of your patience."

He now looked straight into Jehanne's eyes. "Nonetheless, Jehanne, it would be suicidal to your mission and mine if we were to attempt a preemptive attack on the English positions at this time. If you cannot see that, I'll happily explain it to you in private once we're all safely inside the city. Until then, you'll just have to trust me. You do trust me, don't you?"

The girl returned his stare for a moment, then nodded slowly.

"Good, then we'll talk some more later." He put his helmet back on, mounted, and rode away to join the others.

For the moment, Jehanne would have to content herself with the safe return of her friends and household.

Dear God in heaven, I'm doing everything wrong. I don't know what to do. Please have mercy on my ignorance. Please, dear Lord, help me know what to do and say!

Within minutes, she greeted the Duke of Alençon whom she hadn't seen since April 26th, Jean d'Aulon, de Metz, and de Poulengy, followed closely by her brothers. The girl had forced herself not to think about how much she missed them all until this very moment and now had a hard time concealing her feelings of joy and delight.

Unknown to Jehanne, the Bastard and the other French captains had made covert arrangements to have a second large supply convoy advance to Orléans along the southern banks of the Loire—the route the Maid had followed when she first arrived. The French knew the English would closely monitor their large troop movements, but felt reasonably confident that they lacked the manpower and inclination to intercept this latest delivery of livestock, food, and provisions.

When Jehanne, La Hire, and the others encountered the advancing reinforcements from Blois, they were still too far west of Orléans to observe the latest supply column that had already arrived in Chécy. What the Bastard failed to mention to Jehanne was that he had made arrangements to have these new supplies met by a small armada of barges and boats to replicate the crossing of the Loire by Jehanne's supply convoy. This operation began at dawn and would take the rest of the morning and well into the afternoon—following the apparently "safe" eastern trail into the city, just north of the Bastille Saint Loup, and then into Orléans through Porte de Bourgogne.

Meanwhile, Jehanne, the Bastard, and a majority of the new troops entered the city through Porte Renard on the western side. Again, the French marched between the Bastilles Saint Laurent and la Croix-Boissee, and, again, the English did and said nothing—much to Jehanne's frustration and surprise. Her stomach roiled and grumbled, still expecting an English attack at any moment, but it never came.

The new troops occupied themselves with finding lodging, and the citizens of the city took great joy in making sure the new supplies had been distributed to suit everyone's needs. They were now one people trying to get used to the idea that their lives might now become more than just an exercise in survival.

After a joyful reunion with her returning friends and household, Jehanne made her way back to the Boucher home where she exchanged the suit of armor for her original traveling clothes, then shared a late-morning meal with d'Aulon and their hosts. Raymond and Minguet took it upon themselves to place her armor and its undergarments on the third floor by an open window where they would have a chance to dry out.

After their meal, she and her steward met in private. Learning from d'Aulon about the blatant treachery of Regnault de Chartres and his cohorts in Blois brought Jehanne's blood to boiling; she shook her head in disgust. "I don't understand why my gentle Dauphin permits such treason—from people he's supposed to be able to trust."

"Neither do I," said the thirty-nine-year old d'Aulon, "but I'm glad I went. The Bastard was most wise to travel to Blois when he did, and I'm glad I saw with my own eyes and heard with my own ears the deceit Trémoïlle and his people are prepared to use in order to undermine your mission."

Jehanne paused for a moment, nodding, then sighed. "It certainly is puzzling how these people can do these hateful things and get away with it. The next time I meet with my king, I will most definitely bring this up, but only if I can do so in private. I have to be careful of what I say in front of Trémoïlle and his friends like Regnault de Chartres, but I must pray for them too. I don't understand why God permits their treason."

Later, the Bastard arrived at the Boucher home and met with Jehanne in private—as he had promised. "I now have reliable intelligence reports," he said, "about what the English have apparently known for days—Fastolf is on his way from Paris to reinforce the English with fresh troops and could arrive in the next 24 hours."

Jehanne smiled radiantly. "This is wonderful news. Now we have the perfect reason to attack the English immediately. That's why they've let us come and go into the city without bothering us— they're waiting for Fastolf. This is a gift from our Lord!"

The Bastard smiled. "You may be right about that, Jehanne, but we can't do anything until we have all these new men properly settled and organized."

"And how long will that take?"

"Several hours—maybe the rest of the day."

"Why?"

"There's a lot to do, Jehanne. We've increased the number of troops inside the city walls by almost 100 percent. We're in no condition to effectively fight a battle until we've had a chance to review all our men, equipment, weaponry, and ammunition. Surely you can understand how important that is."

Jehanne smiled and shook her head. "You know me, Bastard, I'm always in a hurry!" A youthful playfulness welled up in her, and she said, "When the English reinforcements finally do arrive, please let me know immediately. I want to send them another letter to let them know that I know exactly how they can leave this city without taking any casualties." She smiled impishly. "I'm sure they'll be just *delighted* to read my every word!"

The Bastard snickered, and they joined in a hearty belly laugh.

Still smiling ear to ear, the Bastard stood and said, "I have to go now, Jehanne, but please rest assured, you will be kept fully informed."

Feeling at ease with the situation—at least for the moment—Jehanne decided to take a short nap. It was now almost noon, and she'd had little sleep the night before. She wanted to be fully rested for any battles that may develop once the fresh French reinforcements settled in. For the moment, everything seemed to be as it should.

Meanwhile, on the eastern side of Orléans, virtually no one had gotten any sleep. Once the second supply train began arriving at dawn the excitement of the people near that gate began to rise. Governor Raul de Gaucourt worried that the English garrison at Saint Loup might launch an open attack against the new incoming supply convoy. He had reports that the Goddons there had been yelling and shouting at all those passing by, apparently spoiling for a fight.

By early morning, the ordinary folk of Orléans had worked themselves into a fever pitch of delusion because of the recent spate of good news: the arrival of the two supply trains which had more than filled the city's storage facilities to overflowing, the safe arrival of the fresh troops from Blois, and the uplifting presence of their Jehanne the Maid in their midst—their long-awaited savior. Now, with her and God at their side, all things were possible. It was time to celebrate.

But, after too much wine for breakfast, many usually well-disciplined citizens felt called to march on the town hall, demanding culverins, scaling ladders, and any other battle equipment they could "borrow" for another diversionary skirmish against the English at Fort Saint Loup. Governor Gaucourt and his staffers met their demands as best they could, but then the governor—upon reflection—decided he needed to supervise these drunken amateurs as their field commander. What made it most attractive for the old soldier was that he had convinced himself that this entire sham attack could take place and succeed in distracting the English without any loss of life or the involvement of the upstart Jehanne. *The English aren't going to attack us just yet,* he thought.

Gaucourt wanted the people of Orléans to understand how they held the future of the city in their own hands. They didn't need any farm girl of dubious virtue from the Lorraine Valley telling them how to defend their city. Jehanne didn't have a minute of battlefield experience—and besides, she was a female. Everyone knows, he reminded himself, women don't know a thing about actual combat. He—the appointed governor of Orléans—had been fighting in this war against the English for forty years.

As the drunken men of the city circled about Gaucourt, now on horseback, shouting and waving their newly obtained weapons of war, plus any swords and shields they could find, the old man tried to get everyone's attention, but failed. Finally in desperation,

Gaucourt shouted an order, and the good male citizens of Orléans charged the Saint Loup Bastille, bellowing and screaming at the top of their lungs.

However, the troops at Saint Loup had been closely watching the city's main eastern gate. They knew their own situation—that they didn't have sufficient men to protect and defend their position. At least 25 percent of their garrison had been reassigned—some to Saint Jean-le-Blanc, some to Saint Augustins, and others to Les Tourelles to make up for the withdrawal of the Burgundy forces.

Moreover, Lord Talbot had left standing orders that each bastille was on 24-hour alert and in no case were they to engage the enemy unless first attacked. The English would wait for their reinforcements.

Still, the troops of Saint Loup wanted revenge for the embarrassment they suffered at the hands of the city's militia when the first supply train arrived with Jehanne. And now, when they saw the same Orléans militia pouring out of Porte Bourgogne and charging across the open field with newly acquired military hardware held high, they decided this was clearly a matter of self-defense and well within the Talbot rules of engagement.

Swords drawn, over half the garrison ran out and met the charging forces midway between their fortifications and Orléans. The English professionals immediately inflicted major casualties on the peasant militia.

The French had little to show for their escapade originally launched for God, country, freedom from tyranny, and to once again to embarrass the English. Worse yet, the invaders quickly exposed Gaucourt as a man whose leadership skills had long since been forgotten. The older man tried in vain to order a retreat, but the battle had escalated out of control. This time, the English were not going to allow the French another quick retreat back through Porte Bourgogne.

180

As the drunken French militia engaged with the English, friends and relatives watching from atop the city's walls immediately realized that the skirmish had been a fatal miscalculation. Many scrambled down off the walls, mounted horses, and rode through the streets yelling for help. Others ran behind them, screaming and pleading for the military to come quickly to the assistance of their overmatched fathers, husbands, brothers, and sons from the swords of English rage.

The sounds of screams and pounding hoofbeats echoing up and down the street outside her second-story window startled Jehanne from her brief nap. Trying to clear the cobwebs, she shook her head. Yes, she was still in the Boucher home, and, yes, it was still the same day, but something unthinkable had begun.

Why hadn't one of her staff awakened her? Jehanne felt rage welling up inside, pulling her out of control. Spotting d'Aulon still asleep across the room, she ran over and shook him. "Listen," she shouted, "something terrible is happening out there!"

The confused steward bolted up, squinting through sleep-filled eyes. Hearing the commotion outside, he tried to focus. "What is it? What's going on?"

He rolled out of bed trying to get his bearings while Jehanne ran down the stairs, where she encountered her brothers, Madame Boucher, and both squires staring out the open front door, frozen by the unfolding frenzy. She saw that Charlotte had stepped out onto the front stoop, watching the mass hysteria—men, women, and children running, shouting, screaming, and keening, while knights on armored mounts galloped and weaved between the throngs, kicking up a hovering cloud of dust in the early-afternoon sunlight. Madame Boucher yanked her daughter inside, slamming the front door. "You stay in this house, little girl. It's much too dangerous out there."

Dear Lord, we don't know if one of the bastilles has launched an attack on its own or if Fastolf and his fresh troops from Paris have arrived sooner than we thought and organized an immediate assault. Please help me know what to do.

"Raymond, saddle my horse for battle," she shouted above outside racket. "And Jean and Pierre, put on your armor—you're going to need it."

All ran off to complete their assigned tasks.

"Minguet, find my standard—right now," she ordered.

Charlotte and Mrs. Boucher stood transfixed by Jehanne'a outburst. "What's wrong with you two?" she barked. "Can't you see I need my armor before I can go into battle? Go find it and bring it down here so we can put it on quickly. I've got to stay here. Everyone's just standing around while French blood is being spilled!"

The boy hurried upstairs, wailing, "Oh no. Oh no!"

Mother and daughter raced up the stairs and searched the two top floors in panic for Jehanne's armor. When they finally located all of it and scrambled back down the two flights of stairs, they found Jehanne pacing the floor like a caged mountain lion.

"Can't you hurry up?" she bellowed, stomping a foot. "The battle will be over before I get there."

Madame Boucher and Charlotte tried desperately to attach the padded undergarments to the thick plates of exterior armor, but fumbled badly, having never done it before under such stress.

Monsieur Boucher ran up the front steps and ripped open the door. "Jehanne, your horse won't be ready for a few minutes yet. Raymond's having trouble with the armor." Seeing his wife and daughter struggling with Jehanne's armor, he knelt down to help. "The secret is strapping the armor to the correct arms and legs in the right order. The legs have to go first and the arms and hands last."

Minguet ran downstairs out of breath. "I heard through the upstairs windows that a battle at Bastille Saint Loup has begun, and we started it!"

"Wretched boy!" Jehanne blurted, barely able to contain her rage at not having been told of the battle by the Bastard. "Go help Raymond. I need my horse right away!"

The noise of people screaming and horses clattering as they rushed past the Boucher home was so loud the girl could barely collect her thoughts.

The Boucher family was now making good progress with her armor, but standing still did not come easy.

"Where's my helmet? I don't see it!"

Charlotte bolted up the stairs. "I know!"

Minguet returned. "Your horse is ready."

"Find my standard!" she barked.

Minguet ran back upstairs, gasping for air.

"And don't forget my sword!" she ordered.

Jehanne clasped her hands together and looked upward in silent prayer.

Please, God, don't let me be too late.

Minguet bounded down the stairs, Jehanne's standard and sword in hand, followed closely by Charlotte waving the helmet.

"We're done with your armor," the Boucher adults announced.

She threw open the front door saying, "To horse, to horse!" and almost knocked over Father Pasquerel coming up the front steps to hear her afternoon confession.

Raymond had waited for her in an alley beside the house, white horse at the ready.

Men and women darted wildly in all directions, bellowing and wailing.

Jehanne mounted her horse, took the standard, thanked all who had helped her, and galloped off in the direction of the screaming crowds—toward the eastern city gate.

Dear God in heaven, please help me!

Moments later, d'Aulon mounted his own warhorse and by the time Jehanne slowed for the Porte Bourgogne gate, he and the rest of her military staff had caught up.

But a new problem awaited. Mass confusion engulfed the gate as fresh French troops attempted to muscle their way outside the city gate to join in the battle underway, while those severely wounded from the abortive attack on Saint Loup required immediate entry back into the city and treatment of their wounds.

Upon seeing a young soldier about her age on a stretcher with blood flowing from arrow wounds to his chest and midsection, Jehanne bowed her head.

Please, God, help him recover and bless his immortal soul.

She had never before witnessed battle conditions where men clashed in mortal combat—to kill or be killed.

"God go with you," she said to the soldier. "And may He keep you safe."

She nodded at the young man and quickly made her way through the bottleneck and out into the open field. D'Aulon, both her brothers, Minguet, Raymond, de Metz, de Poulengy, and La Hire never left her side.

The Saint Loup bastille stood more than a mile in the distance. Jehanne could easily see its belfry tower. At its entrance, pennants belonging to the various French army companies that had already reported to the scene luffed slowly in a lazy eastern breeze.

The English were now employing their newly repaired earthwork fortifications as a launching ramp for cannons. The sound of their vicious explosions echoed off the river and nearby forest as large balls of metal landed close to the retreating men. The girl could also see the flash of swords in the bright afternoon sun as both sides fought hand to hand close to the converted convent fortification.

Astride her white warhorse and dressed in gleaming silver armor and helmet, Jehanne raced toward Saint Loup, her long, white standard held high in defiance. Behind her rode the Bastard, La Hire, de Metz, de Poulengy, and the several other veteran French field captains and their companies.

Jehanne observed that the English, upon seeing her and the 1,500 men with her, now abandoned their hand-to-hand combat with the French militia and beat a hasty retreat to the hoped-for safety of Saint Loup.

The once-retreating French troops under Gaucourt, seeing the Maid galloping fearlessly into battle, gave out a huge cheer and followed. Gaucourt tried to save face by staying behind and going through the motions of assisting the dead and wounded.

Jehanne rode straight to the entrance of the bastille and planted her standard in the ground just outside its outer moat. The French foot soldiers now ran up and formed a cluster around her.

Jehanne leaned forward in her saddle, helmet visor up.

"Men of France," she began. "You know me. I am Jehanne the Maid. Some of you have been with me since Vaucouleurs; some have traveled with me from Chinon to Poitiers to Tours. We have slept on the cold, damp ground together, and we have all sung psalms and hymns and gone to Mass and communion together.

"Just a few days ago, some of you made your way here with me through a torrential downpour. And just this morning, a great number of you entered this beautiful city having just traveled from Blois."

She nodded slightly in the direction of the Bastard and La Hire.

"But all of you know beyond any doubt that God has sent us all to Orléans to do His work. He has promised us victory, if we will but believe in Him."

She paused and withdrew her sword, then turned in her saddle and pointed it at Saint Loup. "That is where God's mission for us begins, men of France!"

A loud cheer burst forth from the men, and they wouldn't stop.

Finally, Jehanne got the attention of trumpeter and indicated she wanted the men to stop cheering. And when the trumpet blast finally produced quiet, the girl sheathed her sword and spoke.

"Let me remind all of you," she began, "that this bastille has been rebuilt by the English. Before that, it was a church and convent for the Ladies of Saint Loup. The English have tried to turn it into a place of death, but it's still a house of God. So no one is authorized to remove anything from this holy ground for personal use. The only objects any of us will remove from this church and its lands are food and ammunition supplies. No exceptions!"

As those words left her lips, the church bells in Orléans began to peal. It was a warning signal that the Bastard had put in place to indicate large numbers of English troops were on the move.

At that same moment, a rider from the city galloped toward Jehanne and the troops around her, trailing a cloud of dust. After dismounting, the rider handed the Bastard a written message.

A nervous silence fell upon those assembled.

After reading the note to himself, he announced, "Lord Talbot has assembled several hundred troops. They just departed the Saint Pouair Bastille, headed this way."

The Bastard looked in the direction of the Porte Bourgogne gate and saw about 600 fresh French militia galloping toward Saint Loup. He quickly ordered Lord Saint Sévère to intercept those men and lead them in pursuit of Talbot and his advancing forces.

Jehanne rode her horse back to where she had planted her standard in the ground. She pulled it up, raised it high, and pointed it at Saint Loup.

The men-of-war around her began to cheer.

"Onward, men of France!" she yelled above the men's uproar, gripping the pole tightly. "Do not be afraid, for God is on our side!"

Immediately, a lusty roar leapt from the throats of the French soldiers, and they stormed as one into the Saint Loup complex.

For three hours, the battle ebbed and flowed. Jehanne ran from one group of soldiers to another, always encouraging them or leading another charge up a scaling ladder, or pulling up fallen warriors who had been knocked from a ladder by hurled English stones or hot tar. English arrows and cannons landed all about her, but none pierced her armor. Some arrows hit her, but they merely glanced off and fell onto the once-sacred ground.

"Men of France," she kept shouting, "keep up the fight and victory will be ours! God brought us here to do His work, and He will never abandon us."

By now, the French cannons inside Orléans had zeroed in on the Fort Saint Loup, and their large metal balls of destruction began crashing down on the superstructure of the remodeled bastille.

Jehanne paid no attention to the noise and danger falling from the sky around her. La Hire and the Bastard kept one eye on her as the battle raged, and not once did they see her shy away from the destruction, noise, or danger. The other French field commanders and their men noticed that the girl never ran out of energy and never stopped pleading and shouting, "Keep up the fight, men of France, and victory will be ours!"

There were a few moments when wounded English soldiers started to come at her with their swords drawn, but she seemed to ignore them when other French soldiers intercepted her would-be attackers. Not once did she unsheathe her sword. Jehanne never told anyone she never intended to use her beautiful sword— it was only for self-defense in case of an actual hand-to-hand attack.

As the battle raged, the strength and height of the church belfry tower proved a major obstacle for the French—it was too tall and too well-built. And it required little effort by the enemy to simply tip the French attack ladders backward, especially when supporting several soldiers laden inside battle armor. Although outnumbered better than three-to-one, the English held the high ground inside an almost-impenetrable masonry structure. Even when struck with French cannonballs, destruction to the tower usually proved minimal. Despite this, the English soldiers noticed something different: the French were not about to give up. As fast as the English tipped one ladder backward, one or two more took its place.

Eventually, one of the French heavy cannons fired from Orléans struck a fatal blow. No one knew exactly how the fire started, but after one large French cannonball hit the very top of the Saint Loup belfry, the masonry tower began to burn. Dark, dank clouds of smoke suddenly billowed up into the clear spring air.

Soon afterward, many English soldiers decided it was time to surrender. They didn't want to burn to death inside an old French church. The extent and white heat of the fire made it clear they wouldn't be getting any revenge against the French today. Several donned abandoned priestly vestments and filed out from the burning bastille, hands raised and begging for their lives.

"Kill the fake priests," cried several French soldiers. "Kill them all," others yelled. "They deserve to die a painful death after what they've done here. Let's tie them to a stake and set them on fire!"

Jehanne watched and listened to the men. She couldn't understand how men who go to Mass and communion every day and who also knew they had been sent to Orléans to do God's work could act so much against what Jesus taught. She knew she had to say something. "One should not question the bona fides of the men of the church."

The Bastard and La Hire quickly moved to take charge of the

situation to make sure that all French soldiers treated the surrendering English in accordance with Jehanne's instructions for chivalrous behavior.

The Battle of Saint Loup had come to an end, and the French had passed an important milestone—not because it represented a decisive battle, but because it showed that morale in the French army was different now—the men believed they could beat the English.

Under the veteran leadership of La Hire and the Bastard and his fellow captains, the French army took control of the bastille and unearthed great quantities of provisions and essential war supplies: ammunition, cannonballs, and the great iron cannon that prior to Jehanne's arrival had so often wreaked havoc on the inhabitants of the city. Work began immediately on the demolition of the fort. They took down its fences, removed the stakes, and burned the wood posts and slats.

Next, the Bastard ordered all the buildings within the complex burned and reduced to rubble so that the English could never again use them against the French. A preliminary casualty report showed that only two French soldiers had died as a result of wounds suffered during this battle; the English lost 140 dead and forty taken prisoner. The full injury report for both sides would take several days.

Jehanne wept at the loss of life. "Father God," she prayed out loud, "so many Englishmen have died without confession—especially on the eve of the feast of your Son's glorious ascension into heaven. Please, Lord, help me know what to do."

The French marched back to the city with cannon, prisoners, and banners on full display. The day marked the first bit of positive military news the people of Orléans had experienced in a long time and especially since the beginning of the siege last fall.

"In truth," Madame and Monsieur Boucher told their little Charlotte, "this was the first time the French had been on the winning side of any substantive battle against the English since March 21, 1421, at the Battle of Baugé."

By dusk, the bells were resounding and the people rejoicing beyond anything Orléans could recall, including Jehanne's march into the city. She had now become their deliverance—not just a hope of deliverance. And the press of the people struggling and shouldering against each other to get a glimpse of her as she rode through the streets today was so great, she could hardly push her way through to the cathedral for a Mass of thanksgiving.

Afterward, she returned to the Boucher home to change clothes and inform her staff of her plans. "Father Pasquerel and I will be leaving in a few moments to visit the English prisoners we captured at Saint Loup. We plan to offer them confession and communion and make sure they are being properly fed and their wounds cared for. Any of you who would like to join us on this mission is more than welcome."

Her entire staff went with her, including her brothers.

Meanwhile, the Bastard and his two friends, La Hire and de Xaintrailles, gathered in his quarters for a private drink and conversation. All three kept smiling at each other and shaking their heads in disbelief about the events of the day. "You know what?" the Bastard finally said. "This whole day would probably have never happened except for the arrogance and stupidity of Sire Raul Gaucourt."

The other two chuckled and took a gulp of their beer.

"You know what's even more ironic?" said de Xaintrailles. "Fifty-eight-year-old Governor Gaucourt was so determined to show that Jehanne was useless, unnecessary, and should be sent back to

Domremy that he achieved the opposite. Now our men will probably follow her anywhere, no matter what."

"What do you mean 'our men'?" said La Hire. "Hell, *I'll* follow that girl into battle—anywhere!"

The three friends lifted their mugs in salute, and as they did they couldn't help but hear the sounds from outside. The people were giving Jehanne a new name. From their lips it reverberated into the air and echoed along the streets and down the alleys of their beautiful and proud city. They decide to replace *l'Angélique* with *la Pucelle du Orléans.*

"She's not going to like that," said the Bastard.

La Hire laughed. "The people don't care if she likes it or not. That's how they feel. They love her, and nothing Jehanne can do or say will change their minds."

CHAPTER XVI

The Battles for
Saint Jean-le-Blanc
and Les Augustins

ASCENSION THURSDAY, MAY 5, 1429

Before going to bed Wednesday night, although still grieving the loss of the lives of unconfessed English soldiers and her role in their deaths, Jehanne finally found the strength to take a deep cleansing breath and confide to Father Pasquerel, "Tomorrow, I will not go to fight nor put on armor, and out of reverence for the feast day, I will make my confession and receive the sacraments."

And so, Jehanne again rose early and made her confession. Then, dressed in street clothes, she mounted her horse and rode to the cathedral where she attended Mass and received Holy Communion. The priest who celebrated the Mass at the cathedral used the previous day's events as a springboard for his sermon, which he ended with these words: "As Jesus instructed us many times during His brief visit on earth, we are called to pray for all those who lost their lives here in battle yesterday—especially the English soldiers. Why should we pray for English soldiers? Because they are God's people as much as we are. We know that all French soldiers go to daily Mass and communion, but also have reason to believe that the English soldiers do not."

He paused briefly and looked around at the crowded pews. "Please bear in mind, my dear French neighbors and friends, Jesus did not come into this world for a favored few—He came to gift eternal salvation to all men, women, and children. That means the English too."

Afterward, Jehanne repeated to the crowds waiting outside the church that there should be no battles on this feast day, and that all French soldiers should go to confession and remove any and all temptations to sin from their lives. She also repeated that she would not fight alongside soldiers who had not gone to confession, attended Mass, or received communion.

She then rode back through the heavy crowds to the Boucher home. Unknown to her, the Bastard had convened in the Boucher home a secret council of war to plan their next strategy. When Jehanne at long last arrived back inside the Boucher house, her staff explained about the closed-door meeting.

Without a word, she went to her bedroom, deeply hurt at having been excluded. She'd just won a battle for the French the day before—a battle no one expected to win. It had been one the military leaders thought lost, yet she and their Father in heaven had led them to victory. But they still didn't trust her enough to take her into their confidence.

Father, God, please grant me patience and heal my hurt feelings.

When the military leaders finally did invite Jehanne into their meeting, the Bastard asked her to have a seat beside them around the table now covered with maps of the city. La Hire nodded his agreement and pulled out a chair for her.

But Jehanne refused and paced the floor, instead, wringing her chapeau. The field commanders advised her that the plan for the next day was to organize their forces for a violent attack against

Bastille Saint Laurent. They further explained that they now held sufficient numbers to easily overwhelm that particular fort—especially since the latest news about Fastolf indicated that he and his troops were still en route.

Finally, Jehanne had heard enough.

"Tell me what you have really decided and appointed. I should know how to keep a far greater secret than that."

The captains looked at each other, eyebrows raised, but said nothing.

Jehanne started to leave.

The Bastard rose immediately to block her exit.

"Jehanne," he said, "do not get angry. We cannot tell you everything at once."

"And why not?" she snapped.

"Because we're afraid you might get captured and tortured and reveal our plans."

"In other words, you don't trust me. You don't think I'm tough enough to keep a secret—no matter how much they make me suffer. Isn't that right?"

The Bastard looked her squarely in the eyes. "Jehanne, frankly, we don't know what to think. We know you mean well, but you're an inexperienced young woman. You've never been through any of this before." He opened his arms, palms up, and shrugged. "What would you do if our roles were reversed?"

"I'd believe in someone sent by God," she said emphasizing each word. "That's what I'd do. I'd have confidence that God knew what He was doing and would not send someone too weak for the job."

La Hire cleared his throat. "I think we are being unfair to Jehanne—especially in the light of the fact that if it weren't for her leadership and the bond she has with the men, we might easily have lost at Saint Loup yesterday. God knows Gaucourt did his best to make that happen, and we've been trusting him with all our plans since the Dauphin appointed him governor."

The Bastard sighed. "All right, Jehanne. You and La Hire make some good points. So what I'm about to tell you remains in this room. Agreed?"

Jehanne nodded slowly. "Agreed."

He then outlined what their ruse had been and what the real plan was—to try to trick the English into sending reinforcements to help defend Saint Laurent, thereby weakening the garrisons at Saint Jean-le-Blanc and Saint Augustins.

The Bastard further revealed that it was these two bastilles that he and the other French commanders really intended to attack because they were the key outposts defending Les Tourelles, which they knew held the key to quickly raising the English siege. He ended by saying to her in his most conciliatory tone, "We consider this plan good and profitable."

The girl, while clenching her cheek muscles and remembering what the Bastard had told her about her fellow captains, considered what she had just heard and nodded slowly.

The room remained silent for a moment as she cast her eyes into the faces of each man present. "Very well," she said, and then left the war room without another word. She felt her emotions roiling up inside her and didn't want to embarrass the Bastard or further alienate the other captains.

Jehanne went to her room and knelt in prayer and concluded that on this Feast of the Ascension, the Father in heaven would want her to attempt one more act of Christian charity toward the English.

She hoped they would come to realize that it was the will of their mutual God that they leave France and return home—once and for all. She had merely been called to be a living witness to the will of God. She had no agenda other than that. If it were up to her, she would much rather be at home in Domremy on her parents' farm.

She summoned Father Pasquerel and went to confession. Afterward, fighting through her frustration, she dictated the following:

"You, men of England, who have no right to be in this kingdom of France, the King of heaven commands you through me, Jehanne la Pucelle, to abandon your forts and go back where you belong; which if you fail to do, I will make such an uproar as will be eternally remembered. I am writing to you for the third and last time. I shall not write any more.—Jhesus Maria, Jehanne la Pucelle."

Afterward, she inserted a postscript:

"I would have sent you my letter in a more honorable manner, but you have detained my herald, Guyenne, which is against all rules of war. Please send him back to me, and I will send back some of your people captured at Saint Loup, for they are not all dead."

She then fastened the letter to an arrow and rode out of the city along the long masonry bridge that crossed the Loire but had been blasted away from Les Tourelles by the French when the English attacked last October.

Jehanne was accompanied by Pasquerel and an expert bowman. She stopped at the closest point to Les Tourelles and told her bowman to shoot the arrow into a target in plain sight within the English stronghold where it would not injure anyone.

As the sharpshooter pulled back his bow, Jehanne shouted to the English, "Read this. I bring you good news!"

Once the English retrieved the arrow and read its message, they began to yell and laugh. "This is news?"

"More *exciting* news from the Armagnac whore?"

"Go home, cow-wench!"

"I pray I catch you and spend a night with you before burning you to death!"

Jehanne turned her horse and rode back toward the city, sighing and feeling an utter failure. Tears welled up as she rode the rest of the way back to the Boucher home.

Before going to bed that night, she asked Pasquerel to rise extra early the next morning so she could go to confession and Mass before participating in whatever attacks the Bastard and his captains had finally agreed to use against the English.

When Jehanne finally retired that night, she had no idea if the French commanders planned to first attack Saint Laurent (on the northern bank of the Loire) or Saint Jean-le-Blanc and Saint Augustins (on the southern bank).

Friday, May 6, 1429

The day began for Jehanne with Father Pasquerel hearing her confession, and then saying Mass for the entire Boucher household. Everyone, including the Maid, received communion. Throughout the service, Jehanne silently prayed for the combatants she feared might die later that day. She knew the French would go to confession and Mass, but the English would not, and that realization brought her to silent grief. There was nothing more she could do. The Lord knew she tried to warn them, so she prayed that He would have mercy upon them.

During Mass, the loud sounds of horses and soldiers marching along the streets filled the inside of the Boucher home. Sometime later, Jehanne came outside in battle armor, her white horse waiting with most of her military staff. D'Aulon informed her that the soldiers and people of the city needed her immediately at Porte de Bourgogne.

When she finally worked her way through the crowd at the gate, it was closed. The governor of Orléans, Lord Raul de Gaucourt, along with a well-armed but small detail of soldiers and bowmen, awaited her.

"Jehanne d'Arc," the governor said, "you are hereby ordered to remain in the city and under no circumstances are you to leave it for the rest of this day."

"Hah!" she said. "By whose order?"

"By order of the city war council," Gaucourt said. "They have decided not to engage in any battle with the English today."

"Why?"

"I don't know, but that is their final decision," he said, voice rising with annoyance.

"They are wrong. The militia of the city should attack the Bastille of the Augustins," Jehanne answered. "Many of the men-at-arms and the people of this city are of the same opinion. Who are you? You're not even from this city. These people know what's best for them!"

"I have my orders," Gaucourt said. "You are not to leave the city."

Jehanne then said, "Lord de Gaucourt, your procrastination does no good for this city or France. And like it or not, Sire, these soldiers know what they must do, and they're going to do it—with or without your assistance."

With that, the French soldiers surrounding Jehanne forced open the gate and escorted her through the opening.

Gaucourt and his detail had no choice but to step aside. Jehanne and her men greatly outnumbered them. "May I be of service?" he asked as she passed by.

"God's army includes all who believe and are willing to do His will," she answered.

More French troops—militia and professional men-at-arms—now joined forces and hurriedly marched down to the northern bank of the Loire—well ahead of Jehanne. They commandeered small wooden flatboats and tied them end-to-end as an improvised pontoon bridge to the Ile-Aux-Toiles. From there they would cross to the southern bank of the Loire and attack the Saint Jean-le-Blanc Bastille.

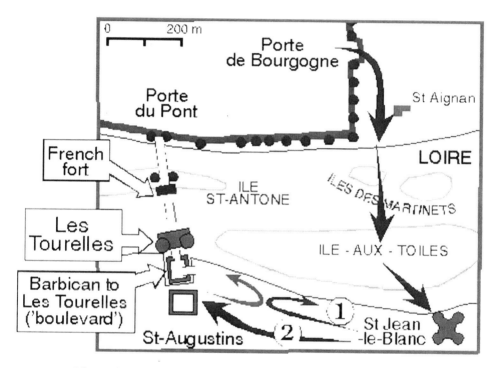

Jehanne's attack movements against Fort Augustins, May 6, 1929

This fort had been hastily pressed into service by the English just a few weeks ago as a lookout post designed to hold a garrison of less than 300 men. Like Saint Loup, this bastille had also been surrounded with buttressed earthworks and a deep trench by the English. But when they saw the noisy French militia now pouring across the Loire headed directly for their position inside Saint Jean-le-Blanc, the English beat a hasty retreat westward to the more secure fortifications of the Saint Augustins bastille.

Meanwhile, mere minutes after the English retreat, the first group of French troops—200 or so—accompanied by de Gaucourt, charged into Saint Jean-le-Blanc, hoping to catch the English unprepared, but found it completely abandoned. Realizing that the English had withdrawn inside Saint Augustins, de Gaucourt ordered these troops to break off their attack and await reinforcements. The remainder of the French forces were still making their way on foot through the bottleneck caused by the narrow makeshift pontoon bridge. Jehanne and La Hire found themselves caught in this disorder because of the difficulty of getting their own horses across the water.

The English garrison that had abandoned Saint Jean-le-Blanc now watched the French troops from the safety of Saint Augustins. But seeing the French milling around the Saint Jean-le-Blanc grounds in a state of disorganization, the former English Saint-le-Blanc forces saw an opportunity and took it upon themselves to charge the French. They poured out of Saint Augustins screaming their bloodcurdling battle cry and engaged the French in a vicious counterattack.

Expecting that the French reinforcements would get there any moment, Gaucourt ordered the men with him to stand ready. But the English came too quickly and attacked before the new troops could arrive. It became clear to Gaucourt that they were about to be overrun. He ordered a retreat, but heavy casualties had already taken place.

Meanwhile, La Hire, Jehanne, and the balance of French men-at-arms had finally completed leading their horses across the makeshift bridge and onto the southern bank. The Maid and La Hire mounted first and, seeing the English in hot pursuit of the French soldiers, fixed their lances and charged straight at their stampeding enemy.

"Go forward boldly in the name of God," Jehanne shouted for all to hear.

A downpour of enemy arrows had already begun to rain upon them, but the girl paid no attention. Nor did she care that the French still had no grand plan of which she was aware. She knew about only one thing: her men couldn't win by retreating.

The troops with her—seeing her disregard of the danger—immediately raised their voices with their own primordial battle scream and raced into the battle alongside Jehanne, La Hire, and the other French captains.

When the charging English spotted the fully armored Jehanne on her white horse with her long banner rippling in the breeze, they began yelling.

"Come to me, French whore! I hear you're pretty good at your trade."

"Hurry up and let me take you down. I need something to keep me warm tonight."

"Farm-wench, go home!"

"Rotting harlot. You were lucky yesterday, but not today!"

"I wonder how a French witch smells when she's on fire?"

But when the English insults reached the ears of the French fighting men, it made them angry, and they began to congregate around Jehanne.

"Follow me, men of France," she shouted. Soldiers who had been in retreat suddenly turned and joined Jehanne's charge.

The English who had so confidently charged out of Saint Augustins expecting to exploit the apparent French confusion at Saint Blanc now stopped in their tracks. Not in their wildest dreams did they ever expected a counterattack in such strength.

As Jehanne, La Hire, and all the French troops bore down, these same charging English soldiers turned tail and once again ran for the safety of Saint Augustins.

Watching the English now in full flight, Jehanne asked for her white pennant from a page and galloped full speed to the Saint Augustins compound. Totally focused on the task at hand, she dismounted, walked to the fosse, and jammed the banner in the ground with sufficient force to ensure that it wouldn't fall from its own weight or the brisk morning breeze now blowing from the east.

Looking side to side for a possible English attack against her person on the way back to her horse, she didn't pay attention to where she walked and inadvertently stepped onto a hidden caltrop—a buried weapon made of two or more sharp nails and built so that one nail always pointed straight up. Designed to cripple both horse hooves and the feet of soldiers, the razor-sharp metal easily penetrated the sole of the girl's boot.

Jehanne uttered no sound but picked up the injured foot for inspection. She balanced on one foot and quickly removed the spike from her foot, tossing it to where it couldn't do any further harm to man or beast.

She could feel her boot filling with fresh blood as small droplets leaked from the bottom of her foot with each step toward her horse. Like most French farm girls, Jehanne had long ago been exposed to physical injury and the sight of blood.

She'd seen her father stab his foot with a pitchfork, and there was the time her father shot at a hungry wolf as he stalked the

202

family cows and the noise startled the cows so that they panicked and ran over her brothers—they certainly bled a lot.

And then there was the time an overly protective buck goat gored Jehanne in the stomach at age twelve. She'd been able to handle the pain, but blood ran all over her clothes, the barn, and the kitchen floor. Fortunately the village doctor lived close and stopped the bleeding with ample use of bandages and lard. Jehanne also remembered how her parents worried that the sight of so much blood might scare her, but she reassured them that she was fine.

Right now, she just ignored the pain from the caltrop and limped slowly back to her horse in silence. After taking a moment to gather herself, she remounted. Just then, La Hire and the rest caught up and gathered around. "We saw what happened," he said. "Are you able to continue?"

She studied the man for a moment and nodded with a twinkle in her eye. "You don't think I'm going to miss the battle for Saint Augustins, do you? They'd have to do a lot more to me than make one foot bleed."

La Hire laughed.

"Trust me, Jehanne, they're going to try as hard as they can to do much more than that to you. You know about that, right?"

She smiled. "I know."

The girl paused and stared at the Saint Augustins complex for few moments.

"Don't you just love it when the English look down their noses at us and think we're stupid cowards who will run away the first time they growl at us?"

La Hire laughed and nodded. "Yeah, I do love it. I love it a lot!"

Just then, d'Aulon rode up, Jehanne's banner in hand. "Do you want me to carry this for you?" he asked quietly.

She smiled. "Good idea, Jean, but I think I'll do it. Thank you, though."

She took it from him and pointed it at Saint Augustins. "Men of France, the Lord is waiting for us to do His work. Right now!"

Just then, Jehanne spotted the Bastard leading a detail to the western side of the Saint Augustins church. By now the pain of her injury had left her thoughts, and she pointed her banner in the direction the Bastard and said, "Men of France, charge!"

D'Aulon, her brothers, La Hire, de Metz, de Poulengy, and the rest of her staff all joined with her as she rode toward the Bastard approaching the newly refurbished fort.

Jehanne's conviction and commitment to an attack seemed to fill the rest of the French troops with a renewed courage. Together with Jehanne, they raced as one cohesive unit toward the bastille.

Ahead, Jehanne saw open land that looked to have once been a garden—spring leaves and flowers had begun to sprout—alongside the now-burned remains of a kitchen. This green patch still had its original retaining wall and a door that opened into the chapel. The French troops ahead of Jehanne ran across the lawn, past the trees toward the door, intent upon taking the chapel. But a giant Englishman with red hair blocked them. Behind him, other English soldiers raced to safety from the charging French by jumping the fence, sliding down to the waterless moat, and then on to the boulevard.

A few French soldiers rushed the giant, only to be felled by the man's huge broadsword. D'Aulon, who had remained at Jehanne's side, saw the carnage and immediately ordered a marksman to fire a culverin at the giant.

The blast from the weapon momentarily deafened Jehanne, but tore a huge hole in the giant's chest. Seeing the downed behemoth, the French troops bellowed another fierce battle cry and raced through the doorway into the yard. Jehanne felt slightly sick to her stomach, but knew she had to keep moving.

Once inside, the French entered the churchyard. The trapped

English forces counterattacked and soon the grass became soaked with blood from the slain and wounded. The able-bodied stepped over the fallen and continued in hand-to-hand combat using shields raised upward for protection against a hail of English arrows from the roadway above.

Meanwhile, Jehanne dismounted and hobbled into the yard, Minguet at her side. She handed him her banner. Seeing so many lying on the ground—dead and wounded—she began assisting those she could, all the while yelling encouragement for the soldiers.

Minguet stayed at her side. In one hand he held her standard and in the other his shield held high to deflect arrows headed her way. The battle lasted several hours—the English slowly losing to the French ferocity.

By dusk, the outcome was no longer in doubt; the French now outnumbered the English. Many English soldiers had sacrificed their lives so others could make their way over the fence, across the moat, and into Les Tourelles. Saint Augustins now belonged to the French. Once again, Jehanne had led a rout—this time of two English fortifications.

As they had done at Saint Loup, the French military searched the newly won bastille and discovered many comrade prisoners for whom they arranged immediate medical attention. The victors also discovered significant stores of food and ammunition, which some of the French soldiers began stealing for personal use.

This lack of discipline angered Jehanne, and she ordered the Saint Augustins grounds—except its original convent—set on fire. She shouted loud enough that all could hear, "Les Tourelles, now filled with frightened English troops, will be our next objective!"

The French soldiers let out uproarious cheer.

The fact that none of the French captains publicly disagreed with her after she made this announcement didn't mean they agreed with her strategy. It simply meant that these captains chose not to discuss the subject in public.

Later that evening, the windblown flames leapt from Saint Augustins and lit the sky, announcing to the people (watching from roughly half a mile away) the tale of the day's French military successes. The Bastard and his fellow field commanders decided to camp for the night in close proximity to Les Tourelles where they could keep a careful watch on the trapped English forces—especially if they decided to launch an evening attack or a desperate escape plan.

With the Augustins battle won and a strong defense perimeter established at Les Tourelles, Jehanne and Father Pasquerel went to visit the wounded French to thank and reassure them as much as possible. In the midst of her visit, the Bastard sent word that he wanted a meeting with her in his tent as soon as possible.

Minutes later, Jehanne limped into view at the Bastard's quarters, Father Pasquerel at her side. D'Aulon, La Hire, and her two brothers had already arrived; all sat around a crackling fire in front of the Bastard's tent. Everyone could see the blood oozing through the hole in Jehanne's boot onto the dirt ground.

She walked slowly, clearly exhausted and in pain. Looking around at the others, the girl scowled. "What's all this?" she said to the Bastard who had already left his stool to greet her. "I thought you wanted to see me?"

"I do," the Bastard said. Taking her hand, he pointed in the direction of where he'd been sitting. "Come sit beside me and warm yourself. The wind is kicking up."

Jehanne allowed her friend to escort her to a stool beside him, and then she took a moment to look about at the others present. "Thank you, Sire," she said finally to her host, "but why are we here? There's so much we should be doing."

"This has been a momentous day for all of us," the Bastard began, "especially you, Jehanne. I just wanted to meet with you and your staff to say that today has been nothing short of miraculous."

Jehanne rubbed her forehead as if she were fighting an urge to say something unpleasant, then took a deep breath, and said, "Well, I thank you, Sire, for your kind words, but I've done nothing. Our Father in heaven has done everything. We should have a Mass of praise and give thanks to Him before everyone goes to bed tonight."

The Bastard nodded thoughtfully. "That's a wonderful idea."

"I will take care of it," Father Pasquerel volunteered.

"And what about all the injured and dead?" she asked, twisting her hands one against the other. "What are we doing about them?"

She began limping back and forth, shaking her head. "We cannot forget them!"

"Luckily," the Bastard said in a calm, soft voice, "the burgesses and citizens of the city want so much to show their appreciation for our victory today that they have volunteered to remove the injured and dead—no matter their nationality—and see to it that they are properly cared for or buried after a proper Mass.

"They also are in the process of bringing food, water, and extra medical supplies for all our troops. They intend to work through the night to make sure the total needs of our soldiers are met. Artisans will also work through the night making new scaling ladders and repairing the old.

"The people of this city want us and—especially you, Jehanne— to know that they consider themselves part of our army and that there's nothing we could ask of them that they wouldn't do—nothing!"

Jehanne slowly nodded her understanding. "That's most humbling, Sire," she said, her voice almost a whisper. "I trust they know how much we appreciate them."

"They do."

"But what about all the injured English who have not yet been to confession? Some of them will surely die this night unconfessed."

La Hire couldn't contain himself. "For the love of God, Jehanne, why do you keep worrying about the bloody English and their rotten souls? They're trying to kill every one of us—especially you. Who cares about their souls? I know I don't!"

Her eyes had begun to moisten as she stared at her questioner, slightly shaking her head again. "Don't you understand, La Hire? All of us here are on a mission for our God in heaven. He cares deeply about all our souls—Englishmen, Frenchmen—everyone.

"If we are to do God's will, not only must we do our best in battle, but then after the battle, we are called to love our neighbors and enemies the same as we love ourselves. That's the message Jesus came to bring us. To not worry about the English and their immortal souls would be to say to God that we only want to do His will when it makes us feel good."

Father Pasquerel nodded. "Well said, Jehanne. God chose you well."

La Hire took a deep breath and sighed, then folded his arms over his barrel chest. "Thanks, Jehanne . . . I guess," he said. "I think I understand, but it sure seems strange—during the day we try to kill these murderers from England in battle, then at night we try to bandage them up and make sure they go to confession in case they die."

Jehanne paused. "I agree, it does seem like two different messages, but please remember this, La Hire. I have tried to explain to the English many times how they can save themselves and their souls, but they laugh and call me names.

"Jesus told us that we are called to love and forgive our enemies—seventy times seven times. No one said doing God's will would be easy. Of course it's hard, but Jesus told us that's what we should do. And that's why we're here—to do His will."

No one spoke for a few moments.

"Jehanne," said Father Pasquerel, "for your information and peace of mind, I and my fellow priests have already heard the confessions of all living English prisoners and any French soldiers who asked to have their confessions heard."

The girl flashed a weary smile. "Well, that's certainly wonderful news."

"However, Jehanne," Pasquerel concluded, "there is one more important task that needs to be done and only you can do it."

"What is that?" she asked.

"You need to go back to the Boucher home, have your wound tended to, take a bath, eat some solid food, and get a good night's sleep. Without you well rested and your foot properly cared for, you will be of little value tomorrow."

She scowled. "I'm not going to do that," she said, clearly taken aback. "I need to stay with the troops. They need to know I haven't abandoned them. They need to know they can count on me!"

"They already know that, Jehanne," La Hire added. "After Saint Loup and today, there is no doubt in the minds and hearts of French soldiers that they can count on you. What you need to think about is . . . Will you be at full strength for the next battle? If you're not, your mission could easily fail. The first two battles, we caught the English off guard. But the next one, they'll be more than ready. They still think they're invincible. There will be no surprising them in our next battle."

"And when will that be?" she asked.

"We haven't decided yet," the Bastard replied smoothly, "but rest assured you will be included in our discussions. The main thing for you to focus on right now is proper care for your foot and getting enough rest."

Jehanne turned silent for a moment—deep in thought. "But it's so far away, Sire," she said, looking at d'Aulon, her voice soft and barely audible. "I don't really feel up to riding all that way by myself."

D'Aulon cleared his throat. "All your staff and I will go with you," he said. "We would not have you make such a trip alone, Jehanne. Besides, I'd much rather sleep in a warm Boucher bed than on the cold ground out here."

The men chuckled.

"You may be right," she said, sighing. "All right, you've talked me into it."

By the time Jehanne got on her horse and reentered the Porte de Bourgogne with her staff, it was 9:00 p.m., but a sizeable crowd awaited with their endless questions.

"Welcome, la Pucelle. We love you!"

"Are you okay? Did you get hurt?"

"We heard that the English ran away. Is that true?"

The questions wouldn't stop.

Jehanne held up one gloved hand for quiet, and the people quieted for a moment. "What happened today is that we defeated the English and sent them running back to Les Tourelles."

Her voice sounded weak and scratchy.

"France now holds Saint Jean-le-Blanc and Saint Augustins. I'm sorry, everyone, but I'm very tired. It's been a long day. Please excuse me, but I need to get some rest. God is with us. We will be victorious!"

Her words brought cheers of unrestrained jubilation and soon the streets overflowed with men, women, and children almost hysterical in their celebration. But they also saw the exhaustion on the face of their Maid and escorted her back to the Boucher home before continuing their revelry throughout the night.

Inside the Boucher home, the family knew of her coming long before she arrived. They gave her a hero's welcome once inside, but immediately felt saddened by the anguish on her face and the exhaustion in her eyes. By now, Jehanne felt almost like one of their family.

Madame Boucher took charge and told the girl to sit down on a stool in the entranceway. She instructed Raymond and Minguet to remove Jehanne's armor while she went into the kitchen and ordered the cook to locate a bundle of bandages and to heat several buckets of water.

Pasquerel sank to his knees beside Jehanne and assisted the two pages in removing Jehanne's protective covering. Then, he started removing her armored boots—first the right, then the injured one. Much of the blood had dried into sticky red glue around her left foot, making it impossible to remove the boot.

Madame Boucher returned a few minutes later with the cook, carrying jars of ointment mixed with herbs and myrrh, and three buckets—one empty, one filled with warm saltwater, and one filled with plain warm water. She told Jehanne to place her left foot in the empty bucket. Madame Boucher then slowly poured the plain warm water down into the girl's boot and told Pasquerel to gently rotate the boot around the girl's leg.

Jehanne grit her teeth in agony, but made no sound.

Finally, they were able to remove Jehanne's foot from the boot, and bright red fluid oozed and dripped into the bucket.

The two pages and Father Pasquerel turned white with nausea.

Jehanne winced from the pain as Madame Boucher carefully peeled off the girl's sock in order to fully expose the wound. She then placed Jehanne's left foot into the bucket of warm saltwater. The girl grabbed the sides of her stool with both hands and squeezed until her knuckles turned white. She never uttered a word, but her breathing came in short bursts.

After some moments, Madame Boucher removed the girl's foot from the bloody saltwater and began rinsing it with the clean warm water. Once satisfied with the foot's cleanliness, she applied the ointment to the wound and finally wrapped Jehanne's foot in fresh white bandages.

Those who saw and heard Madame Boucher attend to Jehanne's injury knew from the swelling and loss of blood that this puncture was more serious than they had thought. It had become clear that a good chance existed for more swelling and infection.

Charlotte then brought a small cup of wine, from which Jehanne sipped, then closed her eyes in silence. After a moment, the color started to return to her face, and she opened both eyes. "Many thanks to you, Madame Boucher, and your husband and all your family," she said, "for taking such good care of me."

She looked at the faces of her staff, looking down at her with great concern.

"And heartfelt thanks to each of you and to the Bastard and La Hire for talking me into spending the night here. You couldn't have been more correct, and I couldn't have been more wrong to think otherwise."

Those there smiled and Raymond and Minguet helped her get up and limp to the family table, where the cook had spread out an evening meal. Jacques Boucher then led everyone in a prayer of thanksgiving, and all sat down at table.

Still, Jehanne maintained her fast because it was Friday. She would only eat small pieces of bread soaked in wine.

Most of her staff had been with Jehanne since the day the Dauphin announced that all his investigations into her background had been concluded, and that she could now proceed to join the troops in Blois for the relief of Orléans. However, fourteen-year-old Louis de Contes—Minguet—was slightly different. He had been assigned to Jehanne beginning with the first day she arrived at the Chinon castle—March 8th. Yes, he reminded himself, he still wanted to continue his career path as a squire, culminating with eventual acceptance to knighthood, but all that would have to wait. Jehanne was his only concern for the immediate future. From their first meeting, Jehanne had become for him the older sister he never had.

Like most boys on their journey toward knighthood, he had been removed from his home at age seven and ordered to serve in the home of Sir Raoul de Gaucourt, whom he had come to despise. The day the Dauphin ordered the undersized fourteen-year-old to serve Jehanne d'Arc instead of de Gaucourt was one of the happiest of his young life.

He took great stock in the fact that she had successfully survived the dangers of this day, in addition to the disagreements she had with the French captains and was now eating food and drink, despite wanting to fast. The boy hoped that one day he would have a chance to share with family and friends about his glorious days with la Pucelle.

Toward that end, he kept careful notes so he couldn't forget or have his mind clouded by adults who would have difficulty believing what he had seen and heard. One thing he knew as a pure certainty: Jehanne and her mission for God were on the lips of every French man, woman, and child in Orléans. It was as if an angel from God had landed in their midst and begun changing everything that was wrong. He prayed every day and night that nothing would happen to la Pucelle—that God would let her complete her mission and set them all free.

Only a few minutes had passed while the Boucher household ate when they heard a knock at the front door. A servant came to the dining area and announced that Jehanne had a visitor. She met him in the Boucher chapel, Jehanne limping there on her injured foot. It was a battle-stained French knight she had never met before. He introduced himself as having been sent to her with a message: "The French captains have gathered and reached a decision not to wage war against the English tomorrow. They told me to convey that there is plenty of food for the soldiers, but the English greatly outnumbered us in total men available for battle.

"The French captains," the messenger continued, "have decided to withhold further attacks against the English until such time as the Dauphin sends more troops."

Jehanne tried to hold her anger in check. From her pew, she glared into the eyes of the exhausted knight and spoke carefully from between clenched teeth.

"Deliver this message back to the war council that sent you: 'You have been to your council, and I to mine,'" she dictated. "'And believe me, the counsel of my Lord will be put into effect, while your council will perish.'"

As soon as the knight left, Jehanne called for Pasquerel. "Send word to the twenty priests still with the troops to have them arise well before dawn, awaken the troops, hear their confessions, say Mass, and distribute communion. Tell them to expect me before dawn."

Later that night in the kitchen, as Jehanne finished her small pieces of bread and cup of diluted wine, she also told Pasquerel, "Tomorrow, rise very early, earlier than you did today, and do what you can to help me do what I must. Please keep close to me all day, for tomorrow I shall have many problems. Tomorrow, blood will flow from my body, above my breast."

CHAPTER XVII
The Battle at Les Tourelles

On this day in Paris, the English regent, Lord Bedford, emphasized in the strongest possible terms to Sir John Fastolf the importance of his immediate departure for Orléans with fresh supplies and reinforcements. In light of the unexpected recent developments there, his administration might now need to give serious consideration to the possibility of an English defeat—albeit an extremely remote one.

"But I still can't see how one illiterate French farm girl could possibly overturn the might of the English army!" Fastolf told Bedford.

"Preposterous!" Bedford said, drawing on his pipe.

However, the regent well knew from last night's intelligence reports that the situation with the people across all France—and especially in Orléans—could be described as one of nervous excitement and growing hope. News and gossip of the surprising French victories over the English, beginning with Saint Loup, had begun to circulate and expand with each new telling.

"You know, Fastolf," Bedford said, "if we lose Orléans, the whole momentum of this war changes. Before that French whore showed up, we stood on the edge of seizing the whole country. Your new troops could make the whole difference!"

Meanwhile, in Chinon, Charles VII received his intelligence reports of the recent French victories in Orléans with his usual stoic exterior, but began drafting a letter to his people explaining the unfolding events.

"Aren't you being a bit premature?" Trémoïlle wondered upon learning of the Dauphin's intentions. "After all, our recent victories there have been nothing but skirmishes. The English barely put up any serious resistance.

"Ever since Burgundy pulled his troops," the obese man continued, "the English have been spread too thin to defend their fortifications around the city. But they have more troops en route from Paris. The only hope we have is to attack Les Tourelles before the new troops arrive. But I know the Bastard: he won't attack that double fortress until he has superior numbers in place. The fresh English troops will arrive before that."

Charles scowled. "So what are you saying—that you believe we're going to lose at Orléans despite the victories of the last two days led by Jehanne d'Arc?"

Trémoïlle slowly shook his bulging head. "I'm saying no such thing, my lord. I am saying that you writing an explanation for what's happening there as we speak will prove a wasted exercise. Moreover, creating a document that includes undue credit to that country wench holds great potential danger. If the people come to believe that she is their savior, your reign—even if we do win in Orléans and you get formally crowned in Reims—could be at great risk."

"What do you mean?"

"After all," Trémoïlle continued, "you wouldn't want a farm girl—along with the hysterical support of the common people of Orléans and all France—trying to tell you how to run your country."

Queen Yolande had always made it her business to receive regular intelligence reports of the situation in Orléans. She had long ago learned the value of professional and trustworthy operatives from her parents and late husband. It would have been impossible for her to govern the family's vast European holdings without such proven gentlemen and ladies working undercover across Europe.

Also, she had long thought that any major battle for control of Orléans might well determine the long-term future of France, not to mention the happiness of her vulnerable daughter and son-in-law. But that was only one of the reasons she had decided to finance the latest fresh troops just arrived in Orléans.

Today, she went to early private Mass in the family chapel. "Dear Lord in heaven," she whispered, "please help our dear little Jehanne and keep her safe. I had a dream that she would suffer great pain and lose much blood this day."

She thought back to her childhood and the first visit to Orléans with her parents. That day she fell in love with its loving and kind people because they made her feel so much at home, even though she was a complete stranger there. "Please, God," she continued, "please be with France. . . especially the beautiful and loyal people of Orléans. They have been cheated by the English for much too long."

In the early of days of Orléans, the lazy waters of the Loire flowed amidst willow beds and birchen thickets, later removed for navigation. Years afterward, a boat sailing down the river from the east would encounter the island Saint Loup, then glide between the two Martinet Islets on the right and L'Île-aux-Toiles on the left. Next, it would pass under a long bridge which spanned an island

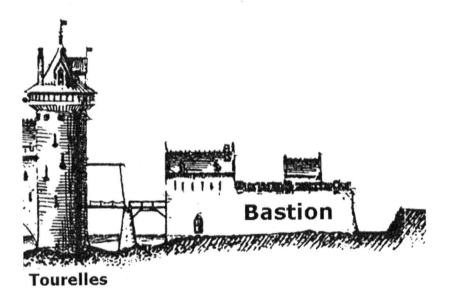

Tourelles

Bastion

Connection between Les Tourelles and Bastion

called Motte-Saint-Antoine. This stone overpass, lined with houses from the north bank, became famous due to its unique engineering and length. Later, its builders extended the buttresses of the eighteenth arch and, on its abutment, erected a little castle called Les Tourelles, formed of two towers joined by a vaulted porch; it controlled access to and from the south bank. Between the nineteenth and twentieth arches, a second drawbridge connected the two towers to the bridge—a fact the people of the city had been closely monitoring in recent days.

Inside the Boucher home, Jehanne and her staff arose in the dark and attended a Mass celebrated by Father Pasquerel. She could now ride into battle in spiritual and emotional peace, knowing that Pasquerel's cleric friends had already awakened the troops and made sure they, too, had gone to confession, heard Mass, and received communion. By the time the girl stepped into her armor, swallowed enough water to quench her thirst, and mounted her warhorse, the spring sun had begun burning off the mists of dawn.

While Jehanne silently retraced her path from the day before, back across the Loire to where her troops had spent the night, she prayed mostly for the souls of the unconfessed English soldiers who would die that day.

Dear Lord in heaven, I'm so sorry to have failed them. Please forgive me.

When she arrived where her troops were readying themselves for battle, she learned that the invaders had abandoned and set fire to the Champ Saint Privé and Ile Charmagne Bastilles. They wanted to make sure the French couldn't use those forts against them. To Jehanne, that meant that Lord Talbot had decided there was no room in Les Tourelles for additional troops. Glasdale and his men would fight to the last man.

The girl carefully inspected the remaining Saint Augustins

structure, now reconfigured as an emergency French field hospital. When finally she and her staff drew within sight of Les Tourelles, it was six o'clock in the morning. In her bones, she knew it was going to be a blazing hot day.

Once Jehanne and her staff had a chance to make an in-depth assessment of the English defenses, she decided to call a council of war within Saint Augustins. She had never done this before, but today it seemed right—to have a chance of defeating the English, all the French captains had to be working together as a team, including La Hire, de Xaintrailles, de Gamaches, Saint Sévère, and the Bastard.

"We have 2,500 men here," she began, as the local medical teams continued to prepare the building for the wounded and dying, "and they're only 700 strong. If we attack within the hour, we will have our best chance. If we wait, Talbot or Fastolf will most likely arrive with reinforcements and our best chance will be lost."

None of the others spoke.

Dear Lord in heaven, please help me find the right words.

She took a deep breath and blessed herself.

"Because Glasdale cannot expect assistance from Talbot until the new troops arrive, he has likely instructed his troops to make Les Tourelles almost impregnable. So, as you know, they have erected multiple defenses guarding the main towers, but please let me finish what I have to say.

"The first is a wooden wall of tree trunks, a palisade, standing ten feet high with only one gate for entry into the interior of their defenses.

"Their second is an earthen ditch, about three meters wide and eight meters deep, separating the palisade from the earthen roadway. When they lower the palisade drawbridge, it extends over the gap. Glasdale has intentionally left the walls of the dry ditch soft

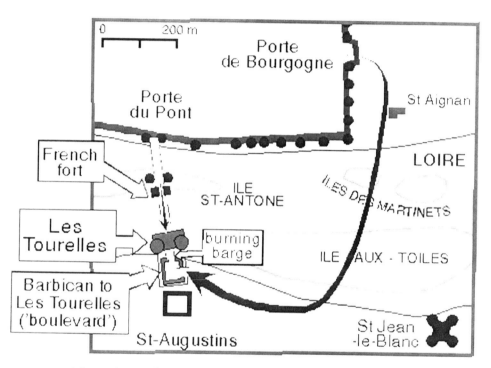

Jehanne's attack movements against Les Tourelles, May 7, 1429

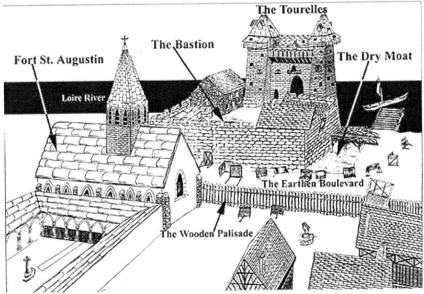

The Forts of St. Augustin and the Tourelles with their defenses.

so we'll slip and slide once we climb up onto the flat earthworks.

"Their third defense is the flat top of the earthen wall, a boulevard, nine meters wide, surrounding Les Tourelles on three sides from where they can hurl down cannon fire, arrows, and hot tar.

"A permanent ten-meter wooden bridge extends out from the end of the boulevard's right side while the bastion's five-meter drawbridge is connected. When these two wooden structures join, it links the boulevard with the bastion.

"As a fourth defense, the English have created a large, dry moat seven meters deep by twelve meters wide. Stone blocks line the descending wall of the dry moat at an angle of 80 degrees. This means we'll have to use scaling ladders to descend the steep angle.

"On the other side of the dry moat stands the fifth defense—the outer stone fortification of the Tourelles. Built from compacted earth and stone, the bastion's wall stands fifteen meters high. The only way to defeat this defense is with more scaling ladders.

"However, once over this wall, we face a sixth defense, the bastion's courtyard where the English will be waiting to attack in hand-to-hand combat.

"The seventh and last defense is on the opposite side of the courtyard—a twenty-five-foot wide, water-filled moat from the Loire which connects the Bastion's courtyard with Les Tourelles.

"And then, after overcoming all this, we will still have to contend with 700 professional Englishmen fighting for their lives. They really do believe that one English soldier can outfight, outthink, and outlast ten Frenchmen every day, all day, let alone one undersized teenage witch."

All the men present chuckled.

"With this review of their defenses, I've probably told you nothing new, but I wanted you to know that I, too, understand the huge and dangerous task ahead. And, based on the message you sent me last night, it seems we have a difference of opinion as how best to proceed. Is that correct?"

The Bastard, La Hire, de **Xaintrailles**, de Gamaches, Saint Sévère, and the other field commanders slowly nodded their heads in reluctant agreement.

"Jehanne, it is true," said the Bastard. "We did send you a message last night."

She smiled. "Good. Then we have a basis for discussion."

Again, none of the men spoke.

"Your plan is to do nothing until the Dauphin sends more troops, right?"

"Correct," said the Bastard.

Jehanne took another deep breath and sighed quietly. "Whatever your reasons for wanting to wait, I'm sure you've given them considerable thought. However, I've prayed about the situation and have concluded that our only real chance to win is if we attack right now: we have many more men than they for a battle right now at Les Tourelles, and they won't expect it."

She paused to look at their faces.

"Do any of you disagree with that?" she asked.

"I do," said de Gamaches. "If you think we're going to surprise them, you're dreaming. They want us to attack."

"That might be true," said La Hire, "but there's a gigantic difference between wanting us to attack and being truly ready. There is no possible way for 700 conceited Englishmen to hold off 2,500 furious Frenchmen—especially when they're being led by a daring farm girl on a mission for God!"

The room became silent.

Jehanne smiled and nodded in La Hire's direction. "Thank you, Sire."

Looking back at the others, she said, "In my opinion, we need to attack right now. Every moment we hesitate is more time for the English to improve their position—more time for them to improve their readiness—more time for them to plan ways to kill good and honest Frenchmen. I vote we do not allow them that chance. I vote we attack now!"

Again the room became silent.

Jehanne looked into each man's eyes. She realized they might think she was totally wrong but that once the battle began, she would immediately be exposed as a hopeless fool. Or, they may think she had made a strong argument for her tactics and were too proud to admit it.

"Then, we're all in agreement?" she said finally.

The Bastard, la Hire, and de Xaintrailles nodded agreement. The others just shrugged their shoulders in reluctant but silent agreement.

"Good!" Jehanne said, stood up from her chair, and quickly limped out into the bright early-morning sunlight.

Minguet had been waiting with her horse and standard.

Jehanne mounted and took her long standard from the young man. She raised it high for all the French troops to see, lowered her visor, and galloped full speed to the edge of the ditch just in front of the wooden palisade, planted her standard, and galloped back.

She then returned her horse to Minguet.

By then, all the French soldiers had begun roaring with enthusiasm. They, too, wanted to get on with the attack. They raised high their scaling ladders, weapons, and shields.

"Sound a general assault," the Bastard bellowed to the trumpeter.

Dear Father in heaven, please help me know what to do. Please let thy will be done here today. Thank you, Jesus; thank you, my sweet Jesus.

It was now approximately seven o'clock, Saturday morning.

Jehanne first ordered the French to destroy the palisade fence and begin down the dirt embankment toward the earthen ditch below. The English then filled the air with arrows and cannon fire from atop the boulevard. Other of their soldiers also charged into the ditch below and attacked Jehanne and her troops as they now made their way down the side of the ditch using ladders.

The English in the trench used axes, lances, lead slingshots, swords—or their bare hands when all else became unavailable. But there were too many French, and the English foolish enough to enter the ditch were soon killed or taken prisoner.

Jehanne and her soldiers next turned their attention to erecting scaling ladders that—if successful—would carry them up to the top of the boulevard. Whoever held this high ground had a tactical advantage because they could—with minimal danger to themselves—unleash an endless barrage of arrows, small arms, and cannon fire on the enemy below. And as the battle continued, the English clearly committed themselves to holding this high ground at all costs. An arrow from that height by an English longbowman could easily pierce any battle armor and kill its victim upon impact.

The Maid and her followers now settled in for the long and bloody task of making their way to the top of boulevard. She and the troops knew that they had to persevere over and over in the day's blazing sun as the English did all in their power to prevent the French from the mounting the steep hill.

Over the course of the morning, the French organized several determined attempts to advance sufficient numbers up onto the boulevard so as to take possession from the English. The French soldiers would scale the earthen walls with great patience and place their ladders with great skill, but the English thwarted each assault, causing high French casualties. Nonetheless, with Jehanne at their side, her troops fought with such abandon and determination, the English wondered if the French thought they were immortal.

Jehanne rushed from one side of the dirt ditch to the other, her standard fluttering high while an endless shower of arrows rained down around her and on her comrades. Although they had no protective armor—only shields—Pasquerel and Minguet followed the girl as close as they dared. Though slowed by her armor and injury, Jehanne remained in perpetual motion, encouraging, assisting soldiers to their feet, and helping others erect yet another ladder; she even aided the badly wounded away from the battle.

"Be hopeful, men, and do not give up," she shouted to any and all within the sound of her voice, "for today God will give us victory!"

As the sun neared its zenith, the French had mounted two cannons, freshly arrived from Orléans, in front of the hole where the palisade fence had earlier stood. Jehanne ducked down and covered her ears as a soldier set them off, the air reverberating with a deafening roar. Dust and smoke filled the ditch, but Jehanne hardly had a chance to catch her breath, scrunching her eyes shut and ducking behind her shield as the English returned fire from high above. When she finally opened them again, she found herself surrounded by more bodies—more blood.

The sun continued to beat down, as did the stream of English air attacks, and Jehanne noticed the resolve of her troops beginning to slacken. Many—their strength depleted or comrades dead—fell back, stumbling across the dirt moat toward Saint Augustins. But they were so close. She could see that the English were beginning to tire as well; her men just had to keep at it! She couldn't let them grow faint of heart. She couldn't let them withdraw. Maybe if she went up one of the ladders . . .

She had to find someone to carry her banner. Spotting a muscular French foot soldier, she spoke loud enough so he could hear her over the din, "Would you please carry this for me?" she said raising her banner high in the air.

"Why do you want me to carry it? I don't know how."

"Just carry it high and don't let anyone take it from you."

"Why?"

"Because I'm going to climb a ladder right now, and when I get to the top, I want you to bring it to me. It shouldn't take that long."

She handed him her standard and told him to keep it flying high where all could see—until she took it back from him. Then, she helped erect yet another ladder and began to climb. "Follow me, men," she yelled. "This day is ours!"

Jehanne had just taken a few steps up the ladder when an arrow—shot by an English longbowman—slammed into her, piercing her armor above the heart and passing through her body and out her back.

The projectile had been shot from atop the boulevard by Sir William de Moleyns, and its force spun and knocked the girl off the ladder. She let out a shriek and landed on her side in a cloud of dust and blood.

I'm hit, dear Lord. Please give me courage and strength for this.

Moleyns saw the girl go down and smiled to himself.

Immediately, his English comrades let out a bloodthirsty roar, confident they had finally killed "the French witch."

"Be sure she's dead!" the young knight shouted for his men to hear.

Several slid down the earthen embankment, determined to kill her if she wasn't already dead.

The French immediately intercepted them.

Pasquerel and Minguet, disregarding the danger, ran to her. Seeing the blood streaming down the front and back of her armor, they picked her up and began racing toward the nearest medical facility.

They'd only run a few feet when a voice behind them shouted, "Stop, give her to me!" It was Sieur de Gamaches—the same man a week earlier who had called Jehanne a "hussy" and refused to take orders from her.

"Let me go," Jehanne said from inside her helmet. "It's just a little wound."

Pasquerel and Minguet glanced at each other and shook their heads.

"Hand her up to me," Gamaches said, "I'll take her to Saint Augustins."

"What are you doing?" Jehanne asked with as much conviction as she could muster. "Put me on my feet, I'll be fine. The men need to know I'm fine!"

Just then, the Bastard ran up from his duties directing ladder assaults, and all three handed Jehanne up to Gamaches, who set her in his saddle.

"Jehanne, you're on a horse with Gamaches," the older man said calmly. "Hold on with your knees. You need immediate medical care."

"We have to stop the bleeding, Jehanne," the Bastard added.

"Don't do this!" Jehanne pleaded, her visor still down as Gamaches cantered toward Saint Augustins with Pasquerel, Minguet, and the Bastard in close pursuit. "It's just a little wound. Why are you taking me away?"

By the time the trailing trio arrived, Gamaches had ordered the girl placed on an operating table. One of several medical "wise women" at the first-aid station was attempting to undo Jehanne's armor.

"Why did you bring me here?" Jehanne shouted, still sitting up. "There's nothing wrong with me. I'm fine."

Minguet and the medical woman kept working on the armor while Pasquerel removed her helmet. Streams of sweat rolled down her face, blood covered her chest.

Seeing Pasquerel, the Bastard, and the others hovering over

her, she began to cry.

In her mind, she was now an utter failure because the battle was still in doubt, and she had left. "We've got to tell the men to keep fighting," she sobbed.

"*You* need to be still and let us help you," the woman said with heavy emphasis. "You're losing too much blood."

Face drained of color, Jehanne grit her teeth to keep control. She couldn't allow the pain and loss of blood to control her, but, try as she may, she couldn't stop the crying.

God, please give me strength.

Fingers shaking, Minguet finally managed to unbuckle her breast and back plates. The medical woman then finished removing them, taking care not to disturb the wound. Blood oozed and ran down everywhere. The long arrow had entered her left upper breast and protruded out through her back.

Pasquerel explained the extent of her wound to Jehanne as he removed her gauntlets.

"We can't stop the bleeding without removing the arrow," the woman said.

"Cut off the arrow point and I'll pull it out," Jehanne gasped between sobs.

"I need two sets of pliers." The woman raised her voice for those within earshot.

Two of her assistants had been working on another soldier nearby; one of them ran and retrieved the pliers.

Using the newly presented tools, Pasquerel and Minguet clipped off the tip of the arrow, trying as best they could to cause the least pain for la Pucelle as she remained in an upright sitting position.

The woman handed her a small piece of wood. "You'll need this."

Jehanne bit into the wood and moaned—tears rolling down her face.

With the metal tip removed, the medical woman gently bathed

the wound with vinegar water where the arrow had pierced the girl's back.

"One of you bring me a cauterizing iron," she said to her assistants.

To Jehanne, she said, "We can't stop the bleeding until the arrow is gone. Are you going to pull it out or do you want me to?"

"Me," Jehanne said.

"Then pull it out right now," the woman said.

Jehanne closed her eyes, spit out the piece of wood, wrapped her blood-streaked right hand around the stem of the wooden arrow, and quickly yanked it out as if making a vicious backhand swipe with her sword. "Help me, Jesus!" she screamed.

Blood and tissue gushed down Jehanne's chest and back. A female assistant brought the cauterizing iron and placed it within easy reach.

"Keep the back wound clean and covered while I do the same with the front one," the woman told the assistant.

The medical woman then looked Jehanne directly in the eye. "Jehanne, do you know what I'm about to do?"

The girl nodded. "Stop the bleeding."

"It's going to hurt—a lot. Are you ready?"

Jehanne nodded.

The medical woman picked up the cauterizing iron and another small piece of wood, and told Jehanne, "Put this between your teeth and bite hard," the woman said. "When I put this hot iron on your wound, you're going to want to jump up and hit me. If you want the bleeding to stop, you can't move—not one centimeter."

The girl took a deep breath.

"I'm ready."

Pasquerel and Minguet both gave the girl one hand to hold.

The boy saw the woman press the red-hot iron on the front puncture. The rancid smell of burning flesh filled the air, and the young boy fought the urge to vomit.

Jehanne stiffened and bit down on the wood, squeezing his hand with all her might.

Minguet thought he might pass out from the pain, but didn't move or say anything. Maybe she had broken his hand.

A muted moan escaped from between the girl's teeth, face ashen. The boy worried she might pass out.

"That's a good girl, Jehanne," the woman said. "We're halfway there. Would you like a drink of water?"

Jehanne nodded her head, but didn't release the boy's hand.

"Are you going to be all right sitting up like that?" the woman asked.

The girl nodded, still squeezing Minguet's hand. By now, it was completely numb.

The woman partially filled a cup with fresh water. "You need to drink some of this," she said. "Without it, you may lose consciousness."

The woman moved the cup to Jehanne's lips, and the girl took several small sips.

With that, Jehanne released the boy's and the priest's hands and closed her eyes, color slowly returning to her cheeks.

The woman wiped some of the sweat and blood off the girl's face and neck. "Does that feel a little better?" she asked.

Jehanne nodded and opened her eyes.

"Are you ready for me to fix the back wound now?"

The girl nodded once again and closed her eyes.

The medical woman then repeated the process on the back puncture.

Once again, the rancid smell of burning flesh filled the air, but Minguet held his breath so as not to inhale the putrid fumes.

Jehanne stiffened and bit down on the wood, squeezing his hand so hard it lost all feeling, but the boy didn't flinch.

The girl merely moaned softly.

"Good girl, Jehanne," the woman said. "The hard part is done. Now all we have to do is dress this back wound, and then you can lie down and get some rest."

The woman next began to cover the back wound with herbs, olive oil, lard, cotton, and clean bandages.

"How about another sip of water, Jehanne?"

The girl still had her eyes closed and didn't respond at first. She just sat there squeezing Minguet's hand and that of the priest. But then she opened her eyes and nodded as the woman moved the cup to her mouth.

Sweat covered the girl's ashen face, along with a rush of silent tears. Suddenly her eyes rolled up into her head, and she collapsed backward. The two women caught her before the Jehanne hit her head on the operating table, but it was clear that Jehanne had finally fallen into a state of unconsciousness.

Minguet and the priest withdrew their hands while the two women went about covering the front wound as they had done to the rear one.

"We put something in her cup to help her sleep," the woman said to the priest. "She'll probably sleep for a few hours. She's lost a lot of blood and needs rest."

Father Pasquerel took a deep breath. "She injured her left foot yesterday. Would you mind taking a look at it while she's asleep?"

The older woman nodded.

As the medical women went about their work, the priest crossed himself and knelt down beside Minguet close to where they could watch the girl, but remain out of the way.

At that moment, Jehanne's brother Pierre came rushing into the operating room. "I just heard. What happened?"

Father Pasquerel interrupted his prayers, put one arm around Pierre, and explained the situation. When the friar finished, Pierre seemed reassured and knelt down to pray beside Minguet. The fact that Jehanne had lost so much blood both the day before and to-day weighed heavy on the boy's mind. He suddenly realized that it was highly possible Jehanne might never recover consciousness.

Nonetheless, the boy kept praying.

Father Pasquerel prayed that she would recover soon too. He knew from experience that the fact that she had been administered to so quickly and with such expertise might have saved her life.

The medical woman also shared that since the arrow had pierced her armor cleanly on the front and rear of her shoulder, severe infection might have been averted. And, the woman said, "By passing so quickly into unconsciousness, her body might have taken this opportunity to recover from the shock as well its loss of blood."

"Not to mention," Pasquerel said, "using this time to catch up on much-needed rest."

The whispered voices of men conversing with Pasquerel awak-ened Jehanne later that afternoon. "The people of the city are watching," one soldier said to the friar, "and since la Pucelle fell, the English are getting the upper hand. We desperately need her back."

Another of the soldiers spoke up. "Father, in the past, we've used a 'special magic' we learned from our parents and grandpar-ents. Would you please let us use it on Jehanne so she can heal quickly and rejoin the battle?"

Jehanne opened both eyes and rolled onto her right arm. "No, I cannot allow that, Father Pasquerel," she whispered.

The militiamen he'd been talking with turned and stared at the girl in dismay, her face was still ashen-white.

"I would rather die than have anything to do with witchcraft or something against God's law!" she said. "I know I must die one day, but I don't know when or where; if a salve could be put on my wound without sin, I would willingly allow it."

Hearing this, the soldiers left as did Minguet. He could now breathe a sigh of relief. Jehanne was not going to die.

As soon as they were alone, Jehanne leaned up on her right arm and whispered to Father Pasquerel that she wanted to go to confession.

"What for?" he asked. "You went to confession this morning, then went into battle against the English and almost got killed. What could you have possibly done wrong during that time?"

A flood of tears poured from her eyes.

"Please forgive me, Father, for I am completely unworthy to do God's will. Today was a perfect example of my shame. I moaned and cried when the pain of an arrow came into my chest. I am so very sorry, dear Lord, to have disappointed you."

"Jehanne, you have committed no sin," Pasquerel said. "You're being too tough on yourself. The Lord loves you and wants you to succeed in Orléans, and then to complete the rest of your mission. But He never said it would be easy, did He?"

She wiped her eyes. "No."

"God has faith in you, Jehanne. Otherwise, He would never have sent you here. Why should you lose faith in yourself? You had a physical setback today, but that doesn't mean you're unfit. God sends us challenges to help us grow. Suffering can be a gift. Christ suffered on the cross and gifted all mankind eternal salvation.

"Today you suffered much pain by taking an arrow in your chest for the people of Orléans. Eventually, God and you will use that pain to gift freedom back to all the people of France. Can't you see how proud God is of you—as am I?"

"Really? You're proud of me?" she asked.

"I really am," Pasquerel said, nodding slowly.

The medical woman returned with a warm damp cloth and

wiped Jehanne's forehead and neck. "How are you feeling? Your color's coming back."

"I'm fine. I should be getting up. How long have I been asleep?"

"Several hours," Pasquerel said.

Minguet came back into the infirmary with wine diluted with water in one hand and small pieces of bread in the other. "Would you like some of this?" he said to Jehanne.

"Hah! Thoughtful boy!" Her infectious smile spread ear to ear. "Thank you."

She began to place small bites in her mouth between sips of wine.

Minguet also brought news of the battle, and when she heard that it was not going well, her eyes flashed with intensity. She thought for a moment, then gazed at Pasquerel and Minguet. "I want to thank you both for all your assistance. You've both been a great help and inspiration."

She stopped and smiled—face still pale, but a light now blazed from her eyes. "Now, would you two please help me put on my armor?"

The priest and the page exchanged a look of apprehension.

"What are you saying, Jehanne?" Pasquerel said. "You just awoke from being unconscious and almost bleeding to death."

"That's right," she said. "I was asleep. I was tired and lost a little blood, but now I'm fine. My body may feel sore in places, but my strength is back."

She looked back and forth, one to the other.

"Are you going to help me with my armor or do I have to get these good ladies," she nodded at the medical women, "to do it?"

The priest shook his head and, with the boy, began dressing her in armor.

Outside, the sun hung low on the horizon and the battle for the boulevard still raged without resolution. Many of the French soldiers had witnessed Jehanne being shot off the ladder and her exit from the battle. Nonetheless, their anger and passion to seek revenge on the enemy had been partially diluted by fear that she might yet die. They had also begun to lose heart at their inability to mount an effective campaign against the boulevard from which to launch a fierce attack on Les Tourelles.

The Bastard recognized the situation and, reluctantly, thought he should give orders to the trumpeters to proclaim a retreat. Just then he saw Jehanne ride back onto the field of battle, dismount, and join the French still trying to mount ladders to the boulevard. A huge roar filled the air when they realized what had happened.

The Bastard had no way of knowing that the girl could barely focus her thoughts. Even though her eyes saw the French troops struggling to mount an attack and saw the English fortifications and weapons still in good working order and all the fallen French bodies, she couldn't really identify any of that in her mind.

The Bastard and his fellow captains had already concluded that any hope of carrying Les Tourelles today had ended. It was now eight o'clock and the men had been fighting all day without success. The presence of the wounded Maid wasn't going to change that.

Suddenly, Jehanne grasped what she saw and what was about to happen. Before the trumpets could sound, she rushed to the Bastard. "Please, my lord," she said. "I beg you for just a few minutes."

"No, Jehanne, I cannot do that," the Bastard said. "Our men can do no more this day. They've been fighting in this heat for thirteen hours."

She glanced at the weary and bloody faces around her. "Will you please give me just a few minutes?" she repeated. "Let me pray for just a little while."

The Bastard paced for a moment, shaking his head. "All right,

Jehanne," he said slowly. "But we need to end this before dark."

"I understand. Just a few minutes? Please?"

He nodded.

But before leaving the battlefield, Jehanne left her standard with d'Aulon for safekeeping. Then, remounting her horse, she rode off alone into a nearby vineyard, where she prepared to dismount. The pain in her shoulder and foot dominated her consciousness almost to the exclusion of all else.

She'd never experienced such sharp pain and aching and fought with all her being to stay conscious. Slowly, she lowered herself off the horse to the dirt and onto her knees.

She prayed out loud to her Father in heaven that, if it be His will, He please guide her to the right words and deeds to persuade the French soldiers and captains that victory awaited them right now—this very day.

"Please, dear God, grant me the strength to overcome the pain and lead these men—who have worked so hard to be men of faith—to the victory that is your will!"

Suddenly she stopped praying out loud, closed her eyes, and just listened. Several moments passed, then she began to whisper, "Jesus, Jesus, Jesus. . . ." over and over.

Meanwhile, Monsieur Jacques Boucher from his vantage point atop the city's walls noticed that most all of the people of Orléans had been keeping close watch on the battle. They could see that the English had a distinct advantage by not having to worry about being attacked from behind—via the long bridge that crossed the Loire. The gap the French military had created in the concrete bridge last October—where it had once connected to Les Tourelles—had now become an advantage for the English.

Boucher also observed that the city's carpenter community had taken it upon themselves to design and build temporary bridgework

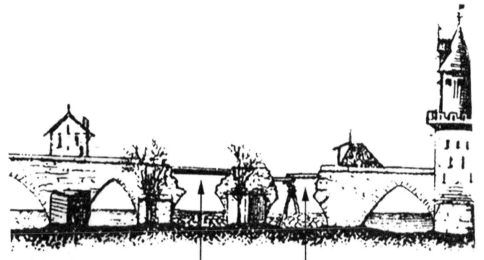

Small wooden bridges quickly constructed by the people of
Orleans so that they could attack the north side of the Tourelles.

that would allow the people of the city to attack the English in Les Tourelles from the bridge.

The people of Orléans also realized that the wooden drawbridge over the water moat that ran between Les Tourelles and the bastion structure on the southern shore provided the English a virtually impregnable exit venue—should the French forces ever fight their way onto the boulevard and into the bastion. Boucher received strong assurances—through neighbors and friends—from the city's boat-building professionals, that they would find a way to eliminate this remaining English advantage.

As dusk fell, the invaders felt certain that victory would soon be theirs. Glasdale looked down at the battle from his command post high in Les Tourelles, still believing his assistant, Sir William Moleyns, had killed the Maid or, at the very least, injured her badly enough that she could not return to fight that day.

Nevertheless, it disturbed him that so many of his soldiers retreated whenever they saw the girl charge onto the field of battle waving her standard. The fact that someone else had recently rejoined the battle for the French dressed in her armor and helmet hadn't fooled him or his men; they recognized the imposter right away. In the first place, the pretender had none of her energy and didn't even bother to hold her own standard; that task had been left to some grizzled French brute who had been waving it back and forth and screaming at his fellow Frenchmen, but had been largely ignored.

As Jehanne knelt in prayer in the quiet vineyard, the battle for Les Tourelles raged on with French soldiers still fighting hard to make their way up the long wooden battle ladders, while the English continued shooting them down with arrows and stones or simply pushing them over backward. The Bastard couldn't help but be impressed with the French plucky persistence and courage. He attributed it all to Jehanne—especially the fact that they'd now just seen her return to the battlefield, then ride away.

D'Aulon kept running back and forth in front of the steep English defenses, trying to exhort the men, trying to inspire them with enough passion to overwhelm the enemy. He had entrusted Jehanne's standard to one of his most loyal, powerful, and battle-tested soldiers—a man known as the Basque. This was the man who now held Jehanne's white standard in his left hand and a broadsword in his right, hacking to death any English soldier who had the misfortune to cross his path.

When Jehanne finally galloped back onto the battlefield and saw who held her standard and how he was using it as a lure for English soldiers, she decided to take it back. Her standard had never been intended by God for such misuse. She eased down off her horse, limped to the Basque, and attempted to take her standard from him, but he'd been given an assignment by d'Aulon and wasn't about to fail in his duty.

At that moment, a wounded English soldier fell down beside the large soldier, sword in hand, and the temporary flag holder turned his attention to view this new danger. Jehanne gave a final jerk on the wooden pole, and the Basque let go.

The French soldiers who witnessed this whole incident thought it was a special signal from the Maid, who had now somehow returned to the battle once again. This time Jehanne wore no helmet and moved as if completely healed from all her injuries.

With a mighty blood-curdling roar, the French now arose from their day-long exhaustion and charged the earthen walls as one; their la Pucelle was with them!

Jehanne helped set one French ladder in place and began to shout while holding her standard high in the air for all to see.

"Courage!" she shouted. "Do not fall back. In a little while, this place will be yours. Watch! When you see the wind blow my banner against the bulwark, you shall take it. In, in—the place will be yours!"

At that moment, Minguet ran to her with her armored helmet, and she put it back on.

Believing that Jehanne had come back to the battle in a state of complete recovery, many of the English began to run in full retreat from their positions atop the boulevard.

The girl now climbed a ladder holding her standard high, silhouetted against the golden light of twilight. Once atop the boulevard, she made her way across the earthwork and down a ladder on the other side. She crossed the dry moat in front of the bastion's stone walls and again raised her standard high.

The easterly wind blew her personal standard straight at the fortress walls. As the long white banner brushed against the masonry structure, the French soldiers let out an ear-shattering roar as if a giant wave had welled up out of the Loire and crashed down on the English. Within minutes, the French flooded into the bastion. Though the English fought desperately, they could not stem the tide.

Jehanne saw that the people of Orléans had completed a temporary walkway made of wood framing and metal gutter-pipes which allowed the French militia to now cross the Loire to Les Tourelles from the north side.

Seeing that victory was at hand, she wanted to be generous and shouted, "Glasdale! Glasdale! Yield to the King of heaven! You have called me a whore, but I have great pity on your soul and those of your men!"

Jehanne also saw that a large boat filled with brushwood, old shoes, bags of sulfur, and manure had sailed under the wooden drawbridge that joined Les Tourelles to the southern bank. Once in position, those men from Orléans set the boat on fire, the flames burning the boat *and* the bridge.

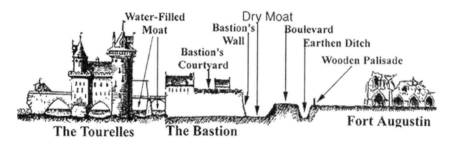

A close-up of how Les Tourelles and Bastion connected to enable troop movements

The English, having resisted with such determination all day long, suddenly broke off their resistance, and the French swarmed into the bastion.

As the English retreated toward the expected safety of Les Tourelles, Glasdale couldn't believe how quickly the battle had changed. He turned to his next in command and bellowed, "I thought you killed that Armagnac whore!"

"So did I," Moleyns shouted back, shaking his head, "But I had forgotten that she's a witch. We can never kill her unless we burn her. How else can you explain our men running away from battle when they see her coming?"

"That's just so much poppycock!" Glasdale screamed. "You can't explain away your incompetence by calling that harlot a witch with supernatural powers. She's a farm girl—that's all. You lied to me about her death!"

With the French in full pursuit, Glasdale now ordered thirty of his best soldiers—including his assistant—to exit the fort and intercept the French. But as they started to do so, Glasdale ran up behind Moleyns and pushed him into the Loire, shouting, "There's one thing I cannot accept—a coward and a liar."

But fire had so weakened the wooden drawbridge that when Glasdale and his full detail of thirty tried to cross together, the wooden structure collapsed, and they all fell into the Loire, sinking and drowning.

Seeing this, once again, Jehanne went to her knees and wept. Her heart mourned the loss of so many unconfessed English soldiers. But this time she especially mourned for Glasdale and those who drowned with him—it had all been so unnecessary.

Also, Jehanne's heart remained broken at the unconfirmed loss of her brave and kind herald, Guyenne. Pasquerel and Minguet thought they understood her tears, but most of the French soldiers and the other captains didn't even try. They were too busy reveling in the moment—the siege of the city had been raised.

Les Tourelles filled with flames, while all Orléans celebrated. The priests and people hugged and cried and sang "*Te Deum Laudamus*," giving thanks to God.

Soon the city streets filled with men, women, and children taking any opportunity they could to indulge themselves in dancing and cheering and shouting. The bells in every church rang and the drinks in every tavern were free. But what the people most wanted was to see their la Pucelle. They wanted to tell her how much they loved her and respected her and were in awe of her incredible courage.

It was no easy feat getting Jehanne's household and their mounts safely onto the long bridge, but because the people of the city wanted so badly to see her, to thank her, to tell her how much she meant to them, the artisans and soldiers made it happen. When the girl finally entered the city from the south gate, the people went into unbridled ecstasy.

Jehanne rode helmetless beside the Bastard and La Hire. Her brothers, Pasquerel, her pages, d'Aulon, de Poulengy, de Metz, and Ambleville, all rode close behind. Each of them, she thought, deserved immense credit and appreciation for the enormous help they had given her—even from their first meetings. Nonetheless, she also wanted to show her great appreciation to the people of Orléans who had—each in their own large and small ways—paid such a high price for this incredible victory.

Jehanne kept balance with her knees and waved back at the jam-packed and screaming crowds with her uninjured arm. She laughed as tears of joy and thanks and pain streamed down her face—her left shoulder and foot kept pounding and throbbing with each new step of her white steed. The more the crowds cheered and cried for and with her, the more she realized how much love and delight she felt for them.

In many ways, Jehanne realized that the citizens of Orléans and she had much in common. From the beginning, no one gave either the city or Jehanne any chance against the English. Each had been mocked and underestimated by their countrymen, as well as the enemy. Both had been forced to endure long periods of waiting, frustration, and torment, but in the end, God had blessed them all, well beyond their wildest dreams.

As she rode through the streets, she offered up one more prayer of thanks to God, who had brought her and these people, so far. *Jesus, Jesus, Jesus* . . .

CHAPTER XVIII

One Last English Trick

Long before dawn, the Orléanais could hear and see through the darkness that the English were mustering out of their still-intact bastilles, arranging themselves in battle formation, facing the western walls of the city—especially Porte Renard.

Per standing instructions from the Bastard, the church bells rang out to awaken the whole city. Madame Boucher awakened Jehanne in the dark and told her the news. The girl immediately began to dress, but because of her wounds it was too painful to wear her upper-body armor. But she could still ride. So she wore a long tunic of chain mail over her steel leggings.

The girl left the safety of the city walls through the Porte Renard accompanied by her hungover military retinue, including Father Pasquerel. There, they joined the assembled French men-at-arms and many of her fellow captains of the recent battles: the Bastard, La Hire, Gamaches, maréchal de Sainte-Sévère, Gilles de Rais, Ambroise de Loré, Poton de Xaintrailles, Florent d'Illers, Charles de Bourbon, and Governor de Gaucourt. Several of the other French captains and their men had remained on the south bank of the Loire to guard Les Tourelles from possible further vandalism by the English or their rogue agents.

The two armies now stood in deadly silence, staring at each other through the early dawn. Less than fifty yards separated them.

Jehanne saw the danger and ordered that the French should not charge the English unless first attacked. She expected a number of her fellow captains would be most unhappy—especially La Hire—but felt sure no one wanted to challenge her today. She summoned Pasquerel and asked him to organize two Sunday Masses: one for the English and one for the French to be celebrated in the open space between both armies.

By the time both services had ended, another hour had passed and now the sun stood high enough in the sky that the stars were no longer visible. Still, both sides remained facing each other in stony silence. Neither side held a numerical advantage—each had approximately 4,000 men on the field.

La Hire rode up beside Jehanne. "We're never going to have a better chance to destroy these English—there they stand, just asking for it. They owe us for Rouvray and who knows for how many more."

Jehanne barely shook her head side to side without a word.

Now Gamaches rode up and joined the conversation. "Jehanne, we're going to have to fight this English army a lot more before you can achieve your mission. Why not demolish them right now? We're never going to have a better chance."

Jehanne just kept shaking her head.

The Bastard rode up, but just listened as more and more of the French captains came forward, trying to convince the Maid to attack the English right away.

Finally, she took a deep breath, body aching. "Gentlemen," she began, "we are all Catholics and sworn members of God's army. Sunday is the day God rested at the beginning of the world. We'll have plenty of opportunities in the next few weeks to attack the

English army, but not today. Sunday is the Lord's Day!"

Those words had barely passed her lips when an English trumpeter sounded an order from the rear of the enemy lines. Their troops, in unison, turned their backs on Orléans and marched in tight formation to the west.

Jehanne looked up and heard a thunderous cheer sounding from high on the ramparts of the city. The people of Orléans were once again celebrating—hundreds waved hats and jumped up and down on the walls. She knew everyone would attend Mass that day; they had much to be thankful for.

"Come on, men, after them!" shouted La Hire, aiming his sword forward.

"Let them go," Jehanne said. "It is not God's will they should be attacked today."

Once the English had marched well out of sight, the French military organized a search in each of the abandoned bastilles. They discovered huge stores of food stuffs, ammunition, weapons, and cannons. They also found injured and dying English soldiers, French prisoners, and Jehanne's long lost Guyenne. He had been seized by English soldiers, starved, beaten, tortured, and left chained to a metal stake at the center of a stack of wood ready to be set on fire at a moment's notice.

The French captains immediately summoned all the priests and medical people available. Father Pasquerel brought Jehanne the news at a grotto for the Blessed Virgin Mary close to the Croix-Boissee bastille well outside the western city walls. The girl had been on her knees, thanking Mary for her intercessions for victory and safety.

When Jehanne heard the news, she pulled herself to her feet and began limping and sprinting as best she could to Saint Laurent where the man rested on a bed of improvised blankets, bandaged and exhausted from his ordeal.

Jehanne cradled Guyenne's head in her arms, sobbing with joy. "I'm so sorry," she whispered over and over to the overwhelmed herald as her tears dripped onto the man's bloodstained cheeks. "I'm so very sorry," she said. "Please forgive me, my kind, brave Guyenne, *mea culpa, mea culpa, mea maxima culpa*. And please, God, have mercy on my ill-tempered and arrogant soul. I am such a sinner—such an unholy mess!"

"No, you're not," Guyenne said, his voice weak and raspy. "And the proof is that God helped you beat the English." A small smirk crept into one corner of his mouth. "But the next time you ask me to take a message to the English . . ." his voice now an almost inaudible whisper, "don't be surprised if I suddenly lose my voice altogether!"

Then he winked.

 # Epilogue

ews of the French victory in Orléans reverberated across all
of Europe.

In Germany and Brittany, reports of the Dauphinist troops' successes—led by the teenager from Domremy—became a topic of major political discussion, especially given its long-range implications.

In Paris, where the Anglo-Burgundian party still controlled the city, the news from Orléans arrived May 10th. As recording clerk of the *Parlement*, Monsieur Clement de Fauquembergue saw it as part of his duties to make a record of daily events he considered important and germane to the concerns of that august body. On that day, he wrote that Glasdale and his captains had been defeated by the French, "who had in their companies a maid all alone who held her banner between the two enemy forces, according to what was said." He also drew in the margin of his notes a sketch of la Pucelle and observed that everyone in Paris had her name on their lips.

Over the next two and half months, Jehanne and her captains would march through Jargeau, Meung-sur-Loire, Beaugency, Patay, Troyes, and finally into Reims—as she had always said she would. On Sunday, July 17, 1429, Charles VII was crowned king of France. Regnault de Chartres, who had never visited Reims in his life, celebrated the Catholic Mass and performed the service at the cathedral there.

Breaking with all national and historical precedent, Jehanne stood beside the king during the ceremony, long white standard in hand. Oblivious to how the eyes of those present watched her every move, the girl went to great lengths to observe all other protocols appropriate for such an event. When questioned later as to why she held her standard as she stood beside the king when no other French captains had the same privilege, Jehanne replied, "It had borne the burden, and it was right that it should have the honor."

After Charles VII had finally been blessed and crowned king by de Chartres, Jehanne knelt before her king and embraced him by his knees. "Gentle King," she said, fighting tears, "now is fulfilled the pleasure of God, who wished that the siege of Orléans should be lifted, and that you should be brought into this city of Reims to receive your holy consecration, thus showing that you are true king, and he to whom the kingdom of France should belong."

From the day the farm girl Jehanne d'Arc left for Vaucouleurs with her uncle Lassois for the second time on January 12, 1429, 188 days had passed before Charles became king. Moreover, it had only been eighty-eight days since the Dauphin passed word to all those concerned that preparations for the relief of Orléans could finally begin in earnest and that seventeen-year-old Jehanne would be a major part of that effort.

What in April of 1429 appeared to be an almost certain successful English invasion and takeover of France became in May of 1429 the beginning of an eventual ignominious English defeat and expulsion from France in 1453 by Charles VII and his military forces. France was once again alive, intact, united, and free of foreign invaders.

The people of Orléans never forgot their Jehanne la Pucelle. In the succeeding years, statues of her sprouted up throughout the city. To this day, Orléans conducts an annual Joan of Arc festival during the first week of May. Visitors to this commemoration experience the atmosphere of a 1429 market complete with jugglers, musicians, and dancers as well as displays of falconry, sword fighting, and battle reenactments. Each year, teenage girls of Orléans compete for the privilege to be named Joan of Arc for a day and ride through the streets of the city along the same path la Pucelle followed upon her arrival in late April 1429.

The Burgundians captured Jehanne in 1430 and sold her to the English who tried her before an ecclesiastical court as a heretic and executed the nineteen-year-old in 1431. In 1456—at the request of Jehanne's mother and Charles VII—the French government and the Catholic Church reopened the 1431 trial and found it fatally flawed in several material respects and, therefore, Jehanne was pronounced innocent. The original records of both trials are maintained intact by the French government to this day. She is now one of the patron saints of all France.

On May 30, 1431, as she was burning at the stake in Rouen, the only words Jehanne spoke as the fire consumed her young body were "Jesus, Jesus, Jesus" over and over—no screams of pain and no crying.

The English guards, later sent to remove her remains, found her heart still unburned. They tried to burn it twice more without success. Frustrated and afraid, the guards shoveled her heart and ashes into a burlap bag and threw it into the Seine River.

Most historians credit the Battle of Orléans as the turning point of the Hundred Years War. In less than ninety days during 1429,

Jehanne d'Arc changed the future of France and all Europe in a war that had begun in 1337. Some critics say the outcome of that bloody conflict and its effects on history would have been the same without Jehanne. Others say that she is one of the top fifty women in the history of this planet.

Only God knows what the world would have been like without Jehanne d'Arc.

Appendices

Bibliography

Beckwith, Barbara. *Joan of Arc: God's Warrior: A Seven-day Retreat.* Cincinnati: St. Anthony Messenger Press, 2007.

Burne, Alfred Higgins. *The Agincourt War.* Ware: Wordsworth Editions, 1999.

Castor, Helen. *Joan of Arc: A History.* London: Faber and Faber, 2014.

Charpentier, Paul. *Journal du siège d'Orléans, 1428–1429: augmenté de plusieurs documents, notamment des comptes de ville, 1429–1431.* Orléans: H. Herluison, 1896.

DeVries, Kelly. *Joan of Arc: A Military Leader.* Stroud: Sutton, 1999.

France, Anatole, and Winifred Stephens Whale. *The Life of Joan of Arc.* New York: Dodd, Mead and Co., 1908.

Gordon, Mary. *Joan of Arc.* London: Phoenix, 2001.

Harrison, Kathryn. *Joan of Arc: A Life Transfigured.* New York. Random House, 2014.

Hobbins, Daniel. *The Trial of Joan of Arc.* Cambridge, Mass.: Harvard University Press, 2005.

Ireland, W. H. *Memoirs of Jeanne d'Arc, surnamed La Pucelle d'Orléans; with the history of her times.* London: Printed for R. Triphook, 1824.

Kitchin, G. W. *A History of France: Volume 1 (B.C. 58–A.D. 1453).* Oxford: Clarendon Press, 1899. Fourth edition.

Lake, Deryn, and Dinah Lampitt. *The King's Women: A Novel in Four Parts.* London: Allison & Busby, 2006.

Lowell, Francis C. *Joan of Arc.* Boston, New York, etc: Houghton, Mifflin and Co., 1896.

Lucie-Smith, Edward. *Joan of Arc.* New York: Norton, 1977.

Marcantel, Pamela. *An Army of Angels: A Novel of Joan of Arc.* New York: St. Martin's Press, 1997.

Murray, T. Douglas, Thomas de Courcelles, Guillaume Manchon, and Pierre Cauchon. *Jeanne d'Arc, maid of Orléans, deliverer of France; being the story of her life, her achievements, and her death, as attested on oath and set forth in original documents.* New York: McClure, Phillips and Co., 1902.

Nicolle, David, and Graham Turner. *Orléans 1429: France Turns the Tide.* Oxford: Osprey, 2001.

Noren, Marcia Quinn. *Joan of Arc: The Mystic Legacy.* Santa Cruz County, Calif.: Golden Fields Press, 2011.

Orliac, Jehanne d. *Yolande d'Anjou, la reine des quatre royaumes; avec 8 gravures hors texte.* Paris: Plon, 1933.

Pernoud, Régine, and Marie Clin. *Joan of Arc: Her Story.* New York: St. Martin's Press, 1999.

Richey, Stephen W. *Joan of Arc: The Warrior Saint.* Westport, Conn.: Praeger, 2003.

Rickard, J. "Sir John Stewart, Lord of Darnley, c. 1380–1429." Last modified February 25, 2008. http://www.historyofwar.org/articles/people_stewart_john_darnley_1429.html.

Sackville-West, V. *Saint Joan of Arc: Born January 6th, 1412; Burned as a Heretic, May 30th, 1431; Canonised as a Saint, May 16th, 1920.* Garden City, N.Y.: Doubleday, Doran and Co., 1936.

Scott, Walter, William Baker, and J. H. Alexander. *Tales of a Grandfather: The History of France (second series).* DeKalb: Northern Illinois University Press, 1996.

Seward, Desmond. *A Brief History of the Hundred Years War: The English in France, 1337–1453.* Rev. ed. London: Robinson, 2003.

Trask, Willard R. *Joan of Arc: In Her Own Words.* New York: Books and Co., 1996.

Twain, Mark. *Personal Recollections of Joan of Arc.* Garden City, New York: Nelson Doubleday, Inc., 1896.

Vale, M. G. A. *Charles VII.* Berkeley: University of California Press, 1974.

Warner, Marina. *Joan of Arc: The Image of Female Heroism.* New York: Knopf, 1981.

Xenophon Group Military History Database. "The Relief (1429)." Last modified April 4, 2002. http://www.xenophongroup.com/montjoie/orleans.htm#relief.

 Timeline for
Jehanne la Pucelle

1412: Jehanne d'Arc born and baptized in Domremy.

1425: Jehanne begins to have visits from St. Michael, St. Catherine, St. Margaret.

1428: Jehanne travels to Vaucouleurs (prompted by Saints Michael, Catherine, and Margaret), and asks for a meeting with the Dauphin but is turned away.

1429: Jehanne in Vaucouleurs; still wants meeting with the Dauphin; request granted.

February 13, 1429: Jehanne leaves Vaucouleurs disguised in men's clothing, short hair, and soldier attire and travels to Chinon under armed escort.

March 8, 1429: In Chinon, she asks the Dauphin to help France fight the English and the Burgundians; Charles orders her interrogation by churchmen.

April 1429: Dauphin appoints Jehanne a captain in the French army.

April 27, 1429: Jehanne and her troops set out from Blois to relieve French forces at the Siege of Orléans.

April 29, 1429: Jehanne and La Hire reach Orléans, where they are told to wait for reinforcements.

May 4, 1429: Jehanne leads an attack on the English at Fort Saint-Loup.

May 7, 1429: Wounded, Jehanne still leads a French victory at Les Tourelles.

May 9, 1429: Jehanne travels to Tours, where she asks the Dauphin to go immediately to Reims for a coronation ceremony; he agrees if Jehanne can escort him there.

June 18, 1429: French win Battle of Patay.

July 16, 1429: Dauphin's army and Jehanne reach Reims.

July 17, 1429: The Dauphin is crowned king of France; Jehanne stands at his side.

July 20, 1429: Charles leaves Reims and parades around the region.

August 2, 1429: Charles retreats to Loire.

August 14, 1429: French and English forces skirmish at Senlis.

August 28, 1429: Burgundy and France sign a four-month truce.

September 8, 1429: French assault on Paris begins, but is undermined by Charles and his advisors; Jehanne wounded and French troops forced to retreat; Charles cancels the army.

December 1429: Charles raises Jehanne, her parents, and her brothers to nobility status.

May 14, 1430: Jehanne reaches Compiegne and is captured by the Burgundians.

May 25, 1430: Paris learns of Jehanne's capture

January 3, 1431: Jehanne sold to Bishop Pierre Cauchon who leads the show trial.

January 13, 1431: Jehanne's trial begins; with no counsel, she remains in chains 24/7.

May 24, 1431: Upon the reading of her sentence, Jehanne, frightened and alone, signs a last-minute abjuration.

May 29, 1431: After rescinding her abjuration, Jehanne is transferred from ecclesiastic to secular authority.

May 30, 1431: Jehanne is burned at the stake.

1450: Charles VII orders an investigation into Jehanne d'Arc's trial.

1456: Rehabilitation trial of Jehanne d'Arc concludes (May–July); the English under Bishop Cauchon are found to have conducted a kangaroo court against Jehanne; the Maid is exonerated of all charges.

May 16, 1920: Pope Benedict XV makes Jehanne d'Arc a saint.

What Secret Jehanne Told Charles VII (March 8, 1429): Two Views

(1.) **According to Anatole France:** "It is said that during this private conversation, addressing him with the familiarity of an angel, she made him this strange announcement: 'My Lord bids me say unto thee that thou art indeed the heir of France and the son of a King; he has sent me to thee to lead thee to Reims to be crowned there and anointed if thou wilt.'

"Afterwards the Maid's chaplain reported these words, saying he had received them from the Maid herself. All that is certain is that the Armagnacs were not slow to turn them into a miracle in favour of the Line of the Lilies. It was asserted that these words spoken by God himself, by the mouth of an innocent girl, were a reply to the carking, secret anxiety of the King. Madame Ysabeau's son, it was said, distracted and saddened by the thought that perhaps the royal blood did not flow in his veins, was ready to renounce his kingdom and declare himself an usurper, unless by some heavenly light his doubts concerning his birth should be dispelled. Men told how his face shone with joy when it was revealed to him that he was the true heir of France." (France, page i. 172)

(2.) **According to V. Sackville-West:** "He gave way and took her aside for a private conversation out of earshot, a procedure most tantalizing for the rest of the Court. It was then, apparently, that she revealed something to him far along the road towards belief in the authenticity of her claims. 'Sire,' she said, 'if I tell you things so secret that you and God alone are privy to them, will you believe that I am sent by God?' And then, being encouraged by him to continue, 'Sire,' she said, 'do you not remember that on last All Saints' Day [November 1, 1428], being alone in your oratory in the chapel of the castle of Loches, you requested three things of God?' He answered that he remembered it well. Had he, she asked, ever spoken of these things to his confessor or any other? He had not. Then she said, 'The first request was that it should be God's pleasure to remove your courage in the matter of recovering France, if you were not the true heir, so that you should no longer be the cause of prolonging a war bringing so much suffering in its train. The second request was that you alone should be punished, either through death or any other penance, if the adversities and tribulations which the poor people of France had endured for so long were due to your own sins. The third request was that the people should be forgiven and God's anger appeased, if the sins of the people were the cause of their troubles.' The Dauphin admitted that she had spoken the truth. . . . 'I tell you in the name of Our Lord that you are the true heir of France and the son of the King.'. . . He was clearly impressed. Those who were present noticed the change in his face when he returned." (Sackville-West, pages 116–117 and 119)

The Julian Calendar of 1429

January 1429 (Julian calendar: old style)

1	2	3	4	5	6	7	8	9	10	11	12	13	14	15	16	17	18	19	20	21	22	23	24	25	26	27	28	29	30	31
S	S	M	T	W	T	F	S	S	M	T	W	T	F	S	S	M	T	W	T	F	S	S	M	T	W	T	F	S	S	M

February 1429 (Julian calendar: old style)

1	2	3	4	5	6	7	8	9	10	11	12	13	14	15	16	17	18	19	20	21	22	23	24	25	26	27	28
T	W	T	F	S	S	M	T	W	T	F	S	S	M	T	W	T	F	S	S	M	T	W	T	F	S	S	M

March 1429 (Julian calendar: old style)

1	2	3	4	5	6	7	8	9	10	11	12	13	14	15	16	17	18	19	20	21	22	23	24	25	26	27	28	29	30	31
T	W	T	F	S	S	M	T	W	T	F	S	S	M	T	W	T	F	S	S	M	T	W	T	F	S	S	M	T	W	T

April 1429 (Julian calendar: old style)

1	2	3	4	5	6	7	8	9	10	11	12	13	14	15	16	17	18	19	20	21	22	23	24	25	26	27	28	29	30
F	S	S	M	T	W	T	F	S	S	M	T	W	T	F	S	S	M	T	W	T	F	S	S	M	T	W	T	F	S

May 1429 (Julian calendar: old style)

1	2	3	4	5	6	7	8	9	10	11	12	13	14	15	16	17	18	19	20	21	22	23	24	25	26	27	28	29	30	31
S	M	T	W	T	F	S	S	M	T	W	T	F	S	S	M	T	W	T	F	S	S	M	T	W	T	F	S	S	M	T

June 1429 (Julian calendar: old style)

1	2	3	4	5	6	7	8	9	10	11	12	13	14	15	16	17	18	19	20	21	22	23	24	25	26	27	28	29	30
W	T	F	S	S	M	T	W	T	F	S	S	M	T	W	T	F	S	S	M	T	W	T	F	S	S	M	T	W	T

July 1429 (Julian calendar: old style)

1	2	3	4	5	6	7	8	9	10	11	12	13	14	15	16	17	18	19	20	21	22	23	24	25	26	27	28	29	30	31
F	S	S	M	T	W	T	F	S	S	M	T	W	T	F	S	S	M	T	W	T	F	S	S	M	T	W	T	F	S	S

August 1429 (Julian calendar: old style)

1	2	3	4	5	6	7	8	9	10	11	12	13	14	15	16	17	18	19	20	21	22	23	24	25	26	27	28	29	30	31
M	T	W	T	F	S	S	M	T	W	T	F	S	S	M	T	W	T	F	S	S	M	T	W	T	F	S	S	M	T	W

September 1429 (Julian calendar: old style)

1	2	3	4	5	6	7	8	9	10	11	12	13	14	15	16	17	18	19	20	21	22	23	24	25	26	27	28	29	30
T	F	S	S	M	T	W	T	F	S	S	M	T	W	T	F	S	S	M	T	W	T	F	S	S	M	T	W	T	F

266

Acknowledgements

This book would not have been possible without all of you. Many thanks to:

My angelic wife, Kathy. Her loving and gracious support has been insightful and expert through the decades of tip-toed trips to my computer at all hours of the night;

Emily Maskin and the major role she has played in the development of this book through her ongoing zeal, research, translations, and relentless edits;

Virginia Frohlick who, once she became aware of my efforts to write this book, has been an endless source of ideas, kind assistance, and insights;

My son Matt who has helped raise this book to a new level of professionalism by his inspired critiques of character, plot, and storytelling;

My many brothers and sisters who took the time and trouble to read the whole manuscript and give me honest and impassioned feedback;

Katie Hall, the first publishing industry professional who said she thought this book had the potential to be a player in the world of historical fiction;

Jean Jenkins and her no-nonsense observations, suggestions, and fixes;

Meg Gorham for her enthusiastic interest and willingness to always be there for me;

The loving feedback and loving suggestions from Jim House, Kelly O'Donnell, Meredith Alcock, Jack Webb, Lily Loh, and Katrina Zeno;

The tolerance and compassion from all my children, grandchildren, extended family, and fellow parishioners who have so gracefully listened to my endless stories about the life of Joan of Arc;

The understanding and devoted members of Outskirts Publishers;

And above all, the kind and loving intercession of the Blessed Virgin Mary:

Remember, O most gracious Virgin Mary,
that never was it known that anyone who fled to your protection,
implored your help or sought your intercession,
was left unaided. Inspired with this confidence,
I fly to you, O Virgin of virgins, my Mother;
to you do I come, before you I stand, sinful and sorrowful.
O Mother of the Word Incarnate,
despise not my petitions,
but in your mercy hear and answer me. Amen.

About the Author

Mike MacCarthy

In 1990, Mike MacCarthy co-founded *San Diego Writers Monthly*, which led to his collaboration on 11 published books. He fell in love with Joan of Arc in the hospital at age nine and has since spent so much time reading, writing, and speaking about her that his wife of 34 years lovingly calls Joan "the other woman" in his life.

CPSIA information can be obtained
at www.ICGtesting.com
Printed in the USA
FFOW03n2103050216
21227FF